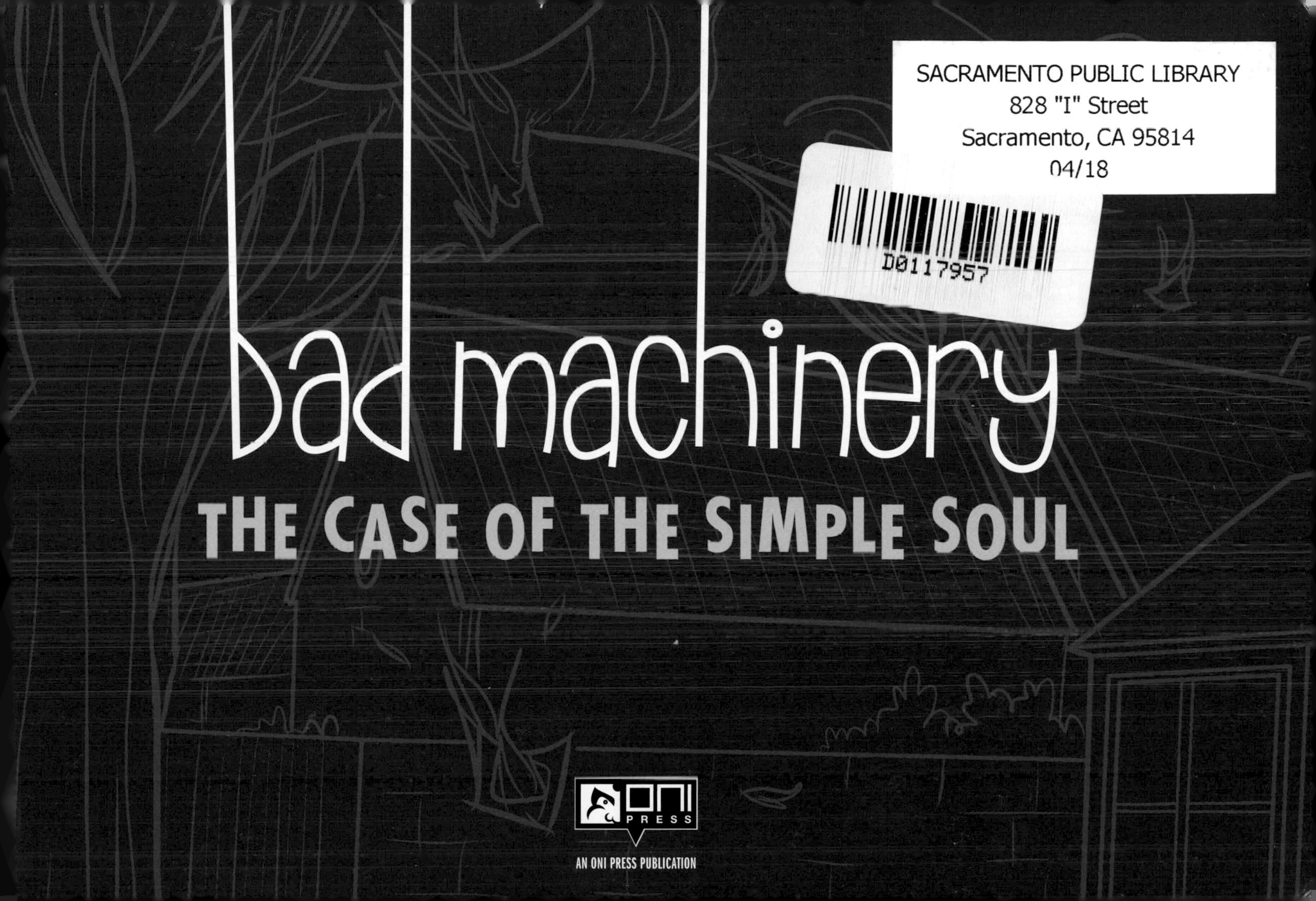

bad machinery

THE CASE OF THE SIMPLE SOUL

ONI PRESS

AN ONI PRESS PUBLICATION

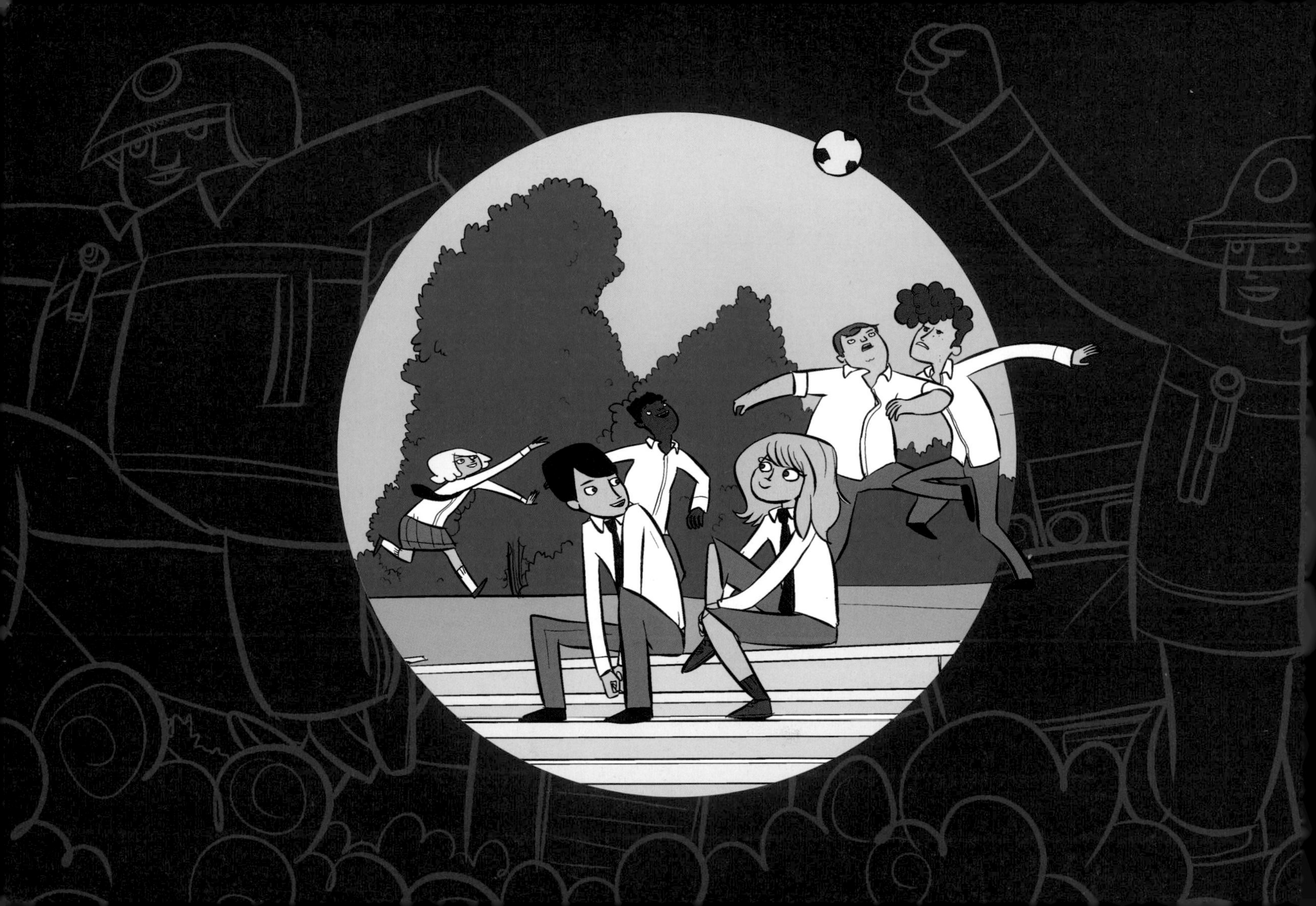

bad machinery
THE CASE OF THE SIMPLE SOUL

by
John Allison

Colour assists by
Adam Cadwell

Edited by
Ari Yarwood

Designed by
Hilary Thompson

PUBLISHED BY ONI PRESS INC.

publisher, **Joe Nozemack**
editor in chief, **James Lucas Jones**
director of operations, **Brad Rooks**
director of sales, **David Dissanayake**
publicity manager, **Rachel Reed**
marketing assistant, **Melissa Meszaros Macfadyen**
director of design & production, **Troy Look**
graphic designer, **Hilary Thompson**
junior graphic designer, **Kate Z. Stone**
digital prepress technician, **Angie Knowles**
managing editor, **Ari Yarwood**
senior editor, **Charlie Chu**
editor, **Robin Herrera**
administrative assistant, **Alissa Sallah**
logistics associate, **Jung Lee**

onipress.com
facebook.com/onipress
twitter.com/onipress
onipress.tumblr.com
instagram.com/onipress
badmachinery.com

FIRST EDITION: DECEMBER 2014
POCKET EDITION: NOVEMBER 2017

ISBN 978-1-62010-443-9
EISBN 978-1-62010-194-0

BAD MACHINERY VOLUME THREE: THE CASE OF THE SIMPLE SOUL, POCKET EDITION, NOVEMBER 2017. PUBLISHED BY ONI PRESS, INC. 1319 SE MARTIN LUTHER KING JR. BLVD., SUITE 240, PORTLAND, OR 97214.

PRINTED IN CHINA.

LIBRARY OF CONGRESS CONTROL NUMBER: 2017938436

10 9 8 7 6 5 4 3 2 1

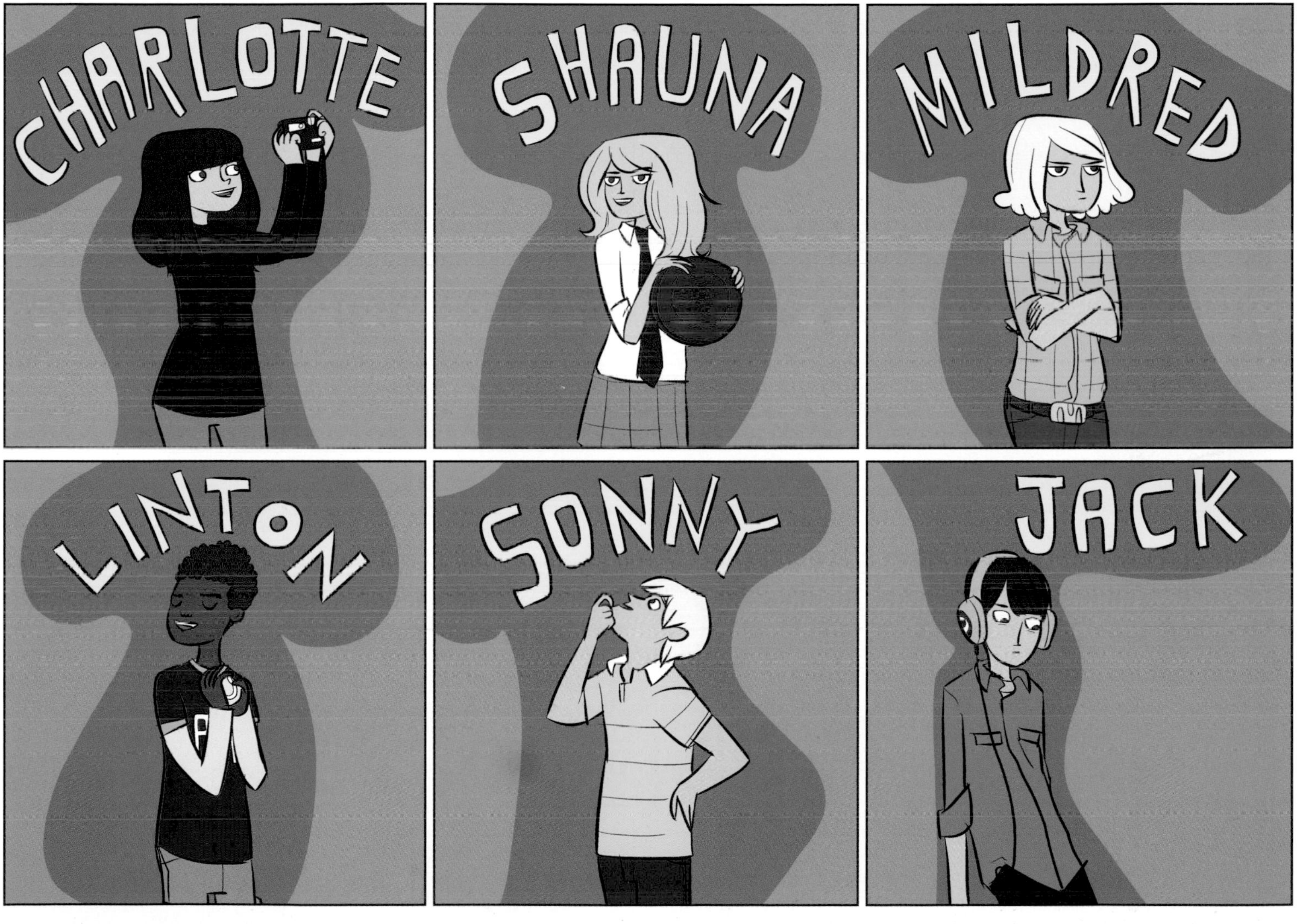
CHARLOTTE
SHAUNA
MILDRED
LINTON
SONNY
JACK

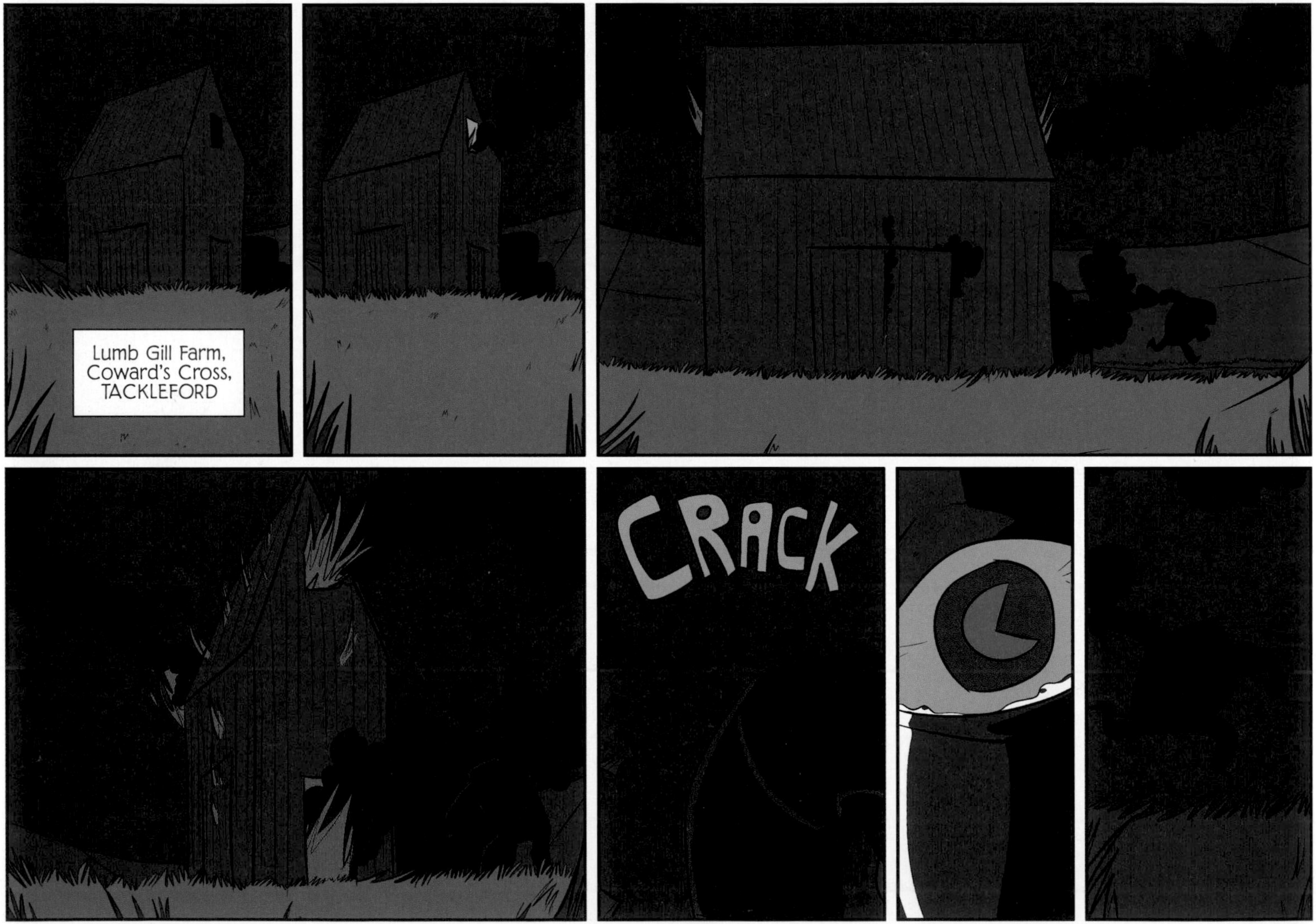
Lumb Gill Farm,
Coward's Cross,
TACKLEFORD
CRACK

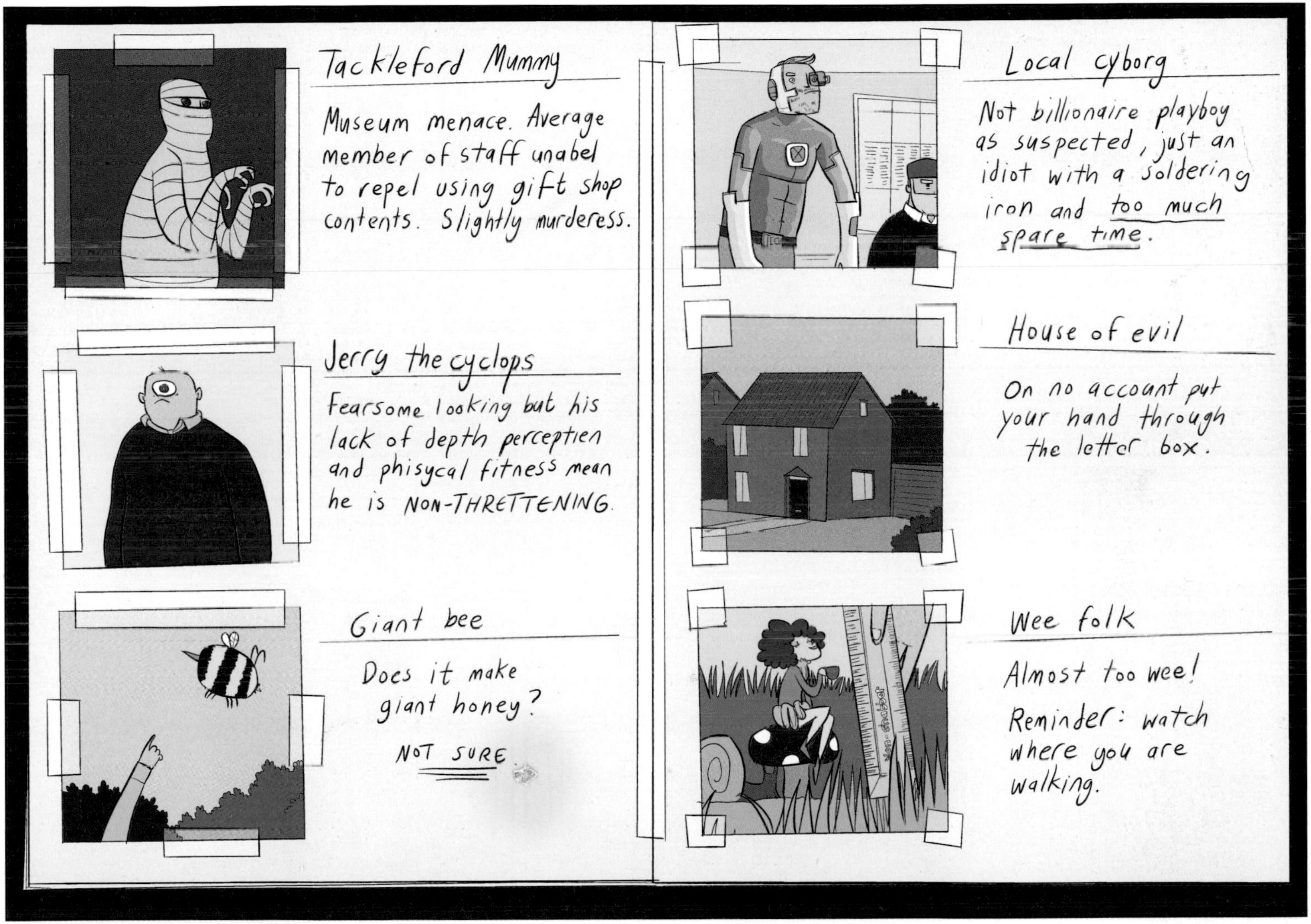
Tackleford Mummy
Museum menace. Average member of staff unabel to repel using gift shop contents. Slightly murderess.
Jerry the cyclops
Fearsome looking but his lack of depth perceptien and phisycal fitness mean he is NON-THRETTENING.
Giant bee
Does it make giant honey?
NOT SURE
Local cyborg
Not billionaire playboy as suspected, just an idiot with a soldering iron and too much spare time.
House of evil
On no account put your hand through the letter box.
Wee folk
Almost too wee!
Reminder: watch where you are walking.

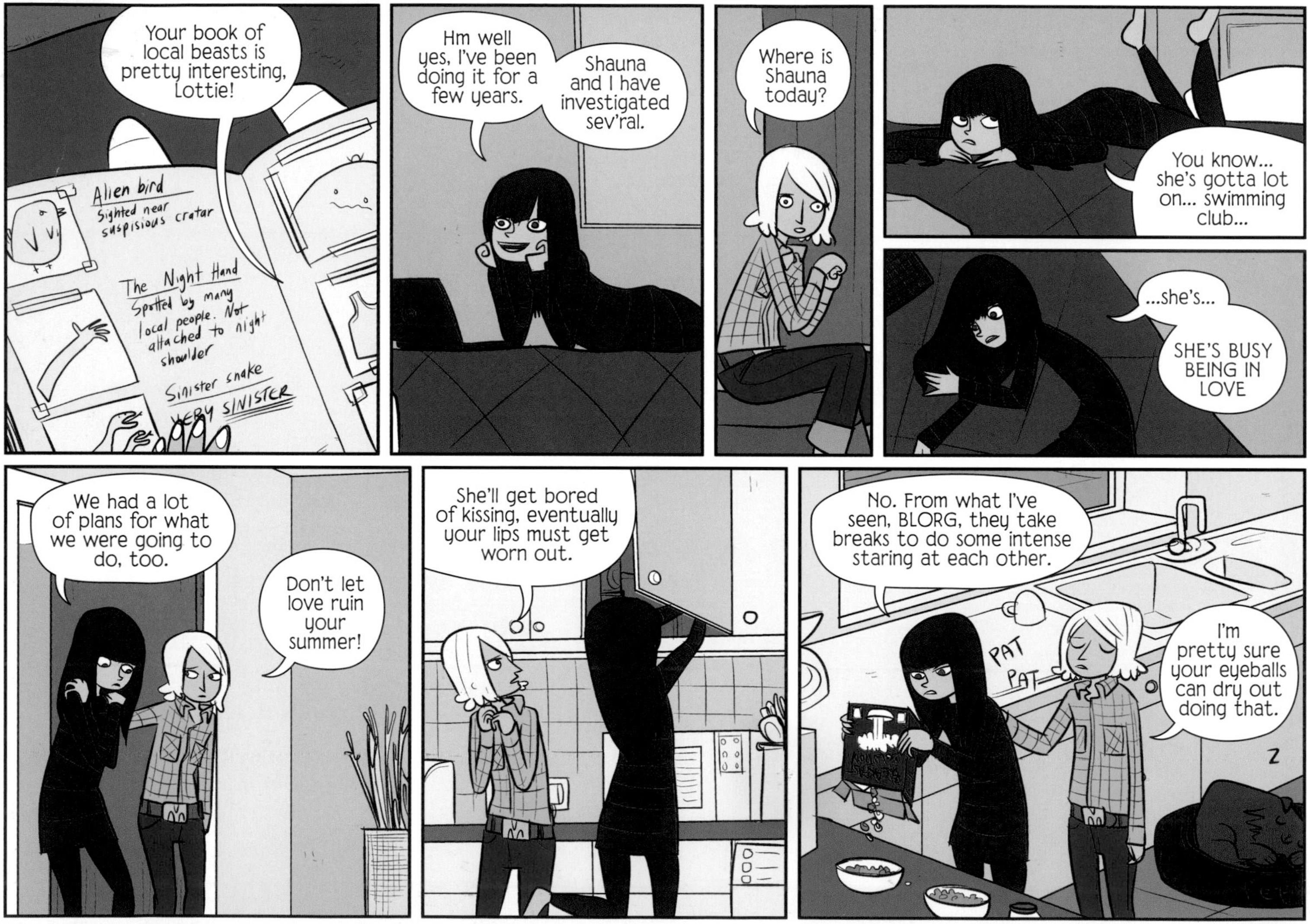
Your book of local beasts is pretty interesting, Lottie!
Alien bird
Sighted near suspisious cratar
The Night Hand
Spotted by many local people. Not attached to night shoulder
Sinister snake
VERY SINISTER
Hm well yes, I've been doing it for a few years.
Shauna and I have investigated sev'ral.
Where is Shauna today?
You know... she's gotta lot on... swimming club...
...she's...
SHE'S BUSY BEING IN LOVE
We had a lot of plans for what we were going to do, too.
Don't let love ruin your summer!
She'll get bored of kissing, eventually your lips must get worn out.
No. From what I've seen, BLORG, they take breaks to do some intense staring at each other.
PAT
PAT
I'm pretty sure your eyeballs can dry out doing that.
Z

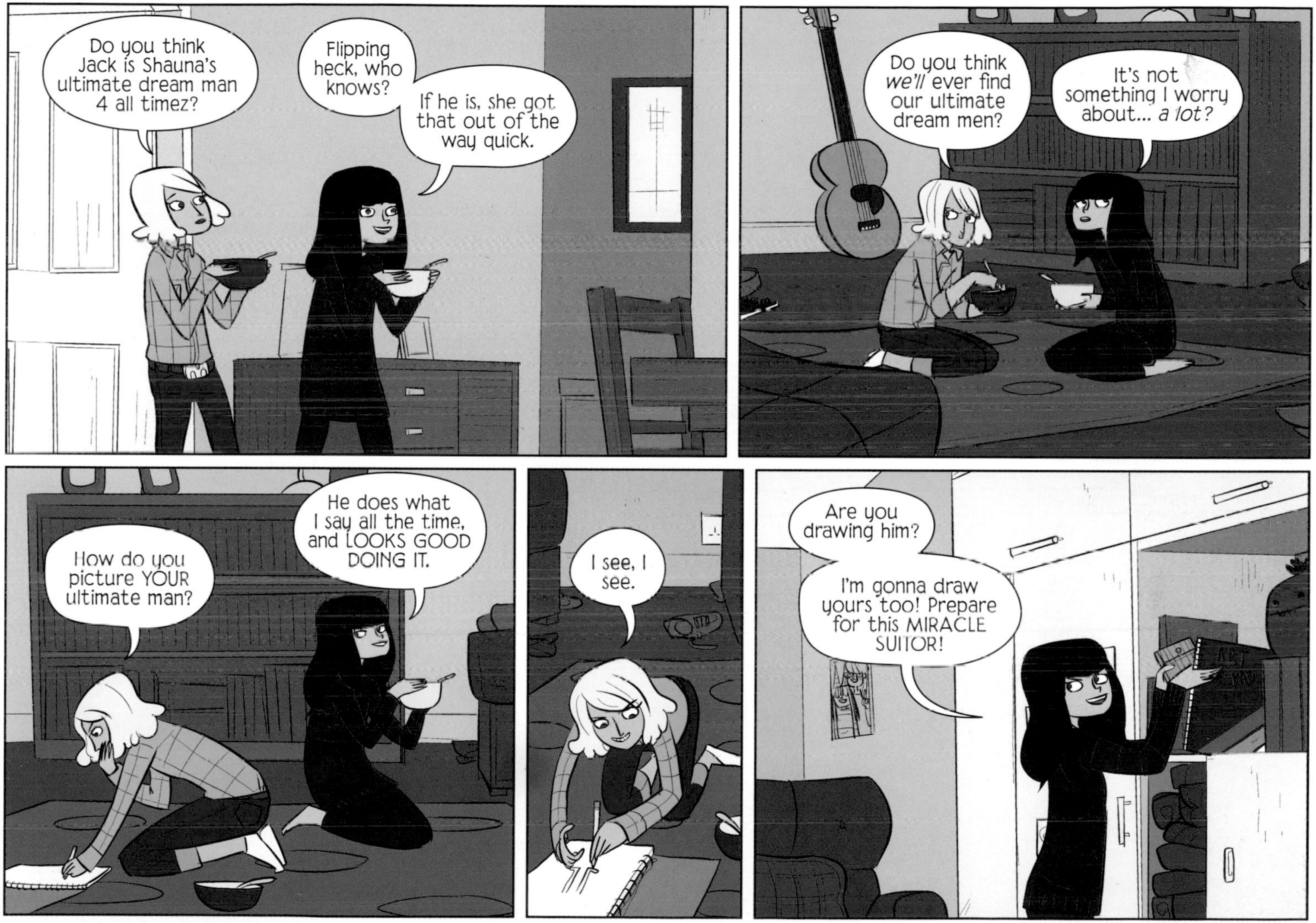

Do you think Jack is Shauna's ultimate dream man 4 all timez?
Flipping heck, who knows?
If he is, she got that out of the way quick.
Do you think *we'll* ever find our ultimate dream men?
It's not something I worry about... *a lot?*
How do you picture YOUR ultimate man?
He does what I say all the time, and LOOKS GOOD DOING IT.
I see, I see.
Are you drawing him?
I'm gonna draw yours too! Prepare for this MIRACLE SUITOR!

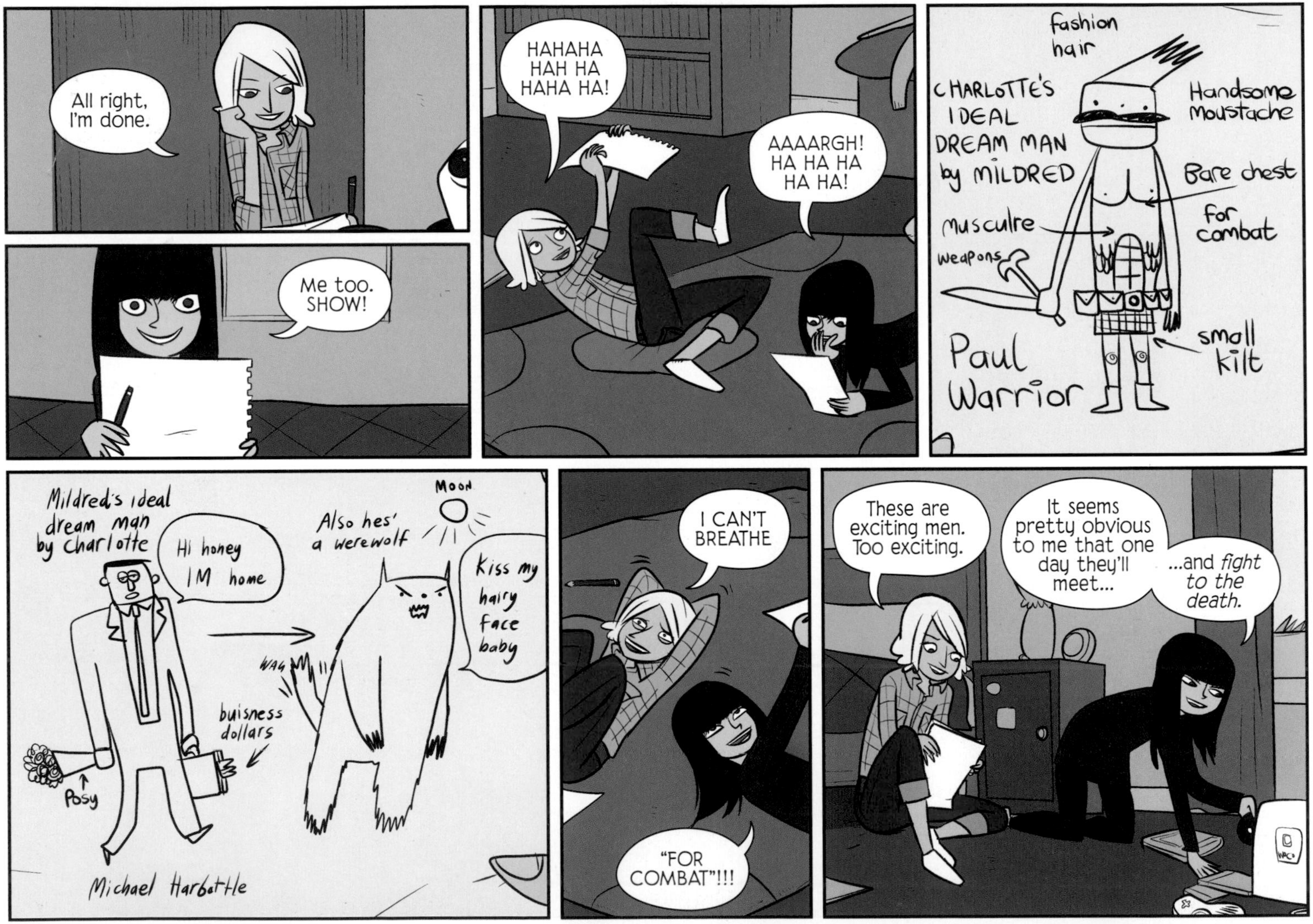
All right, I'm done.
Me too. SHOW!
HAHAHA HAH HA HAHA HA!
AAAARGH! HA HA HA HA HA!
CHARLOTTE'S IDEAL DREAM MAN by MILDRED
fashion hair
Handsome Moustache
Bare chest
for combat
musculre
weapons
small kilt
Paul Warrior
Mildred's ideal dream man by charlotte
Hi honey IM home
Also hes' a werewolf
MOON
Kiss my hairy face baby
WAG
buisness dollars
Posy
Michael Harbottle
I CAN'T BREATHE
"FOR COMBAT"!!!
These are exciting men. Too exciting.
It seems pretty obvious to me that one day they'll meet...
...and fight to the death.

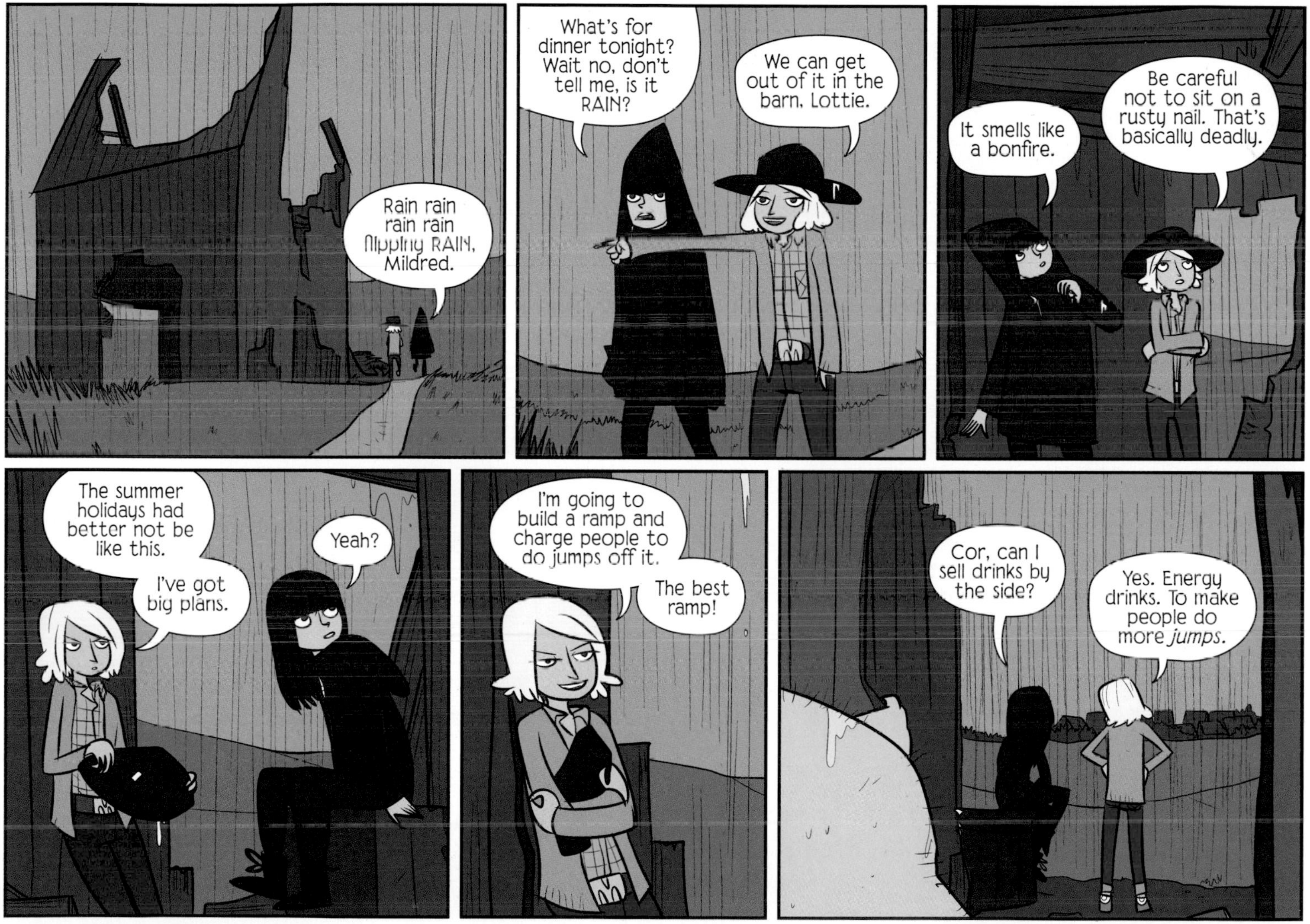
Rain rain rain rain flipping RAIN, Mildred.
What's for dinner tonight? Wait no, don't tell me, is it RAIN?
We can get out of it in the barn, Lottie.
It smells like a bonfire.
Be careful not to sit on a rusty nail. That's basically deadly.
The summer holidays had better not be like this.
I've got big plans.
Yeah?
I'm going to build a ramp and charge people to do jumps off it.
The best ramp!
Cor, can I sell drinks by the side?
Yes. Energy drinks. To make people do more *jumps*.

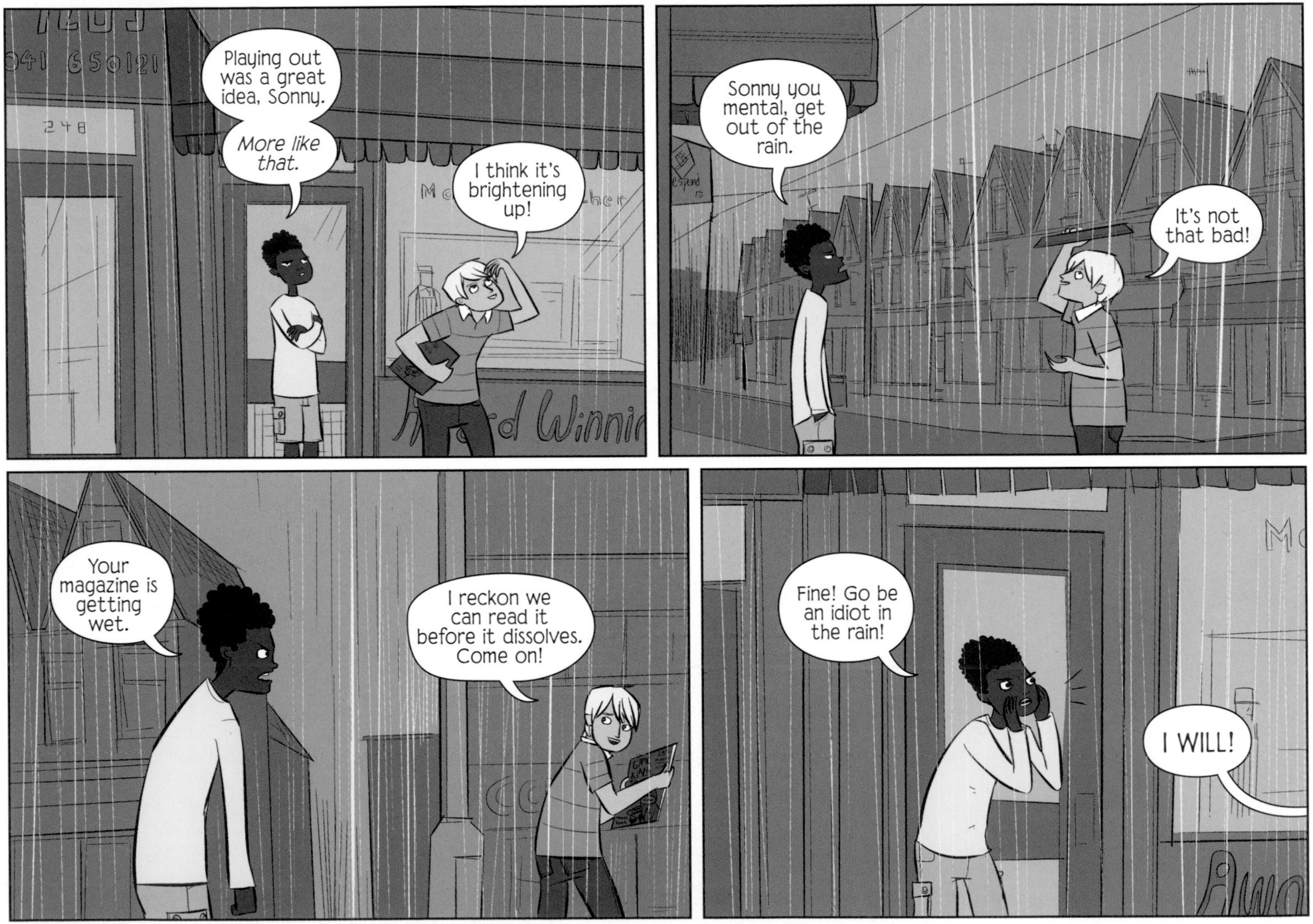
Playing out was a great idea, Sonny.
More like that.
I think it's brightening up!
Sonny you mental, get out of the rain.
It's not that bad!
Your magazine is getting wet.
I reckon we can read it before it dissolves. Come on!
Fine! Go be an idiot in the rain!
I WILL!

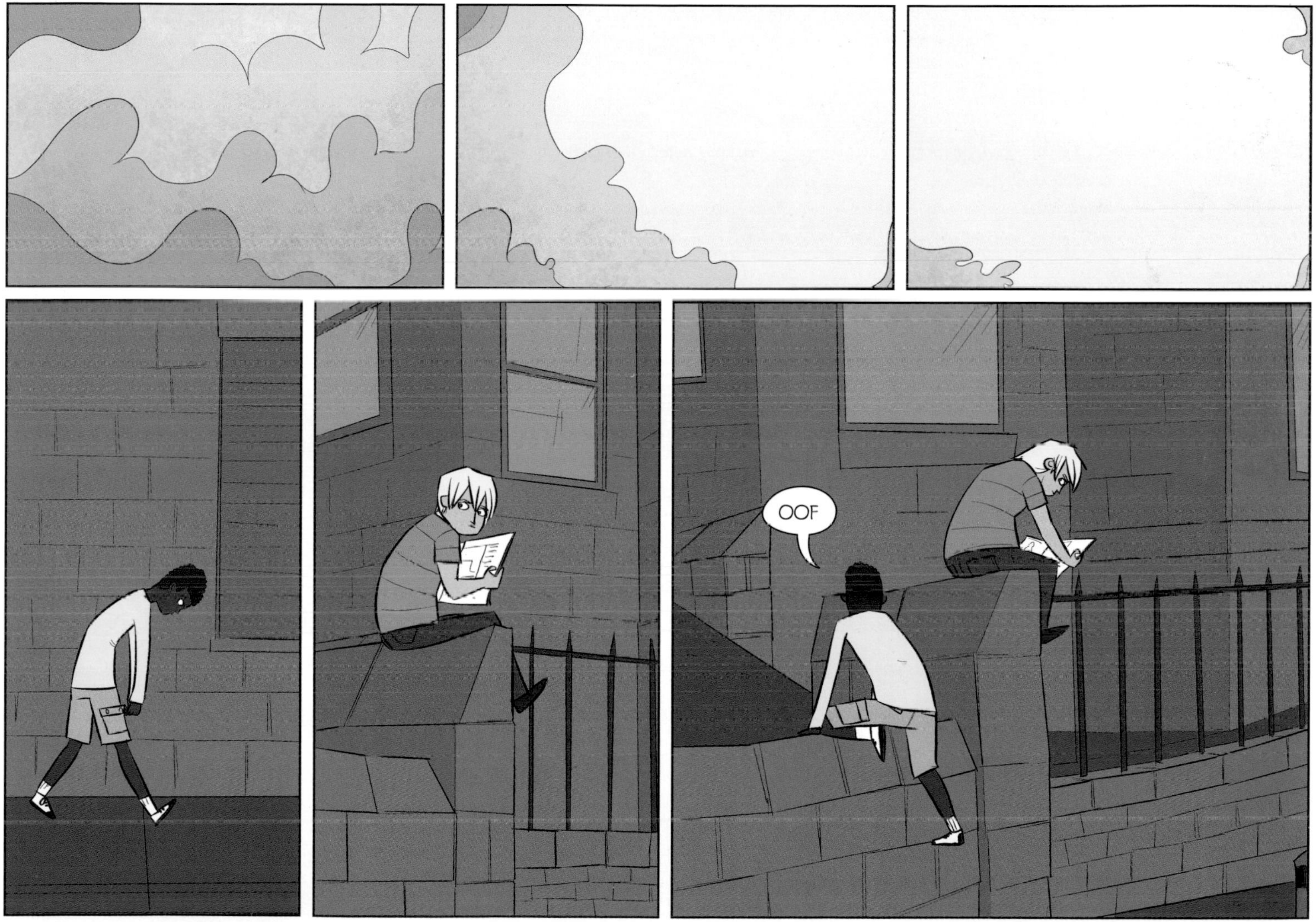
OOF

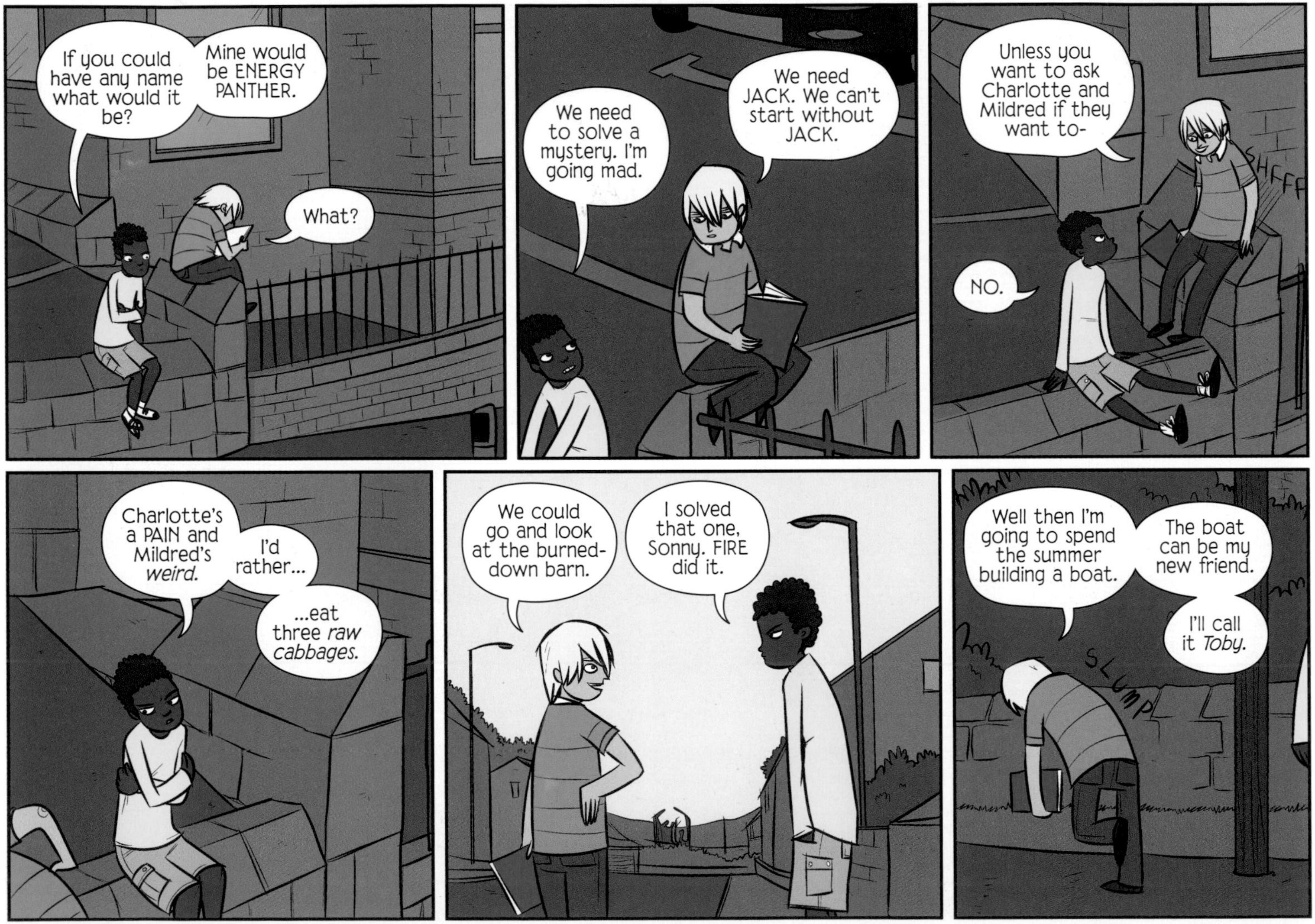

If you could have any name what would it be?
Mine would be ENERGY PANTHER.
What?
We need to solve a mystery. I'm going mad.
We need JACK. We can't start without JACK.
Unless you want to ask Charlotte and Mildred if they want to-
SHFFF
NO.
Charlotte's a PAIN and Mildred's *weird.*
I'd rather...
...eat three *raw cabbages.*
We could go and look at the burned-down barn.
I solved that one, Sonny. FIRE did it.
Well then I'm going to spend the summer building a boat.
SLUMP
The boat can be my new friend.
I'll call it *Toby.*

The Case of the Simple Soul

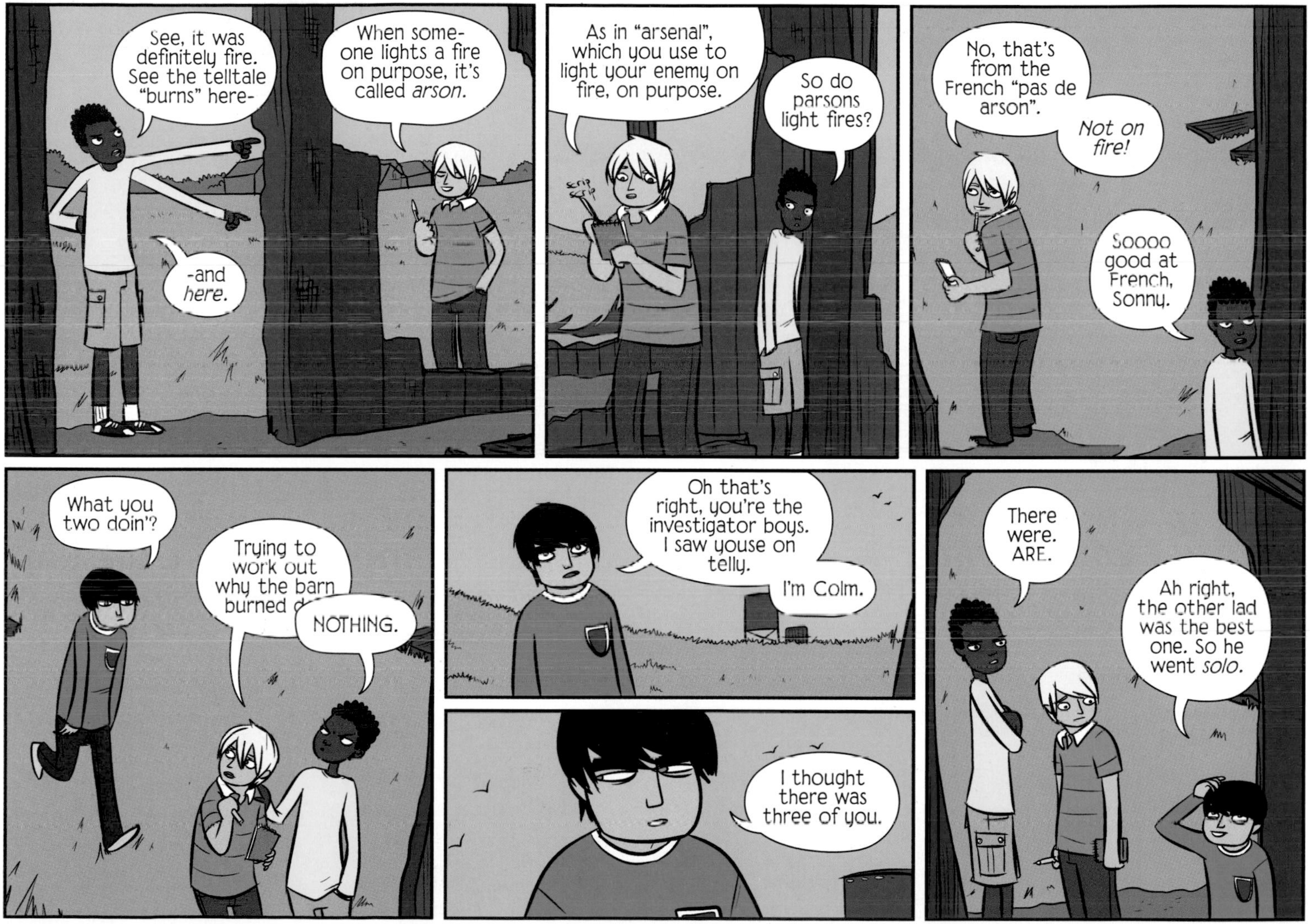
See, it was definitely fire. See the telltale "burns" here-
-and *here.*
When some-one lights a fire on purpose, it's called *arson.*
As in "arsenal", which you use to light your enemy on fire, on purpose.
scrip scrip
So do parsons light fires?
No, that's from the French "pas de arson".
Not on fire!
Soooo good at French, Sonny.
What you two doin'?
Trying to work out why the barn burned d
NOTHING.
Oh that's right, you're the investigator boys. I saw youse on telly.
I'm Colm.
I thought there was three of you.
There were. ARE.
Ah right, the other lad was the best one. So he went *solo.*

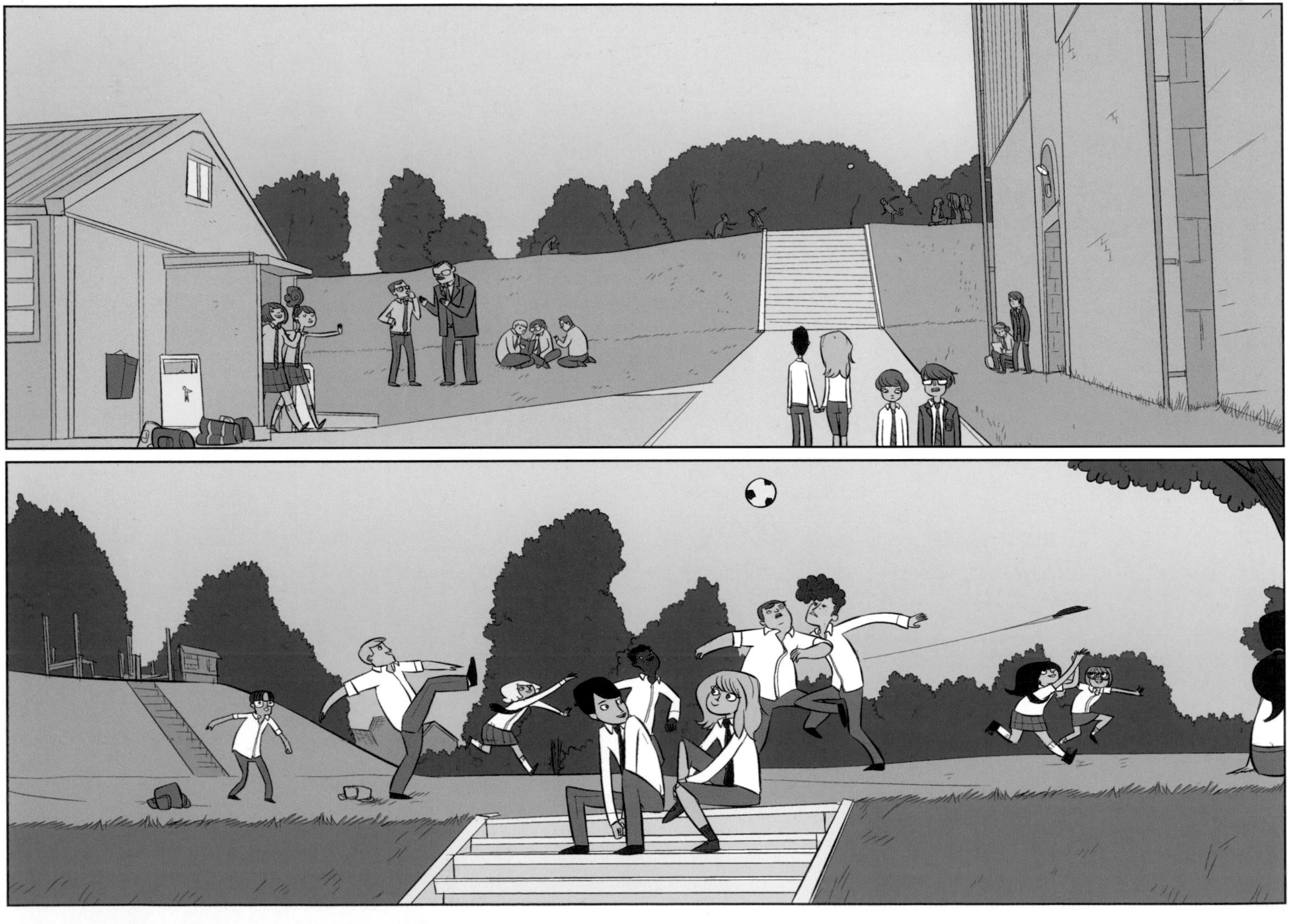

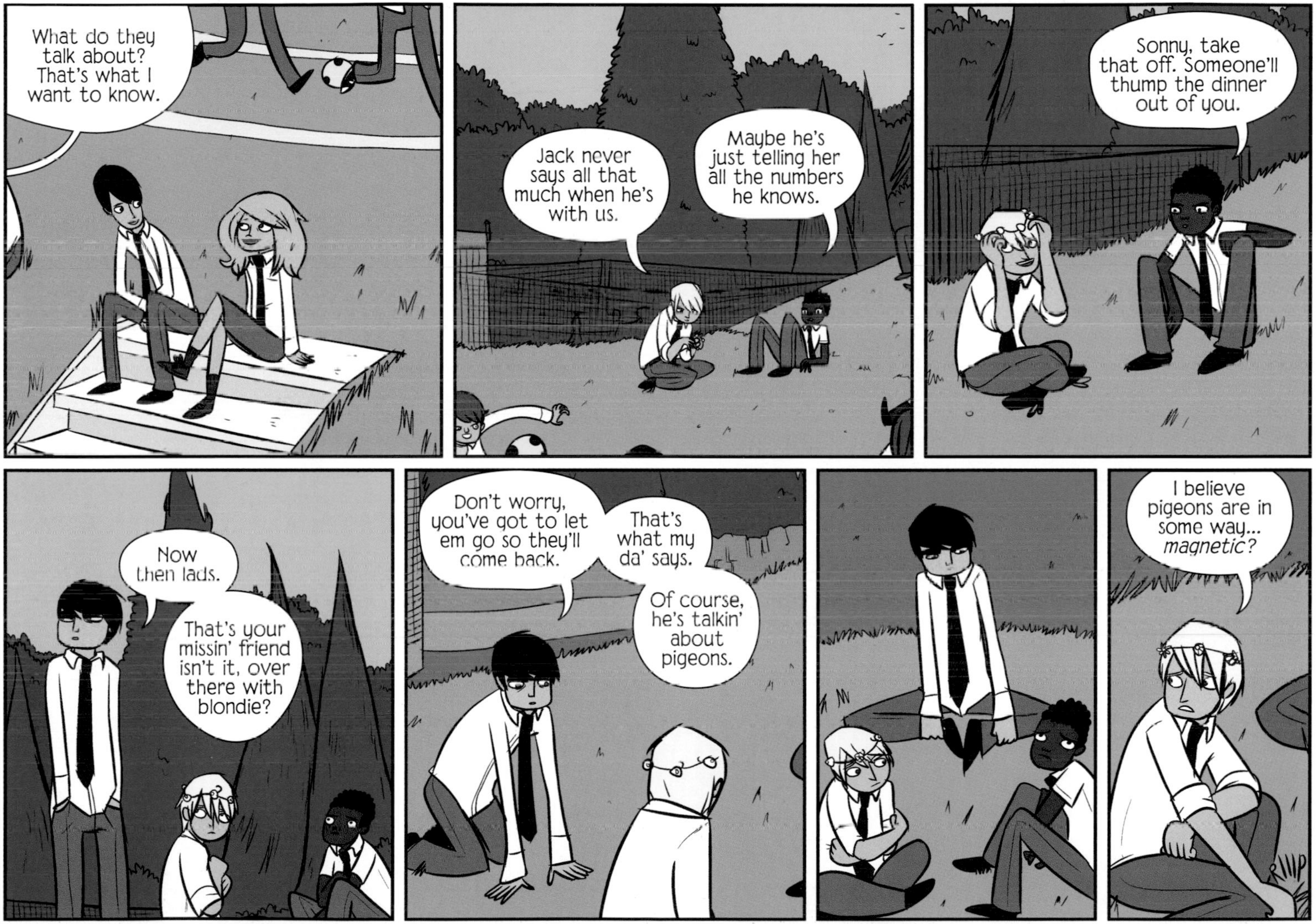
What do they talk about? That's what I want to know.
Jack never says all that much when he's with us.
Maybe he's just telling her all the numbers he knows.
Sonny, take that off. Someone'll thump the dinner out of you.
Now then lads.
That's your missin' friend isn't it, over there with blondie?
Don't worry, you've got to let em go so they'll come back.
That's what my da' says.
Of course, he's talkin' about pigeons.
I believe pigeons are in some way... *magnetic*?
RIIP

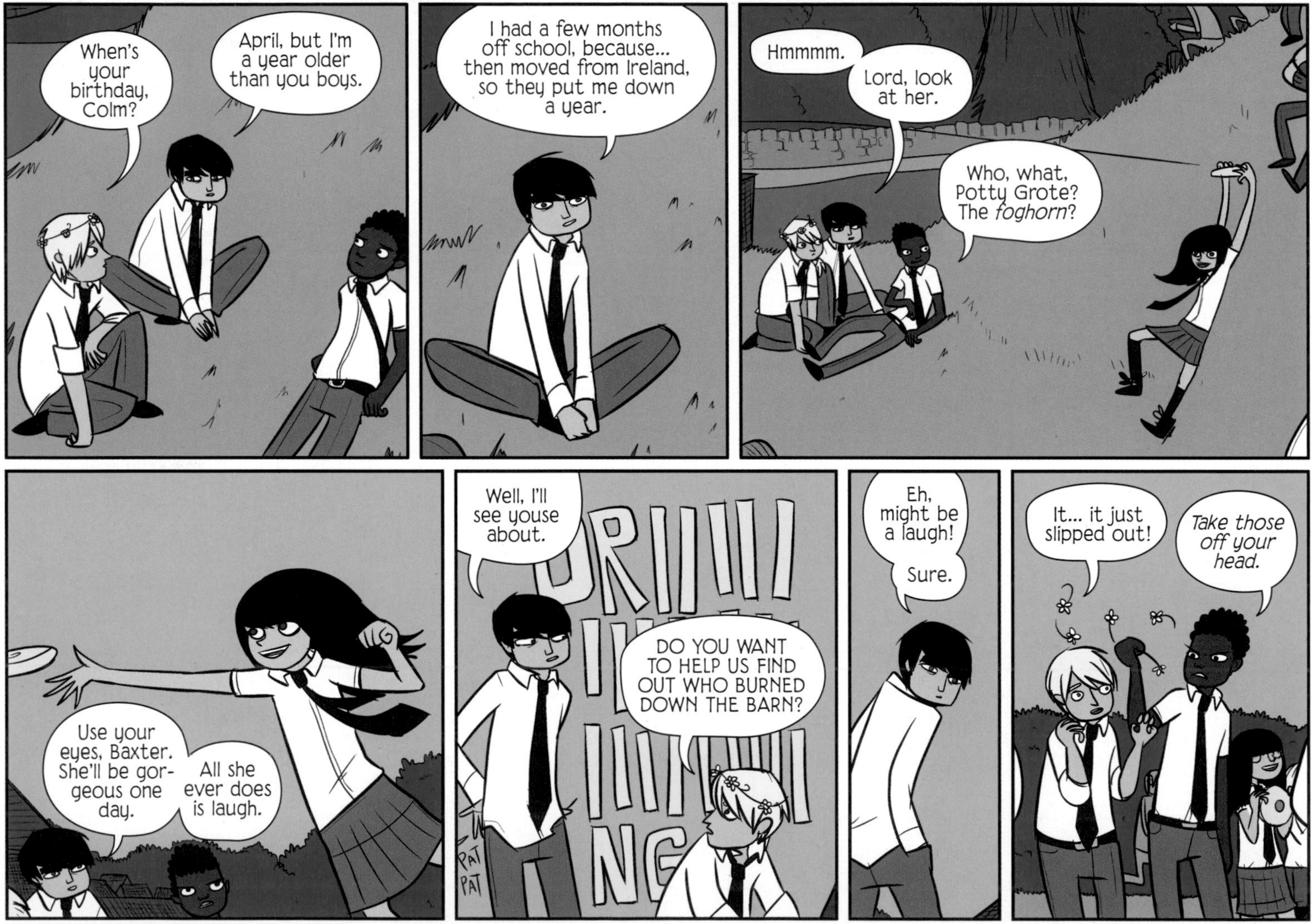
When's your birthday, Colm?
April, but I'm a year older than you boys.
I had a few months off school, because... then moved from Ireland, so they put me down a year.
Hmmmm.
Lord, look at her.
Who, what, Potty Grote? The *foghorn*?
Use your eyes, Baxter. She'll be gorgeous one day.
All she ever does is laugh.
Well, I'll see youse about.
DRIIIIIIIIIIIIIIIIIIING
DO YOU WANT TO HELP US FIND OUT WHO BURNED DOWN THE BARN?
PAT PAT
Eh, might be a laugh!
Sure.
It... it just slipped out!
Take those off your head.

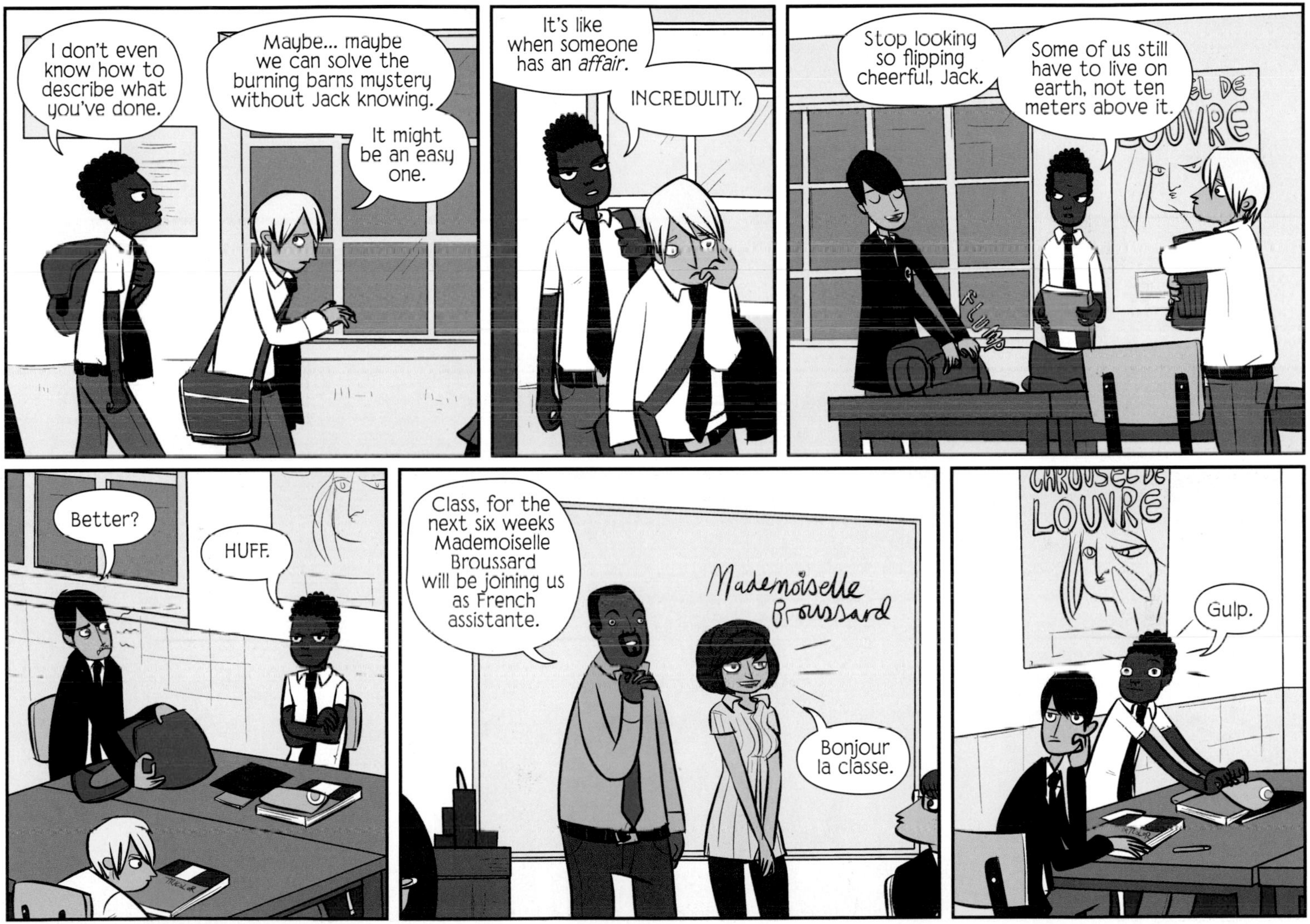
I don't even know how to describe what you've done.
Maybe... maybe we can solve the burning barns mystery without Jack knowing.
It might be an easy one.
It's like when someone has an *affair*.
INCREDULITY.
Stop looking so flipping cheerful, Jack.
Some of us still have to live on earth, not ten meters above it.
FLUMP
Better?
HUFF.
Class, for the next six weeks Mademoiselle Broussard will be joining us as French assistante.
Mademoiselle Broussard
Bonjour la classe.
CARROUSEL DE LOUVRE
Gulp.

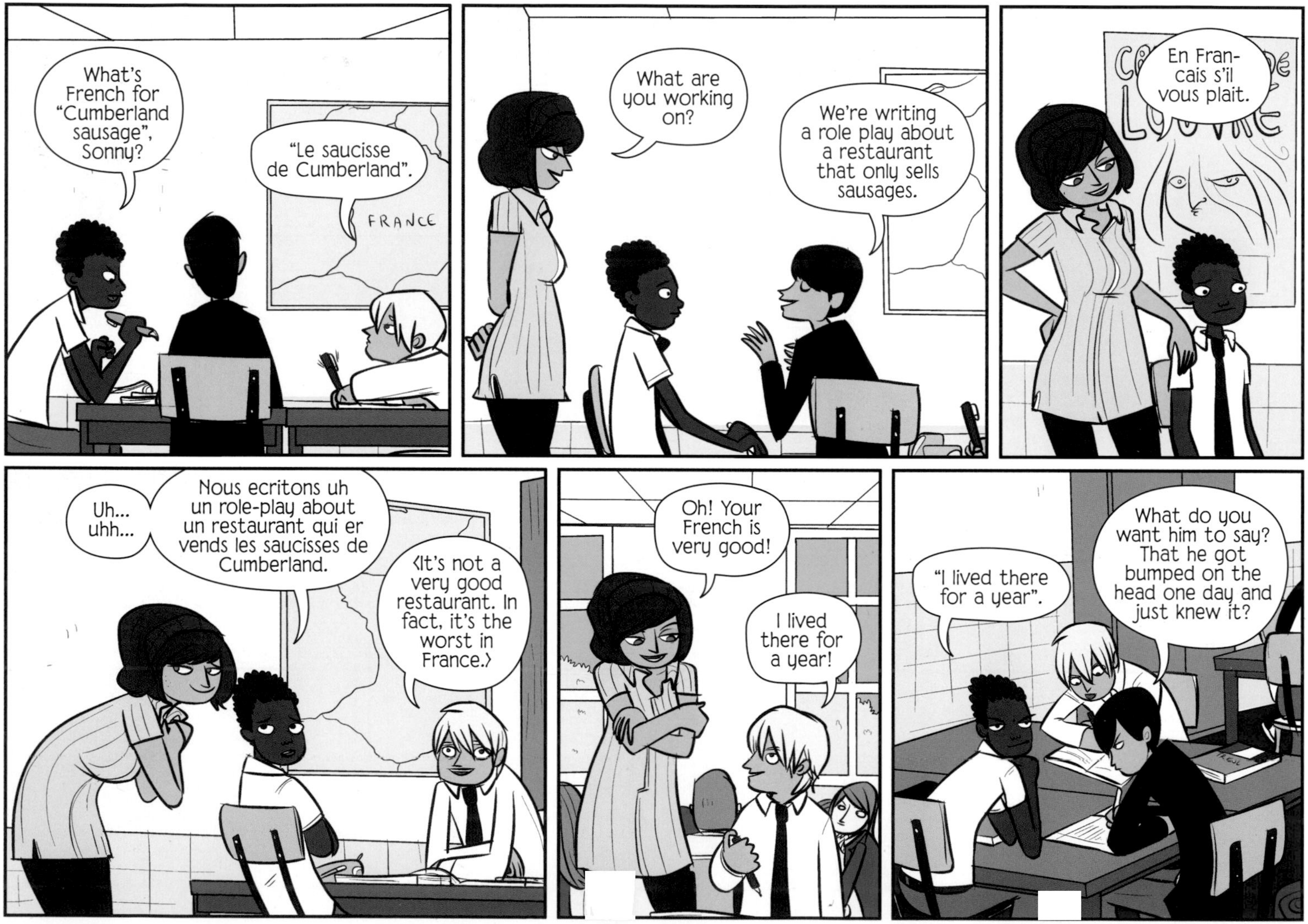
What's French for "Cumberland sausage", Sonny?
"Le saucisse de Cumberland".
FRANCE
What are you working on?
We're writing a role play about a restaurant that only sells sausages.
En Francais s'il vous plait.
Uh... uhh...
Nous ecritons uh un role-play about un restaurant qui er vends les saucisses de Cumberland.
‹It's not a very good restaurant. In fact, it's the worst in France.›
Oh! Your French is very good!
I lived there for a year!
"I lived there for a year".
What do you want him to say? That he got bumped on the head one day and just knew it?

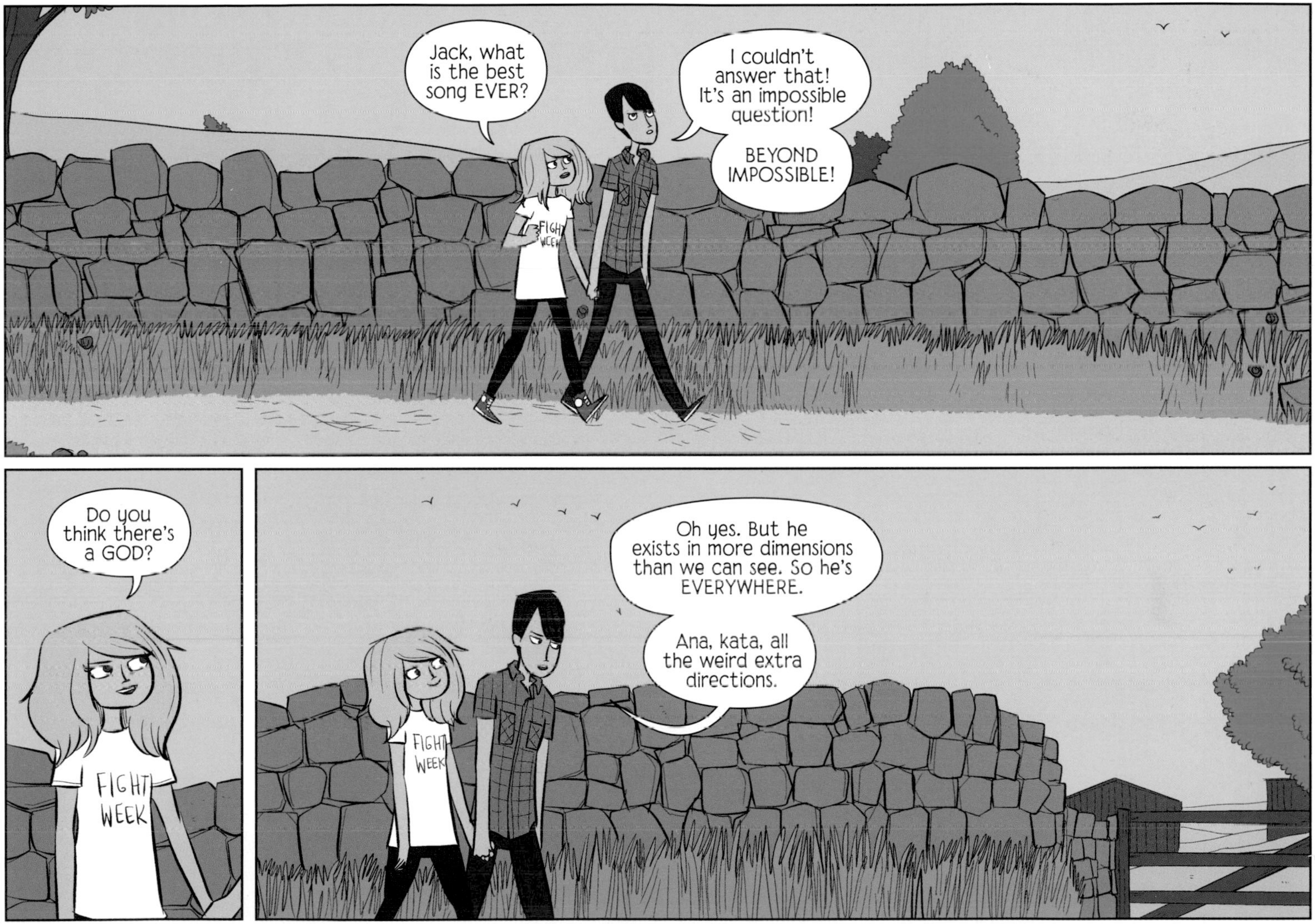
Jack, what is the best song EVER?
I couldn't answer that! It's an impossible question!
BEYOND IMPOSSIBLE!
FIGHT WEEK
Do you think there's a GOD?
FIGHT WEEK
Oh yes. But he exists in more dimensions than we can see. So he's EVERYWHERE.
Ana, kata, all the weird extra directions.
FIGHT WEEK

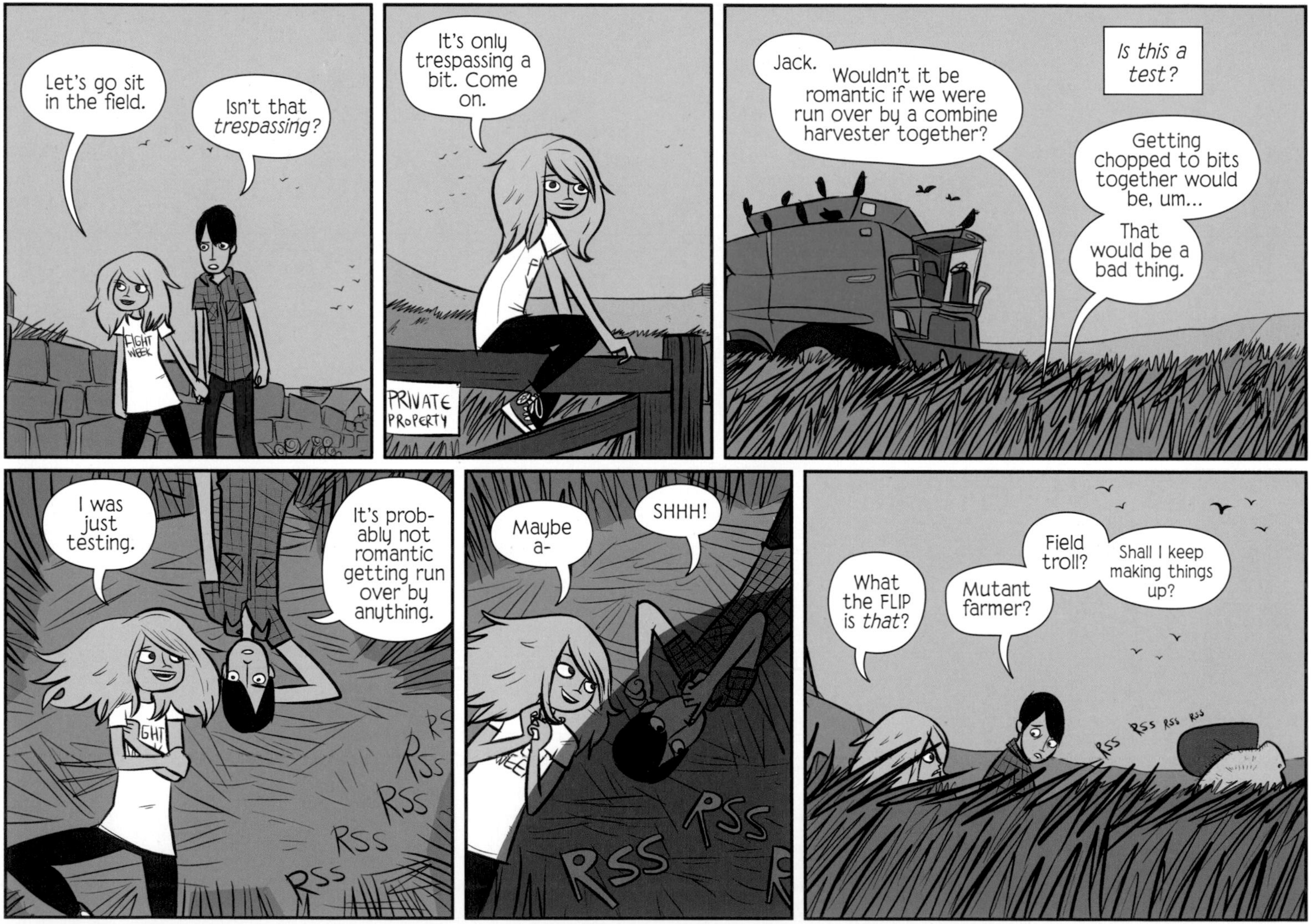

Let's go sit in the field.
Isn't that *trespassing*?
It's only trespassing a bit. Come on.
PRIVATE PROPERTY
Jack.
Wouldn't it be romantic if we were run over by a combine harvester together?
Is this a test?
Getting chopped to bits together would be, um...
That would be a bad thing.
I was just testing.
It's probably not romantic getting run over by anything.
RSS RSS RSS RSS
Maybe a-
SHHH!
RSS RSS
What the FLIP is *that*?
Mutant farmer?
Field troll?
Shall I keep making things up?
RSS RSS RSS RSS

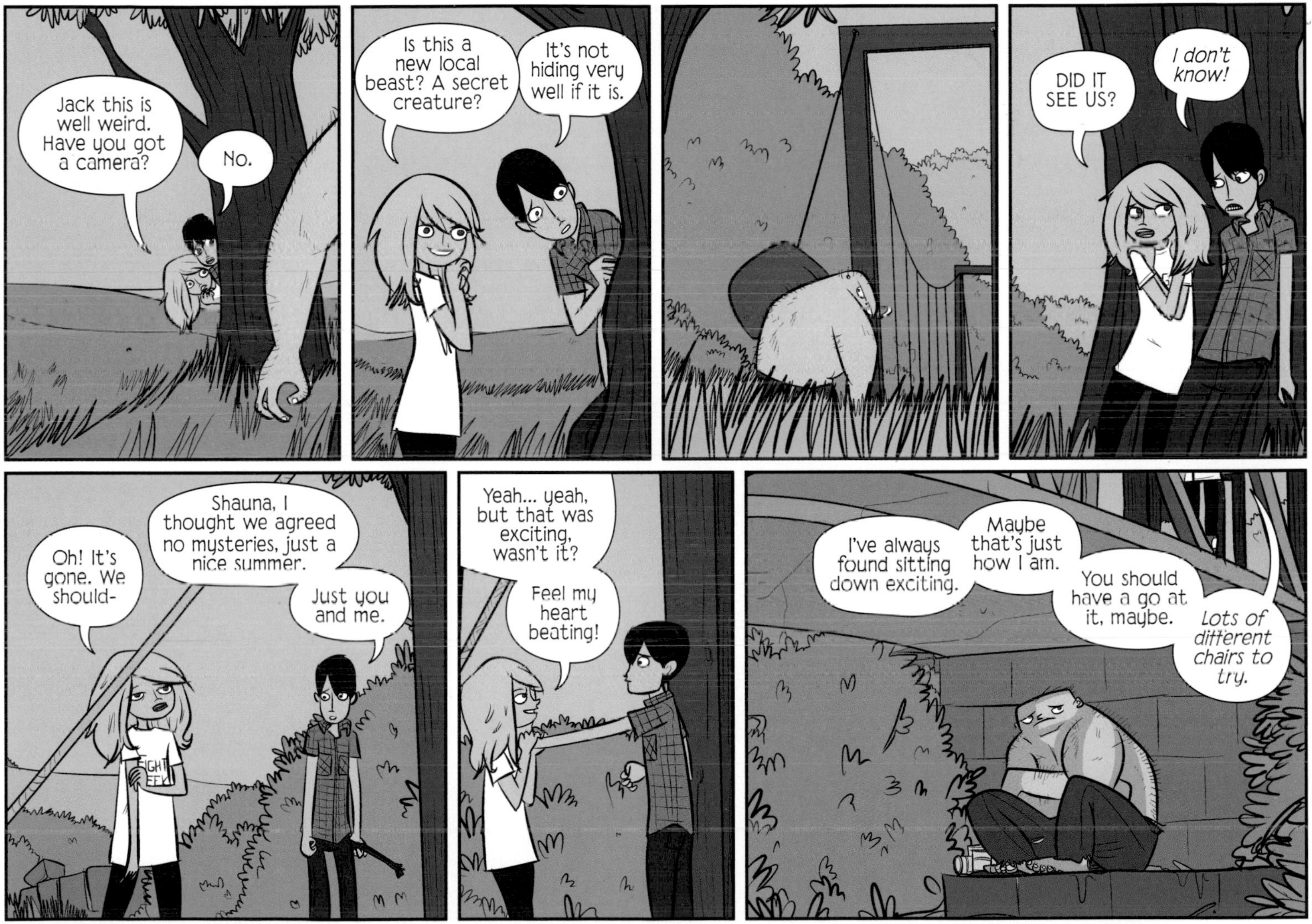
Jack this is well weird. Have you got a camera?
No.
Is this a new local beast? A secret creature?
It's not hiding very well if it is.
DID IT SEE US?
I don't know!
Oh! It's gone. We should-
Shauna, I thought we agreed no mysteries, just a nice summer.
Just you and me.
Yeah... yeah, but that was exciting, wasn't it?
Feel my heart beating!
I've always found sitting down exciting.
Maybe that's just how I am.
You should have a go at it, maybe.
Lots of different chairs to try.

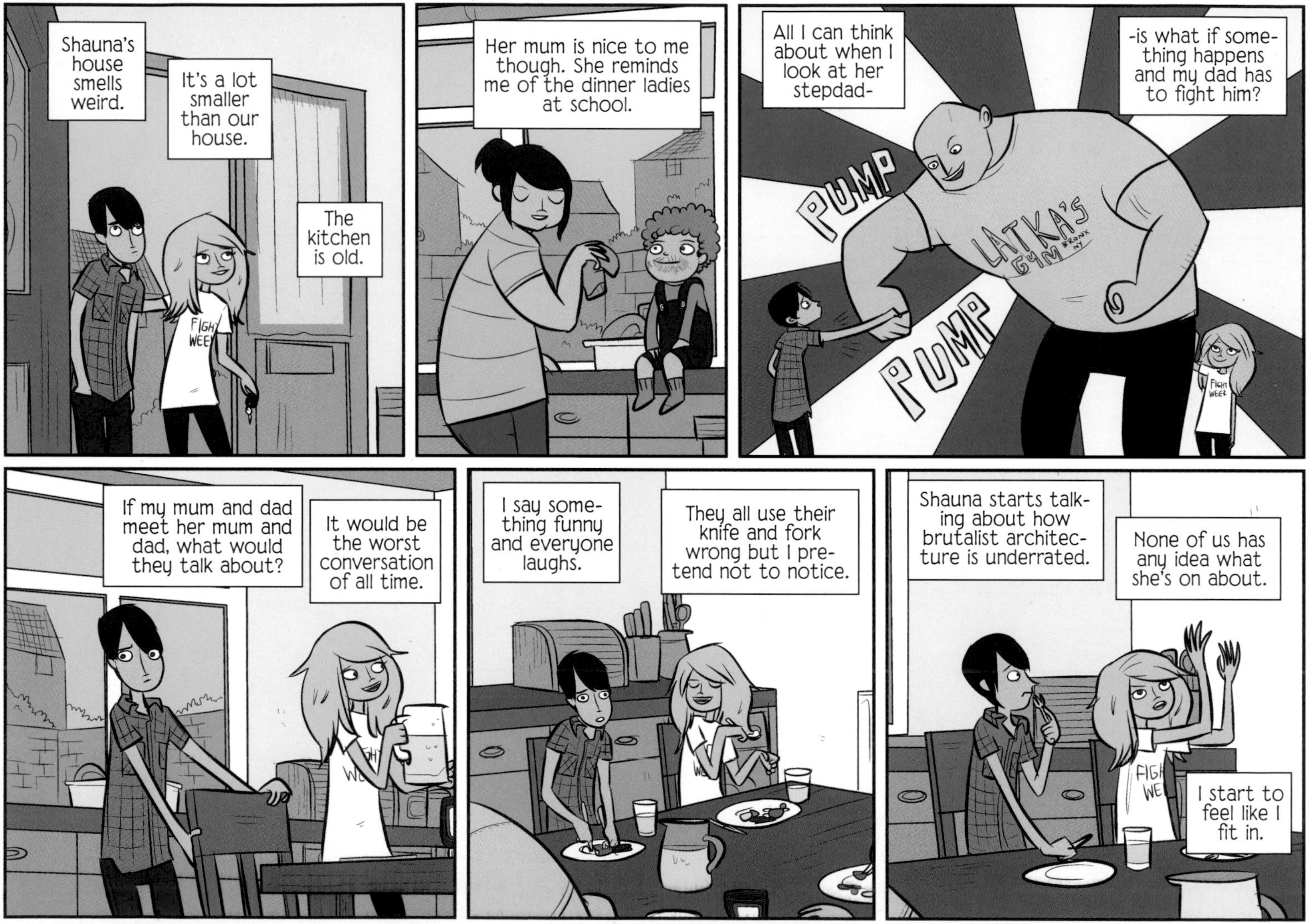
Shauna's house smells weird.
It's a lot smaller than our house.
The kitchen is old.
FIGHT WEEK
Her mum is nice to me though. She reminds me of the dinner ladies at school.
All I can think about when I look at her stepdad-
-is what if something happens and my dad has to fight him?
PUMP
PUMP
LATKA'S GYM BRONX NY
FIGHT WEEK
If my mum and dad meet her mum and dad, what would they talk about?
It would be the worst conversation of all time.
I say something funny and everyone laughs.
They all use their knife and fork wrong but I pretend not to notice.
Shauna starts talking about how brutalist architecture is underrated.
None of us has any idea what she's on about.
I start to feel like I fit in.

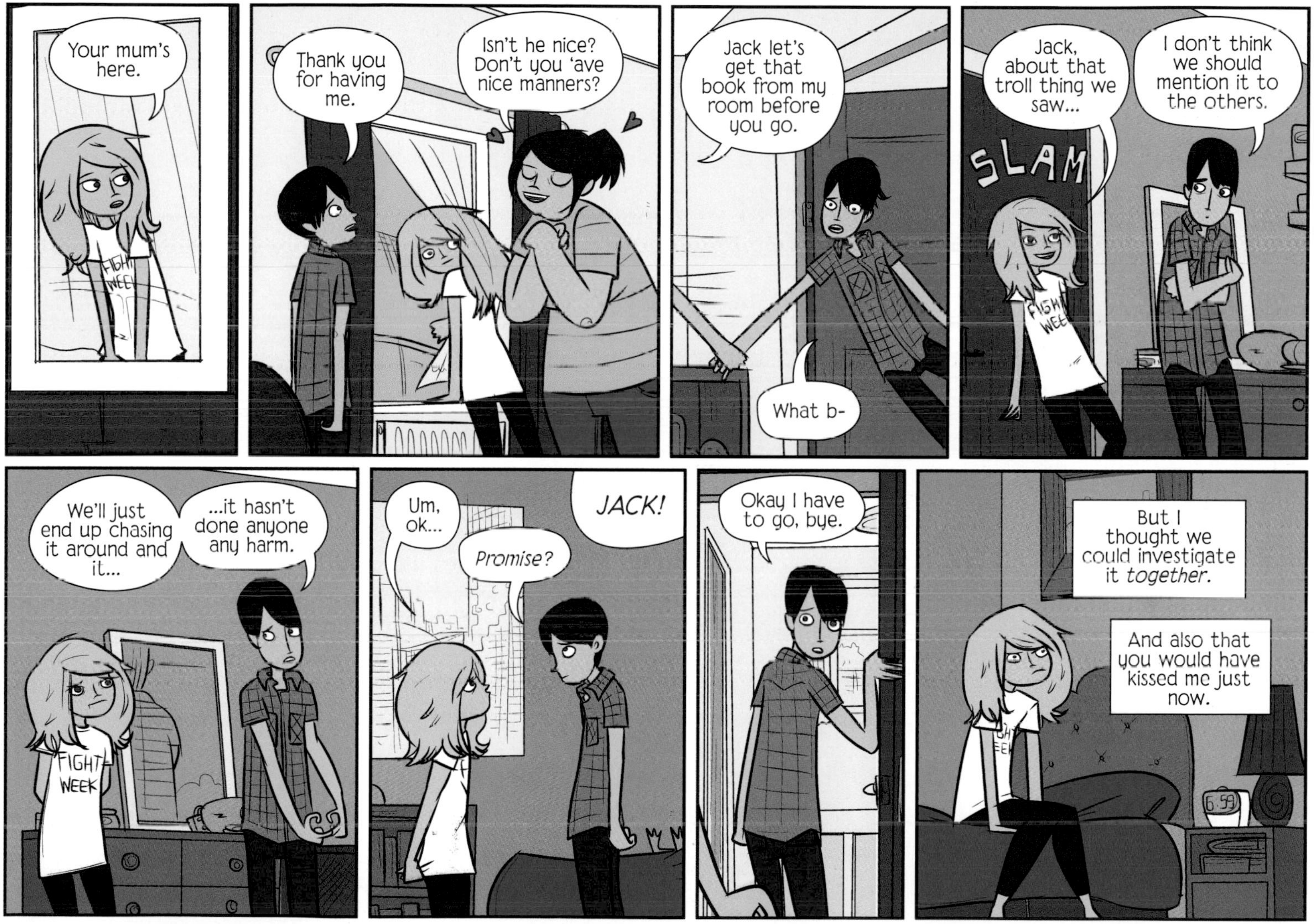

Your mum's here.
Thank you for having me.
Isn't he nice? Don't you 'ave nice manners?
Jack let's get that book from my room before you go.
What b-
SLAM
Jack, about that troll thing we saw...
I don't think we should mention it to the others.
We'll just end up chasing it around and it...
...it hasn't done anyone any harm.
Um, ok...
Promise?
JACK!
Okay I have to go, bye.
But I thought we could investigate it *together*.
And also that you would have kissed me just now.

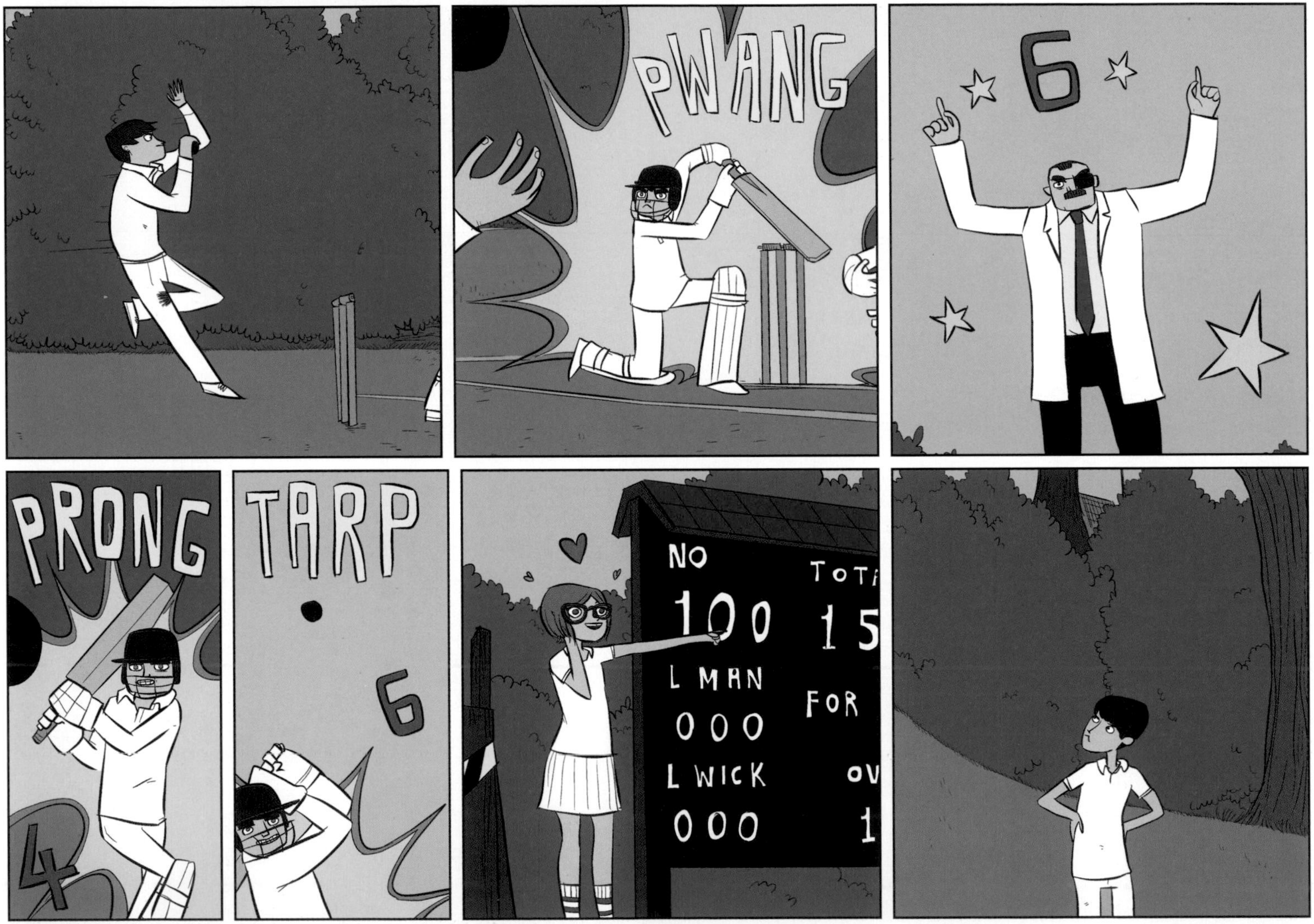
PWANG
6
PRONG
4
TARP
6
NO
100
L MAN
000
L WICK
000
TOTA
15
FOR
OV
1

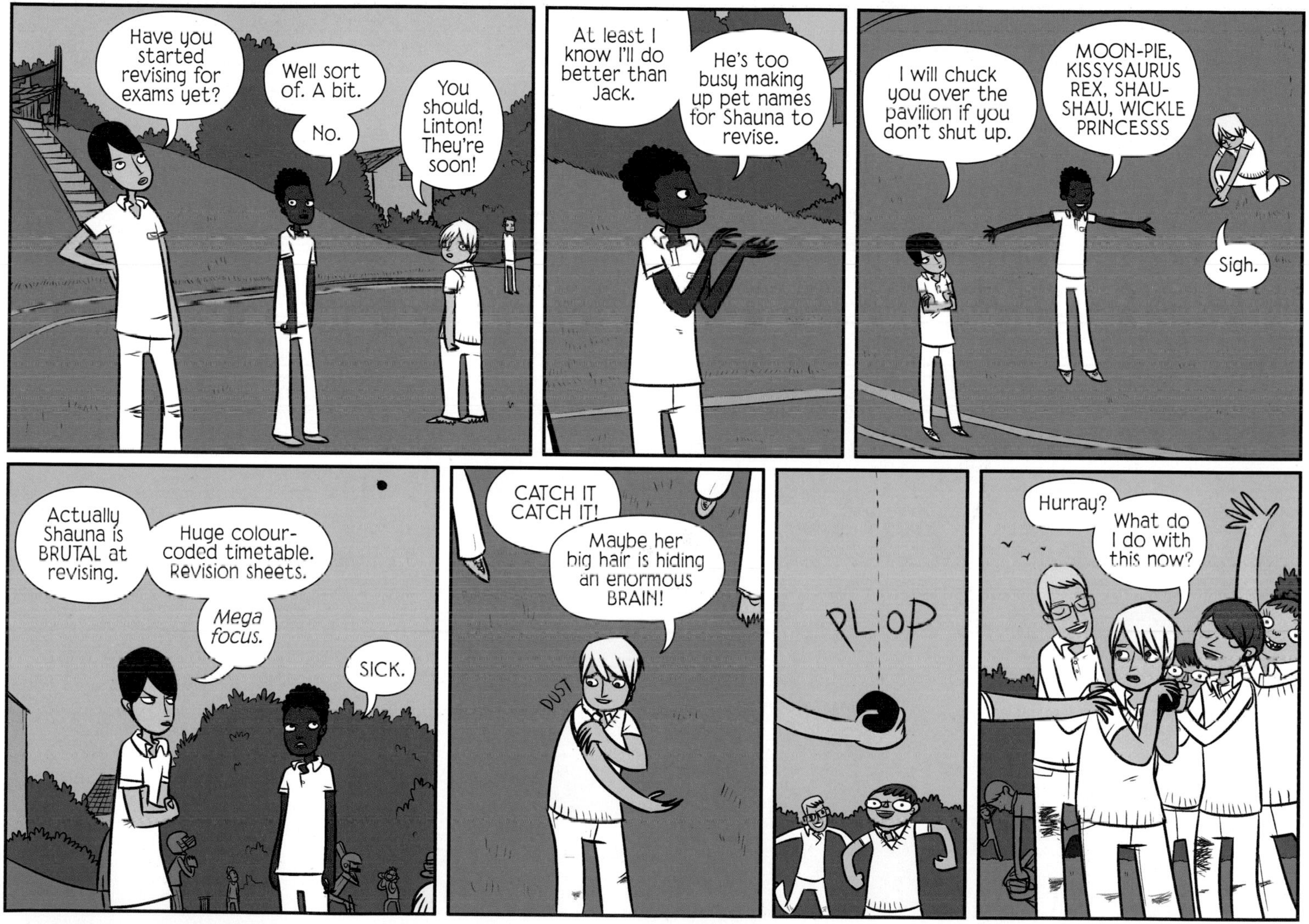
Have you started revising for exams yet?
Well sort of. A bit.
No.
You should, Linton! They're soon!
At least I know I'll do better than Jack.
He's too busy making up pet names for Shauna to revise.
I will chuck you over the pavilion if you don't shut up.
MOON-PIE, KISSYSAURUS REX, SHAU-SHAU, WICKLE PRINCESSS
Sigh.
Actually Shauna is BRUTAL at revising.
Huge colour-coded timetable. Revision sheets.
Mega focus.
SICK.
CATCH IT CATCH IT!
Maybe her big hair is hiding an enormous BRAIN!
DUST
PLOP
Hurray?
What do I do with this now?

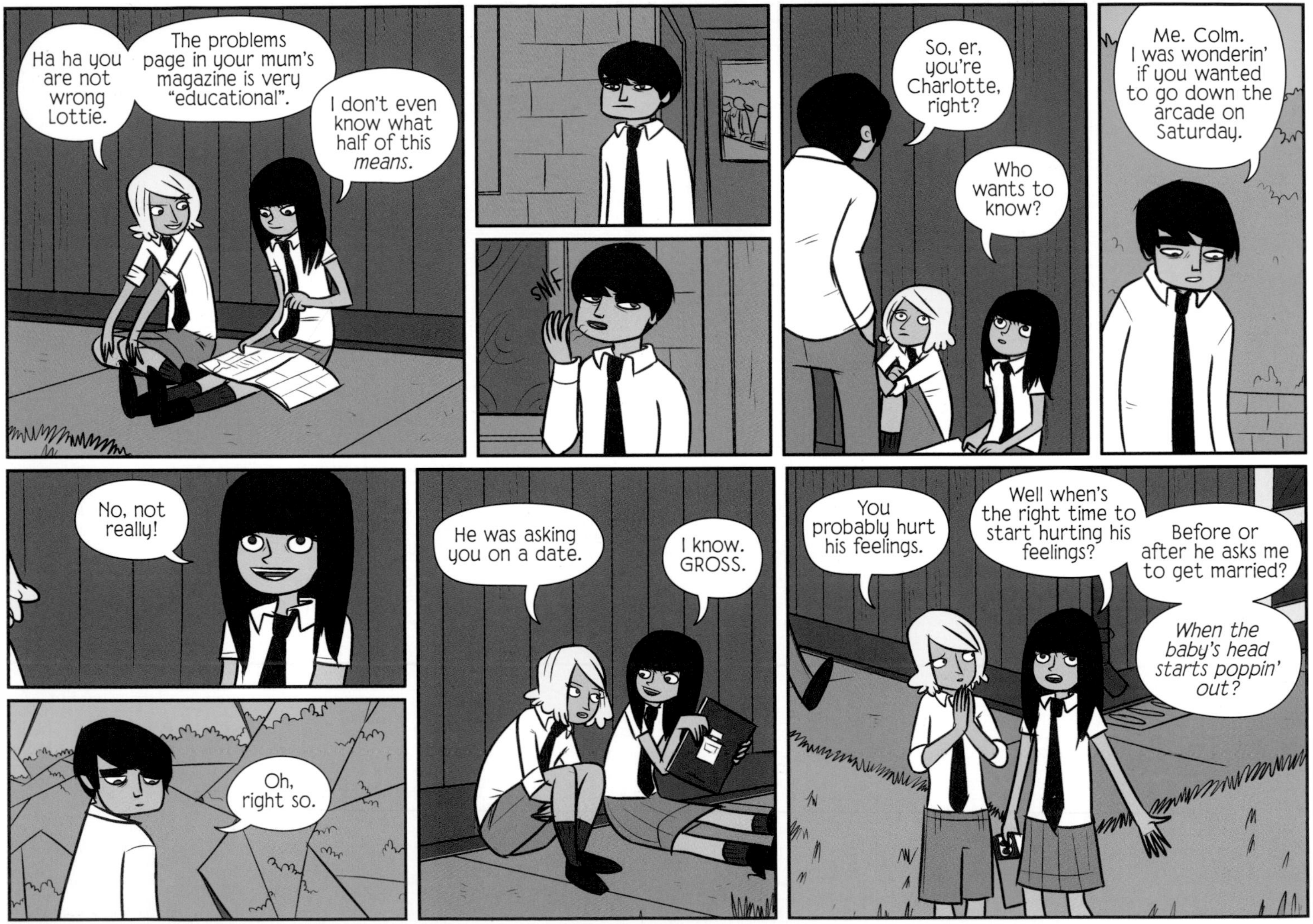
Ha ha you are not wrong Lottie.
The problems page in your mum's magazine is very "educational".
I don't even know what half of this *means.*
SNIF
So, er, you're Charlotte, right?
Who wants to know?
Me. Colm. I was wonderin' if you wanted to go down the arcade on Saturday.
No, not really!
Oh, right so.
He was asking you on a date.
I know. GROSS.
You probably hurt his feelings.
Well when's the right time to start hurting his feelings?
Before or after he asks me to get married?
When the baby's head starts poppin' out?

The Case of the Simple Soul

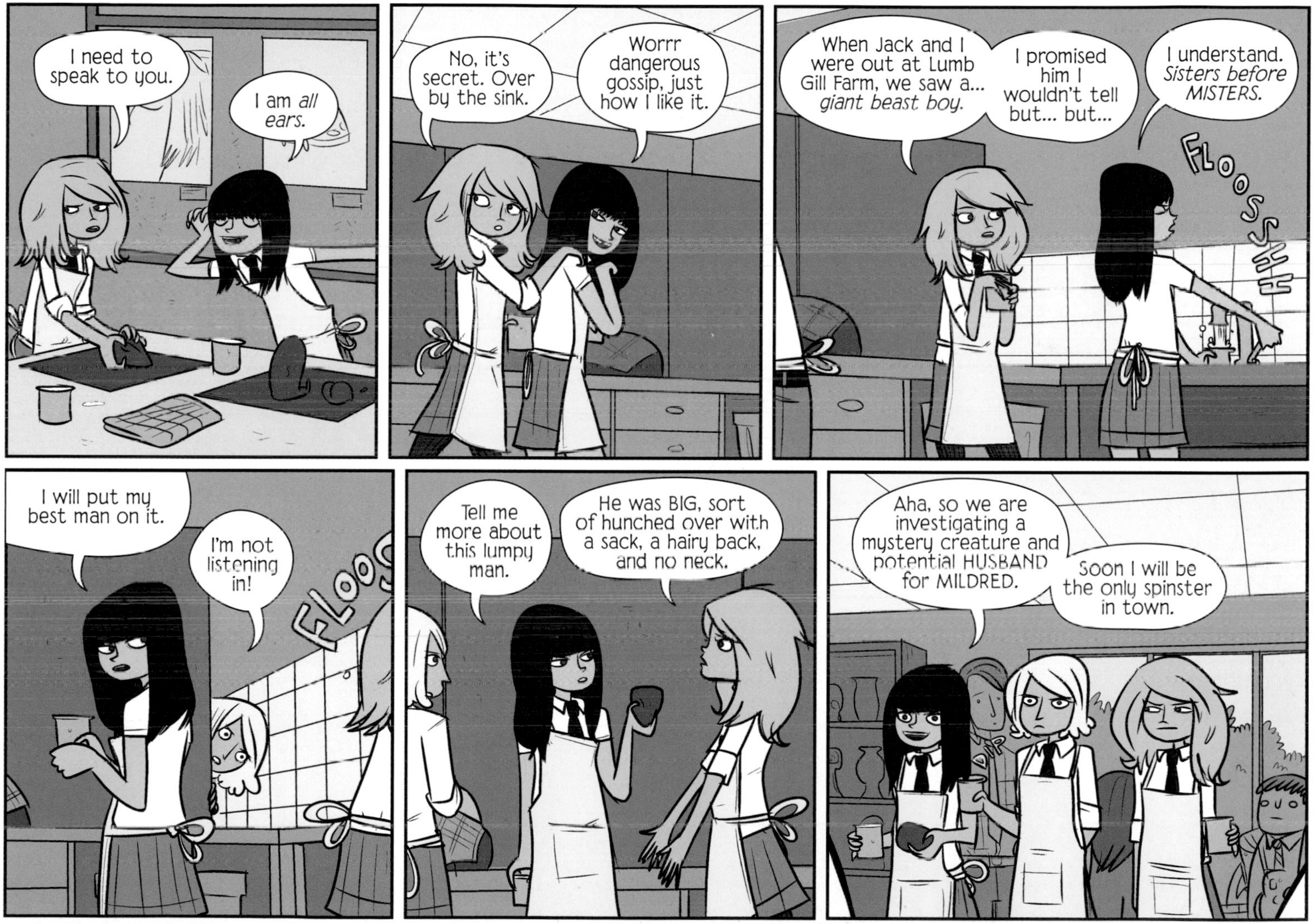
I need to speak to you.
I am *all* ears.
No, it's secret. Over by the sink.
Worrr dangerous gossip, just how I like it.
When Jack and I were out at Lumb Gill Farm, we saw a... *giant beast boy.*
I promised him I wouldn't tell but... but...
I understand. *Sisters before MISTERS.*
FLOOSSHH
I will put my best man on it.
I'm not listening in!
FLOOS
Tell me more about this lumpy man.
He was BIG, sort of hunched over with a sack, a hairy back, and no neck.
Aha, so we are investigating a mystery creature and potential HUSBAND for MILDRED.
Soon I will be the only spinster in town.

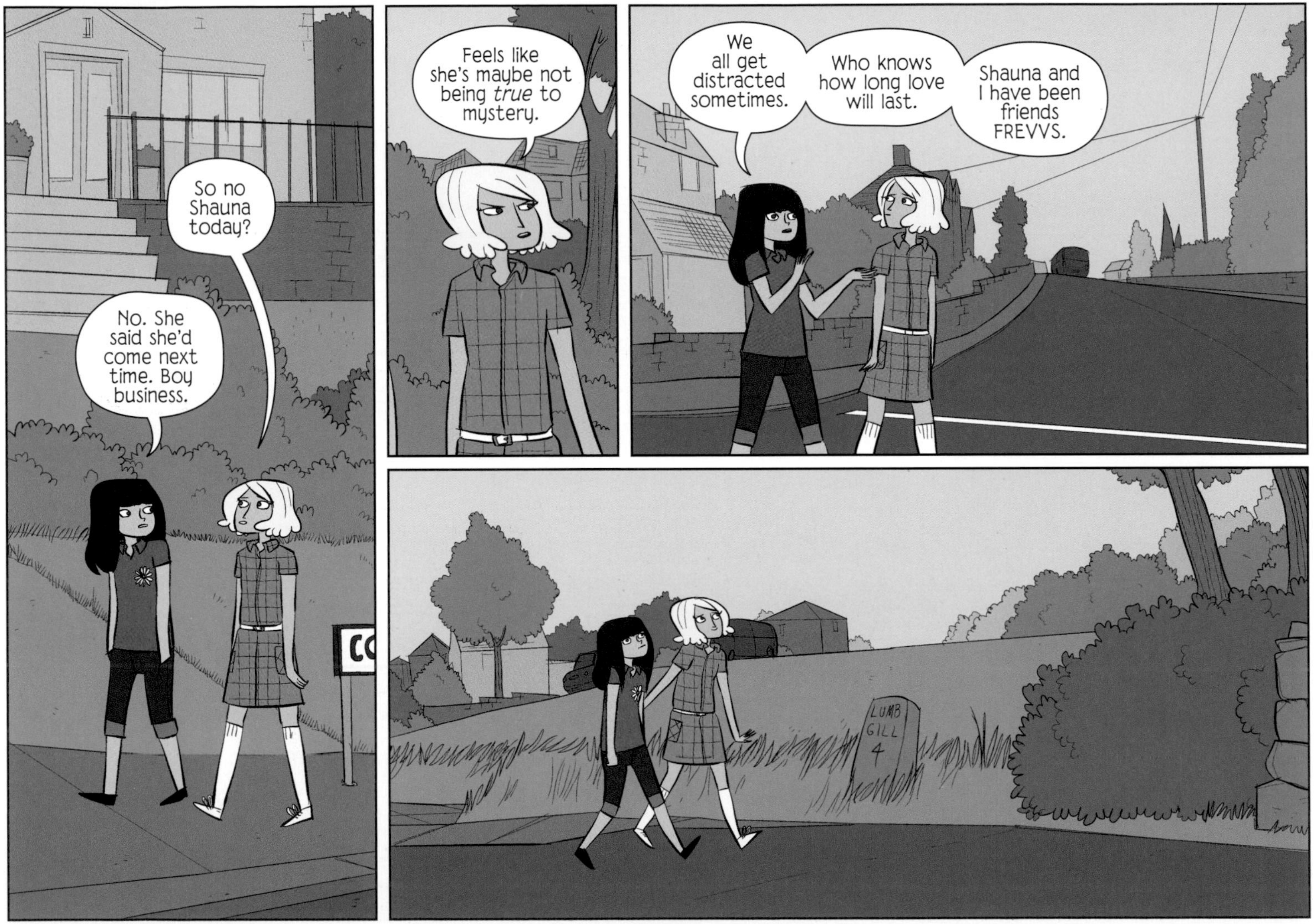
So no Shauna today?
No. She said she'd come next time. Boy business.
Feels like she's maybe not being *true* to mystery.
We all get distracted sometimes.
Who knows how long love will last.
Shauna and I have been friends FREVVS.
LUMB GILL 4

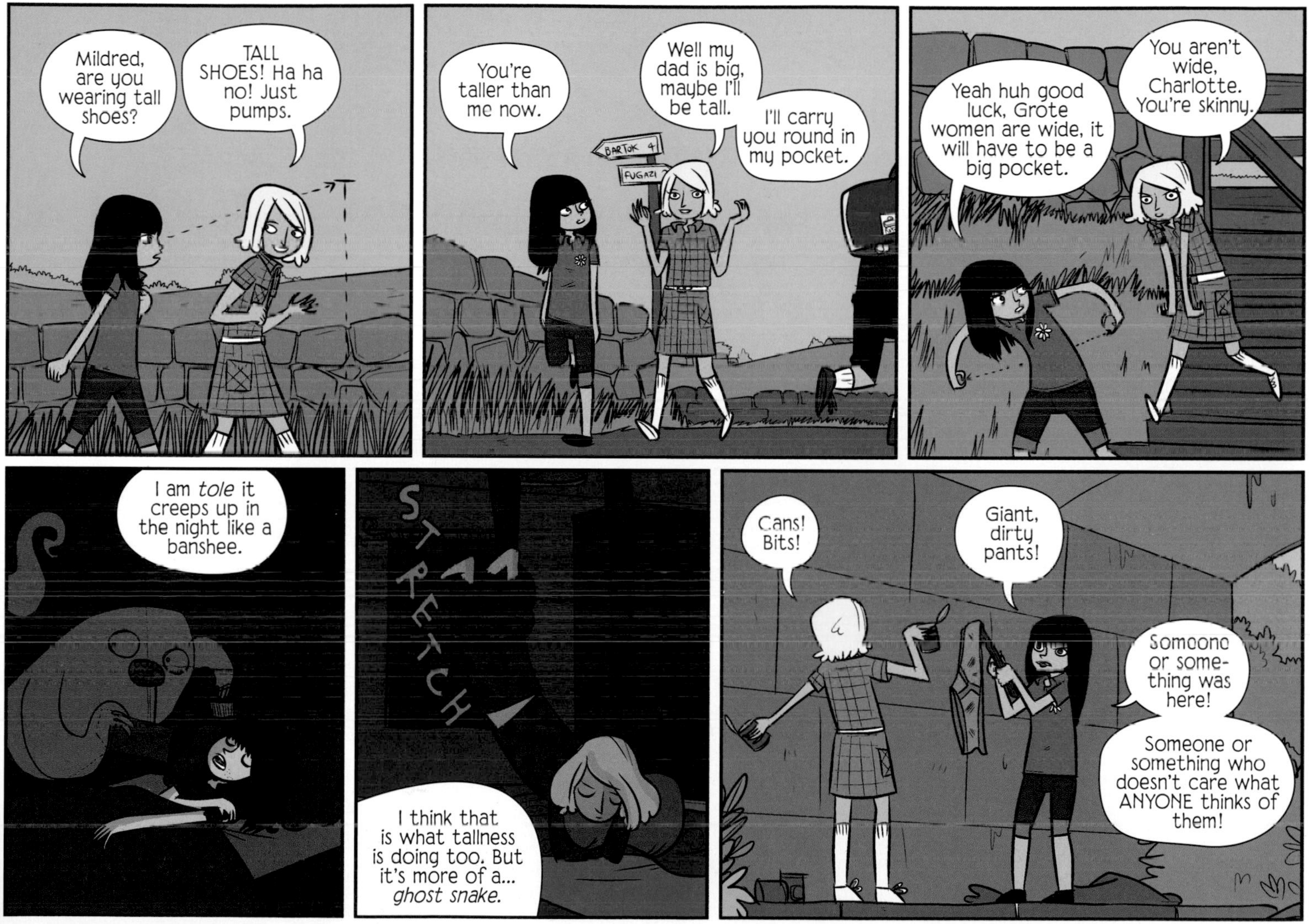

Mildred, are you wearing tall shoes?
TALL SHOES! Ha ha no! Just pumps.
You're taller than me now.
Well my dad is big, maybe I'll be tall.
I'll carry you round in my pocket.
BARTOK 4
FUGAZI
Yeah huh good luck, Grote women are wide, it will have to be a big pocket.
You aren't wide, Charlotte. You're skinny.
I am *tole* it creeps up in the night like a banshee.
STRETCH
I think that is what tallness is doing too. But it's more of a... *ghost snake.*
Cans! Bits!
Giant, dirty pants!
Someone or some-thing was here!
Someone or something who doesn't care what ANYONE thinks of them!

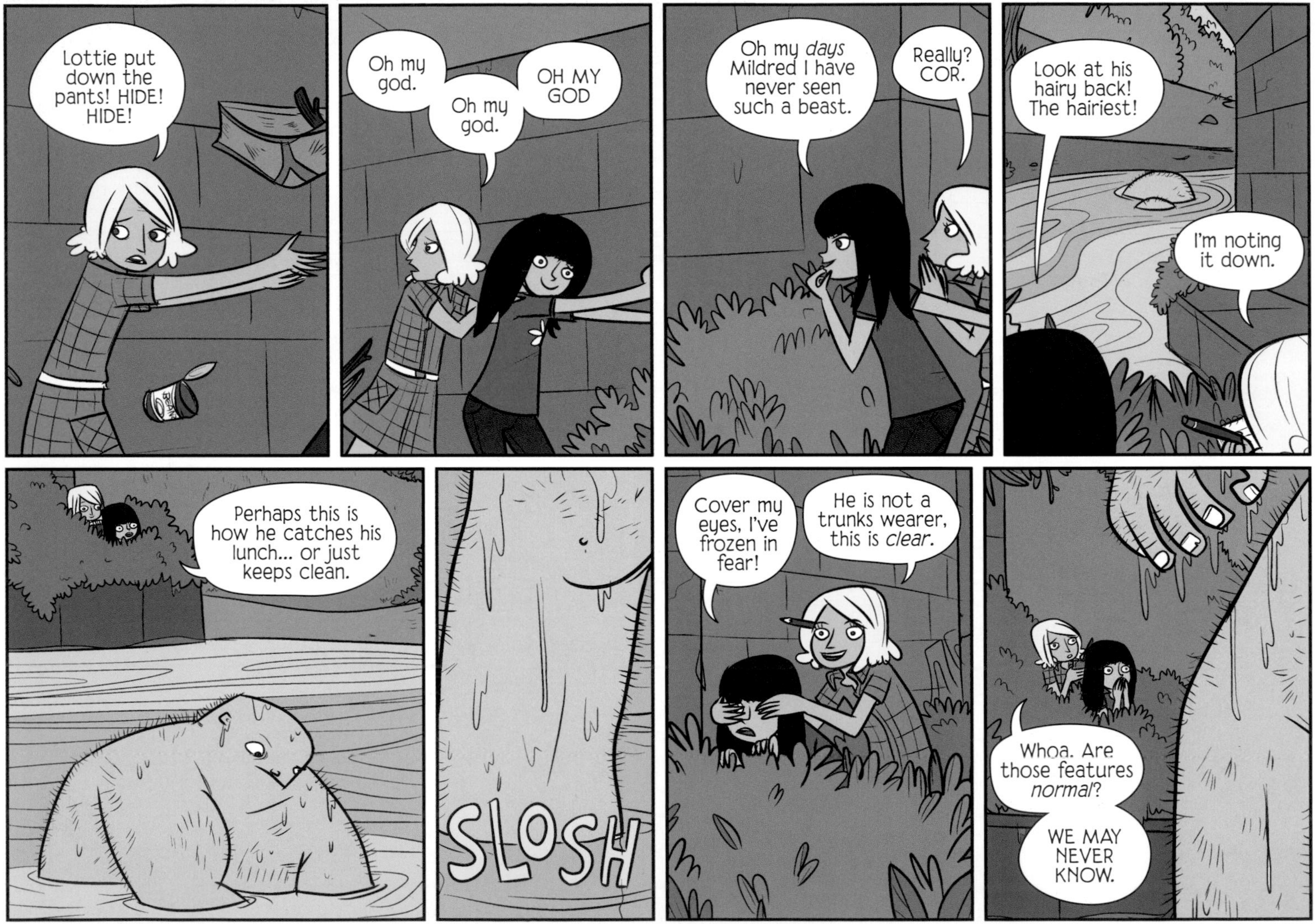

Lottie put down the pants! HIDE! HIDE!
Oh my god.
Oh my god.
OH MY GOD
Oh my *days* Mildred I have never seen such a beast.
Really? COR.
Look at his hairy back! The hairiest!
I'm noting it down.
Perhaps this is how he catches his lunch... or just keeps clean.
SLOSH
Cover my eyes, I've frozen in fear!
He is not a trunks wearer, this is *clear.*
Whoa. Are those features *normal*?
WE MAY NEVER KNOW.

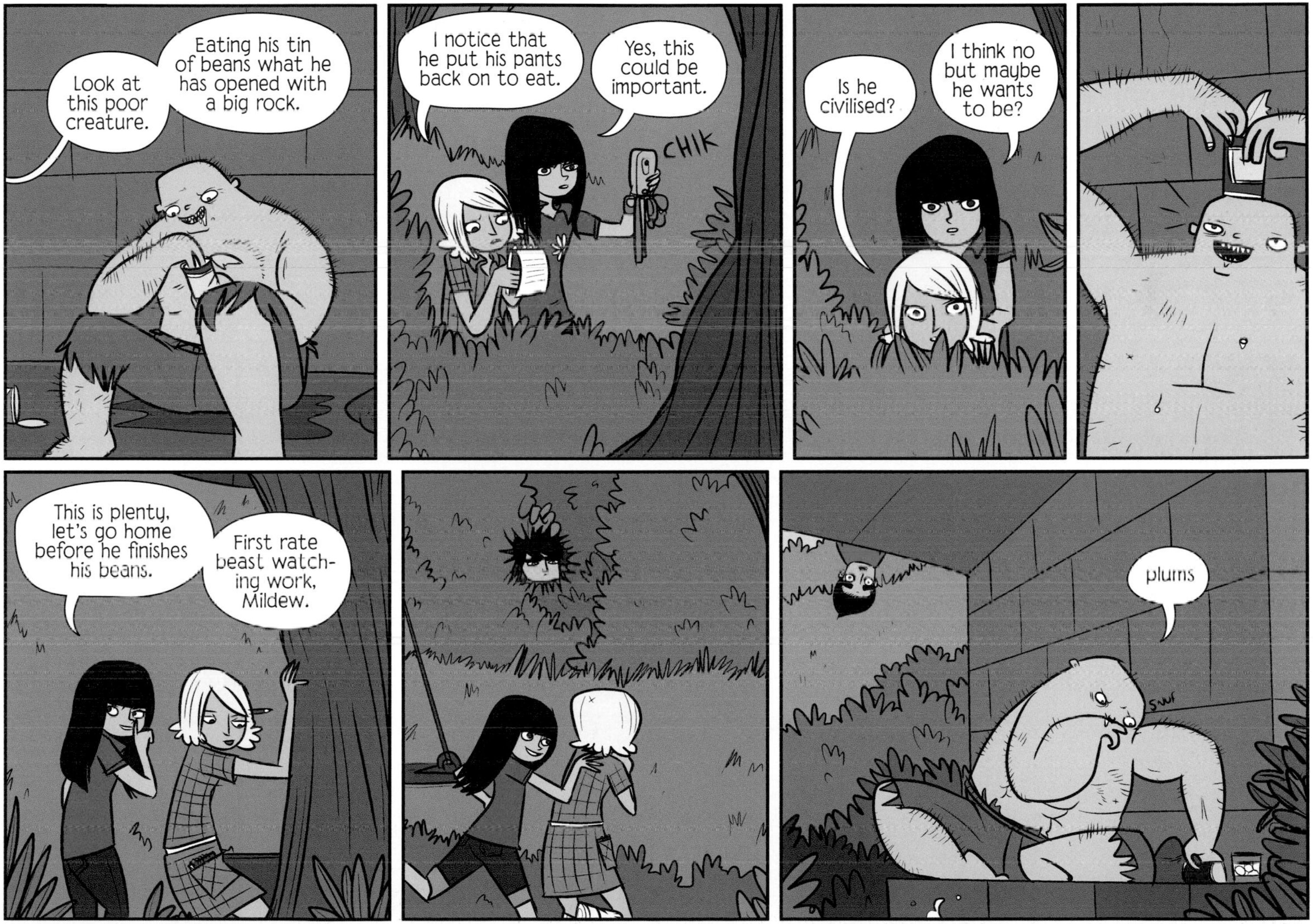

Look at this poor creature.
Eating his tin of beans what he has opened with a big rock.
I notice that he put his pants back on to eat.
Yes, this could be important.
CHIK
Is he civilised?
I think no but maybe he wants to be?
This is plenty, let's go home before he finishes his beans.
First rate beast watching work, Mildew.
plums

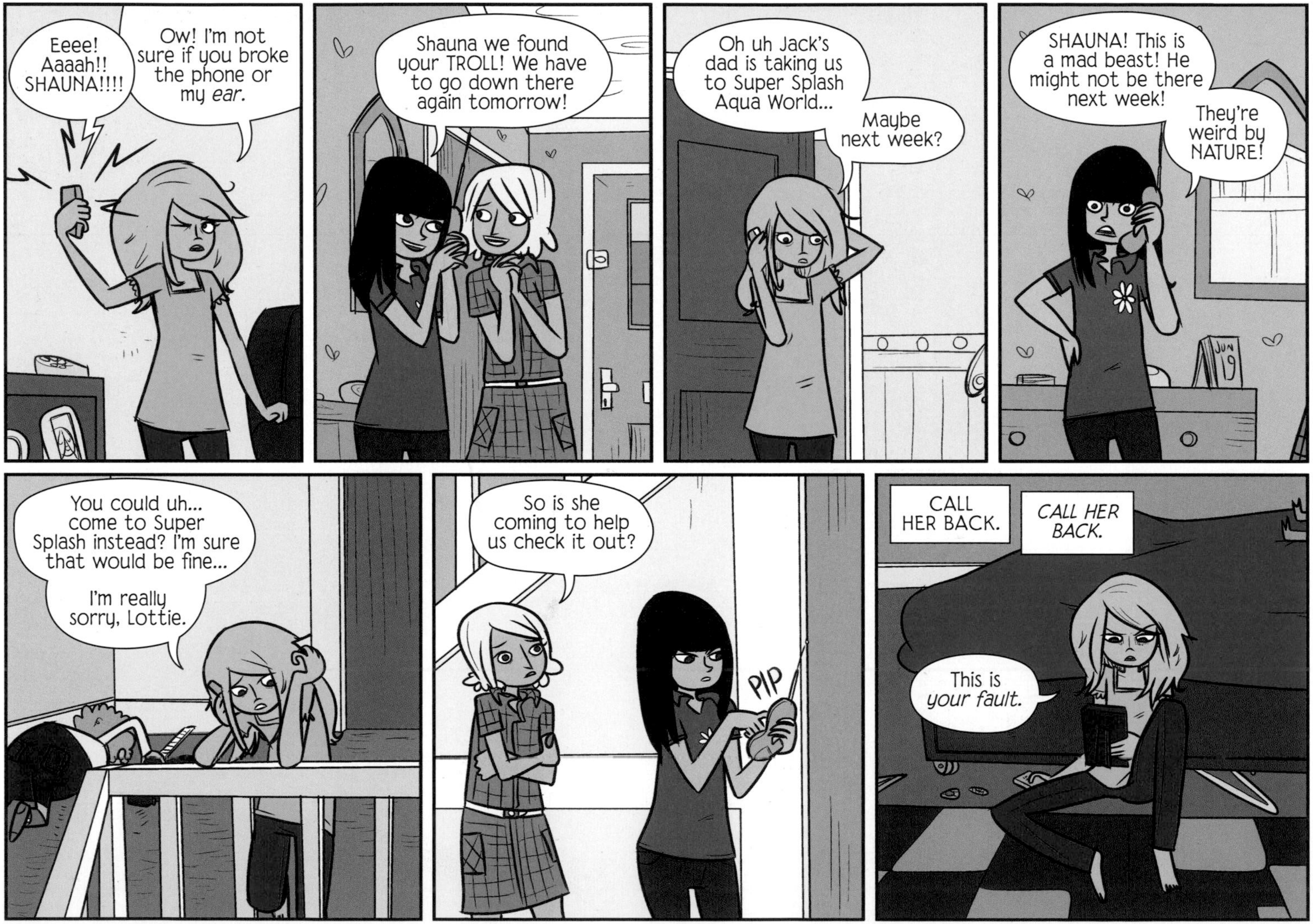
Eeee! Aaaah!! SHAUNA!!!!
Ow! I'm not sure if you broke the phone or my *ear.*
Shauna we found your TROLL! We have to go down there again tomorrow!
Oh uh Jack's dad is taking us to Super Splash Aqua World...
Maybe next week?
SHAUNA! This is a mad beast! He might not be there next week!
They're weird by NATURE!
JUN 19
You could uh... come to Super Splash instead? I'm sure that would be fine...
I'm really sorry, Lottie.
So is she coming to help us check it out?
PIP
CALL HER BACK.
CALL HER BACK.
This is *your fault.*

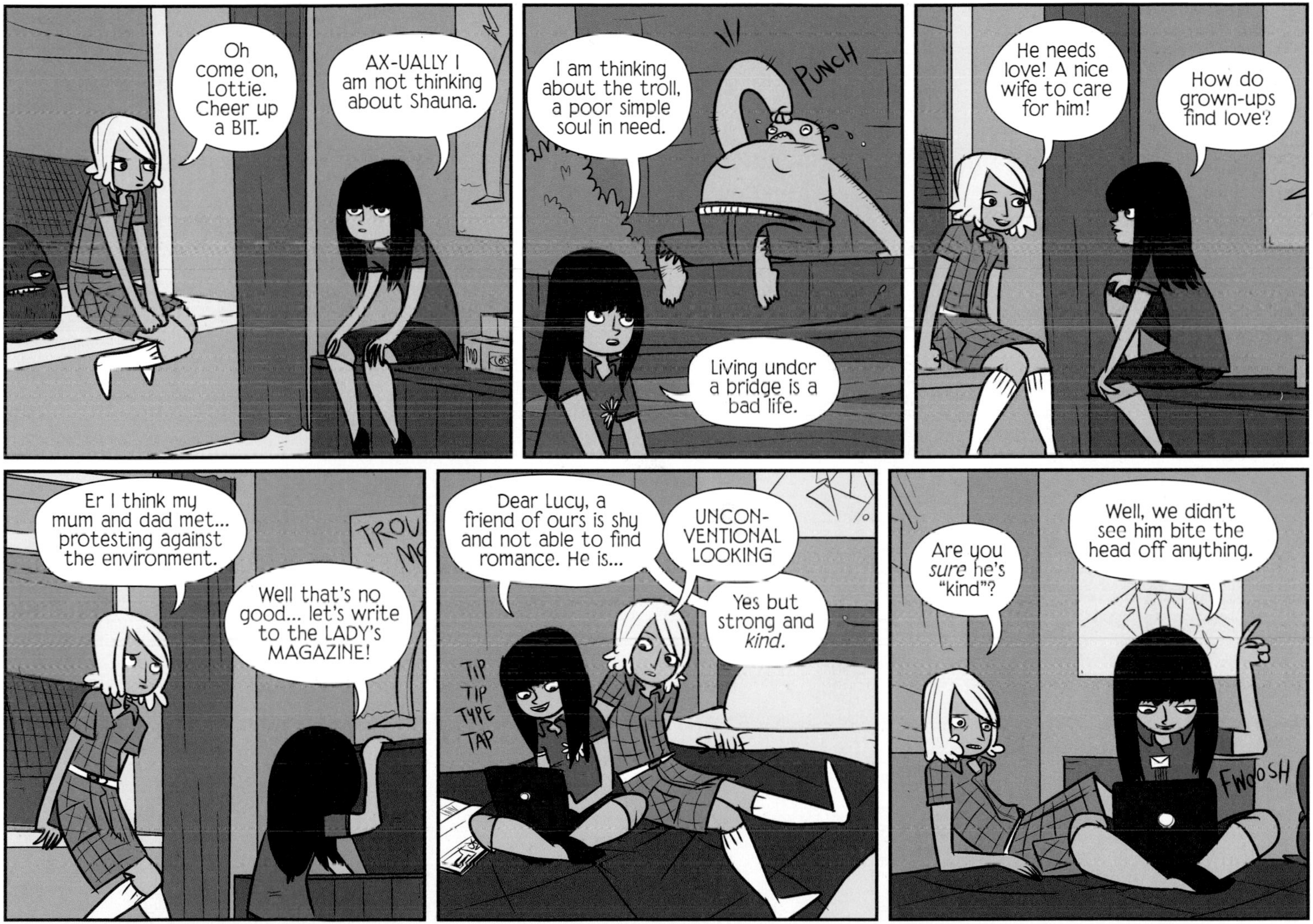
Oh come on, Lottie. Cheer up a BIT.
AX-UALLY I am not thinking about Shauna.
I am thinking about the troll, a poor simple soul in need.
PUNCH
Living under a bridge is a bad life.
He needs love! A nice wife to care for him!
How do grown-ups find love?
Er I think my mum and dad met... protesting against the environment.
Well that's no good... let's write to the LADY's MAGAZINE!
Dear Lucy, a friend of ours is shy and not able to find romance. He is...
UNCON-VENTIONAL LOOKING
Yes but strong and *kind.*
TIP TIP TYPE TAP
SHUF
Are you *sure* he's "kind"?
Well, we didn't see him bite the head off anything.
FWOOSH

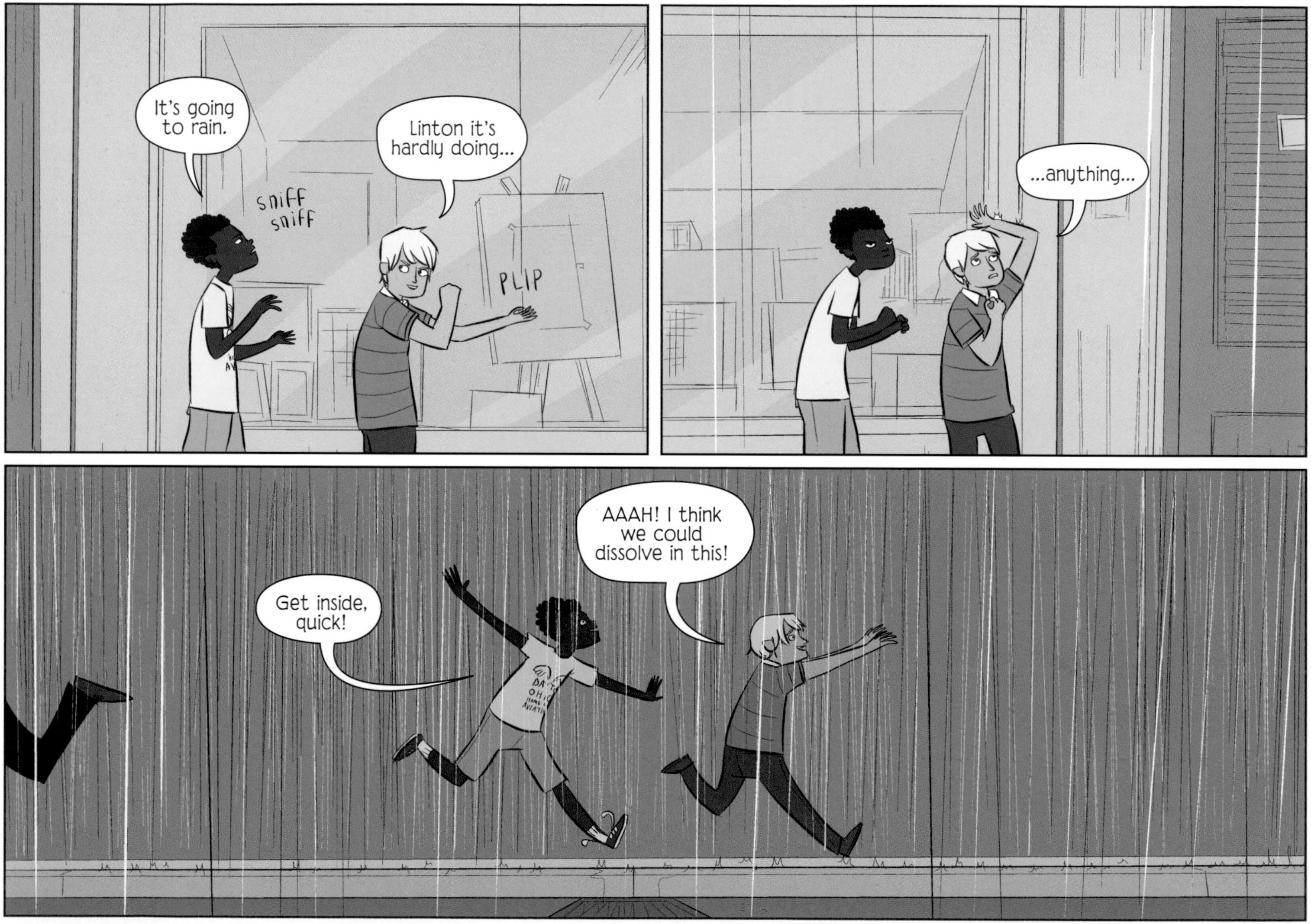
It's going to rain.
sniff sniff
Linton it's hardly doing...
PLIP
...anything...
AAAH! I think we could dissolve in this!
Get inside, quick!

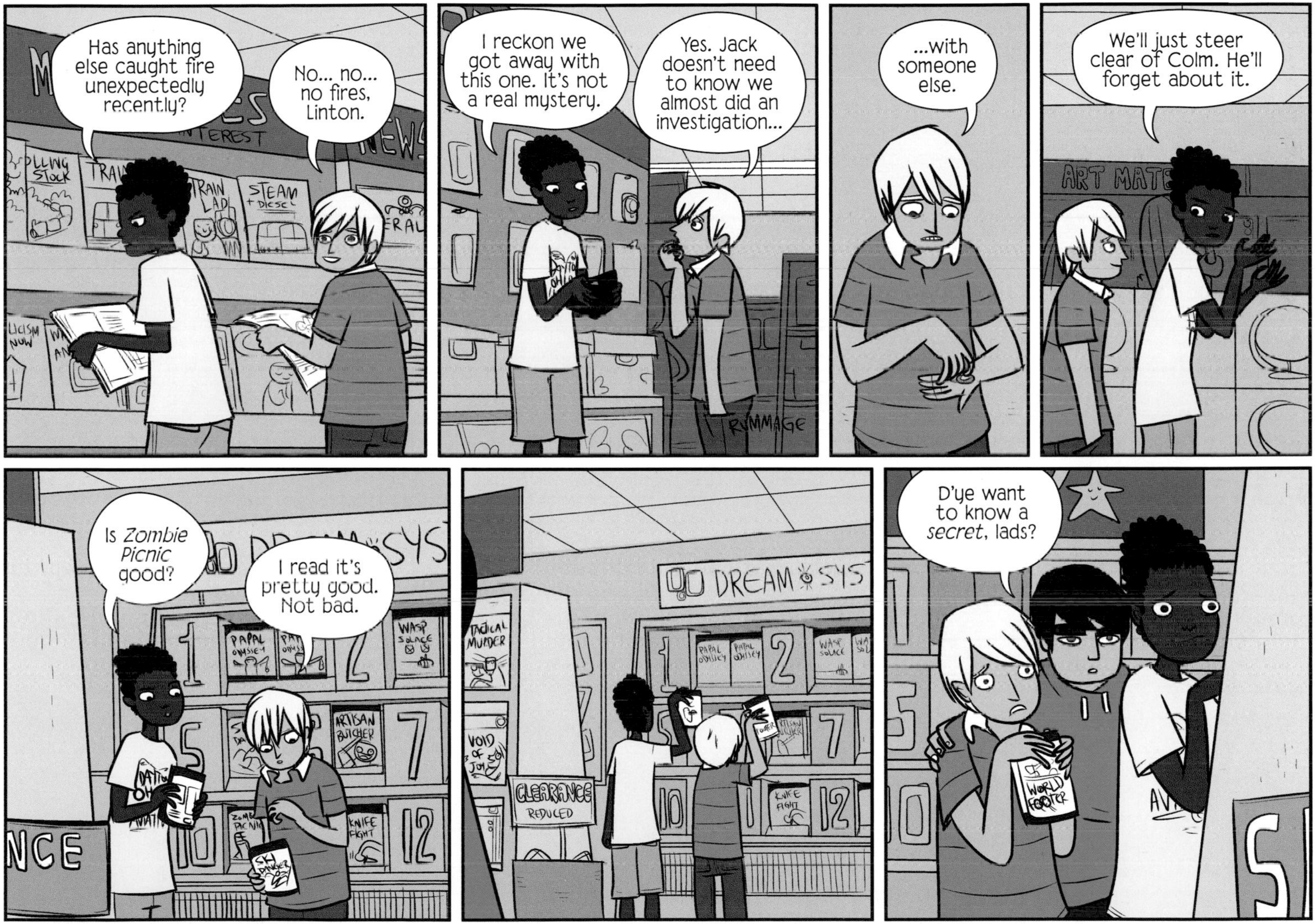
Has anything else caught fire unexpectedly recently?
No... no... no fires, Linton.
I reckon we got away with this one. It's not a real mystery.
Yes. Jack doesn't need to know we almost did an investigation...
RUMMAGE
...with someone else.
We'll just steer clear of Colm. He'll forget about it.
Is *Zombie Picnic* good?
I read it's pretty good. Not bad.
D'ye want to know a *secret*, lads?

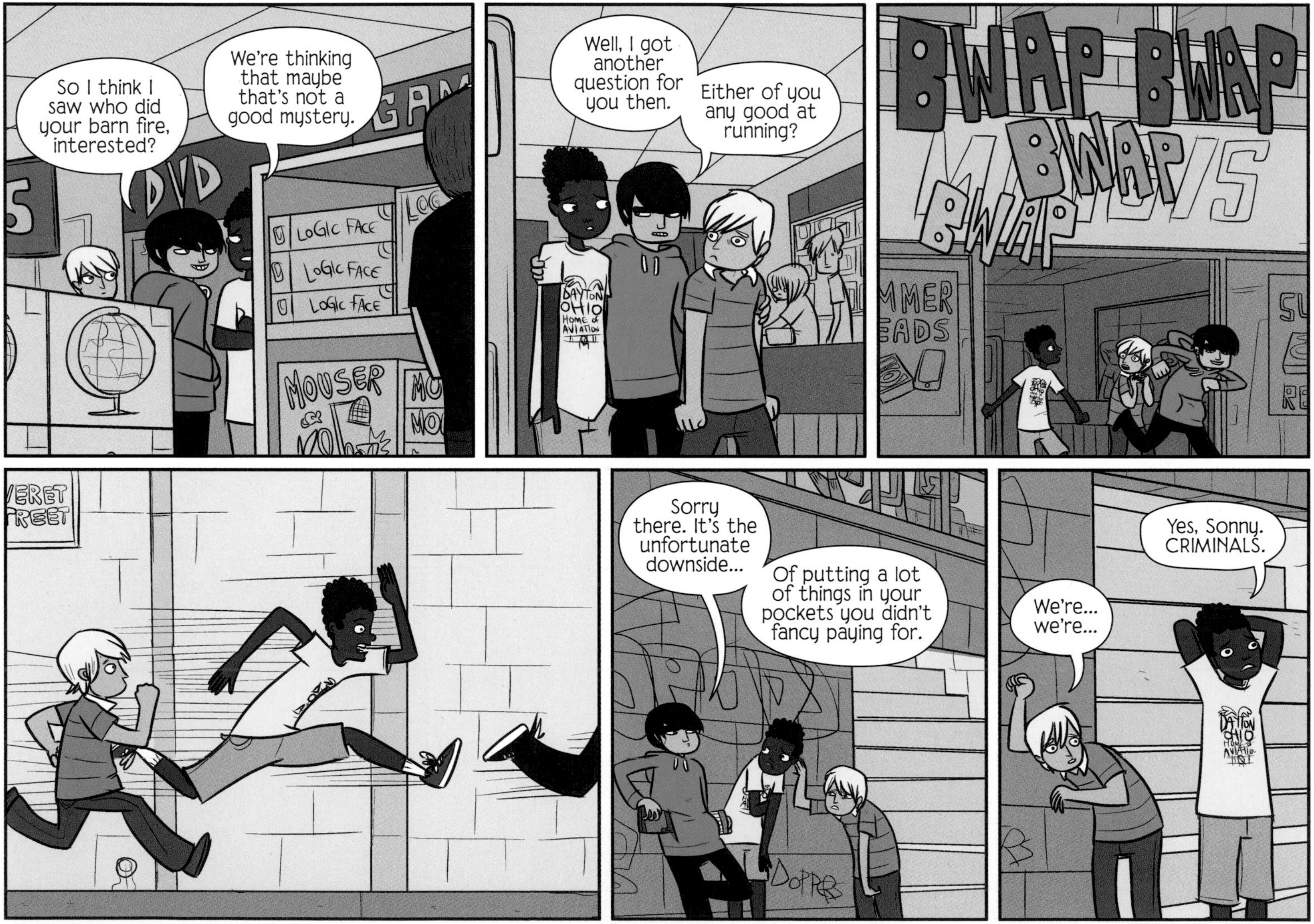

So I think I saw who did your barn fire, interested?
We're thinking that maybe that's not a good mystery.
DVD
LOGIC FACE
LOGIC FACE
LOGIC FACE
MOUSER
Well, I got another question for you then.
Either of you any good at running?
DAYTON OHIO HOME OF AVIATION
BWAP BWAP
BWAP
BWAP
Sorry there. It's the unfortunate downside...
Of putting a lot of things in your pockets you didn't fancy paying for.
We're... we're...
Yes, Sonny. CRIMINALS.

The Case of the Simple Soul

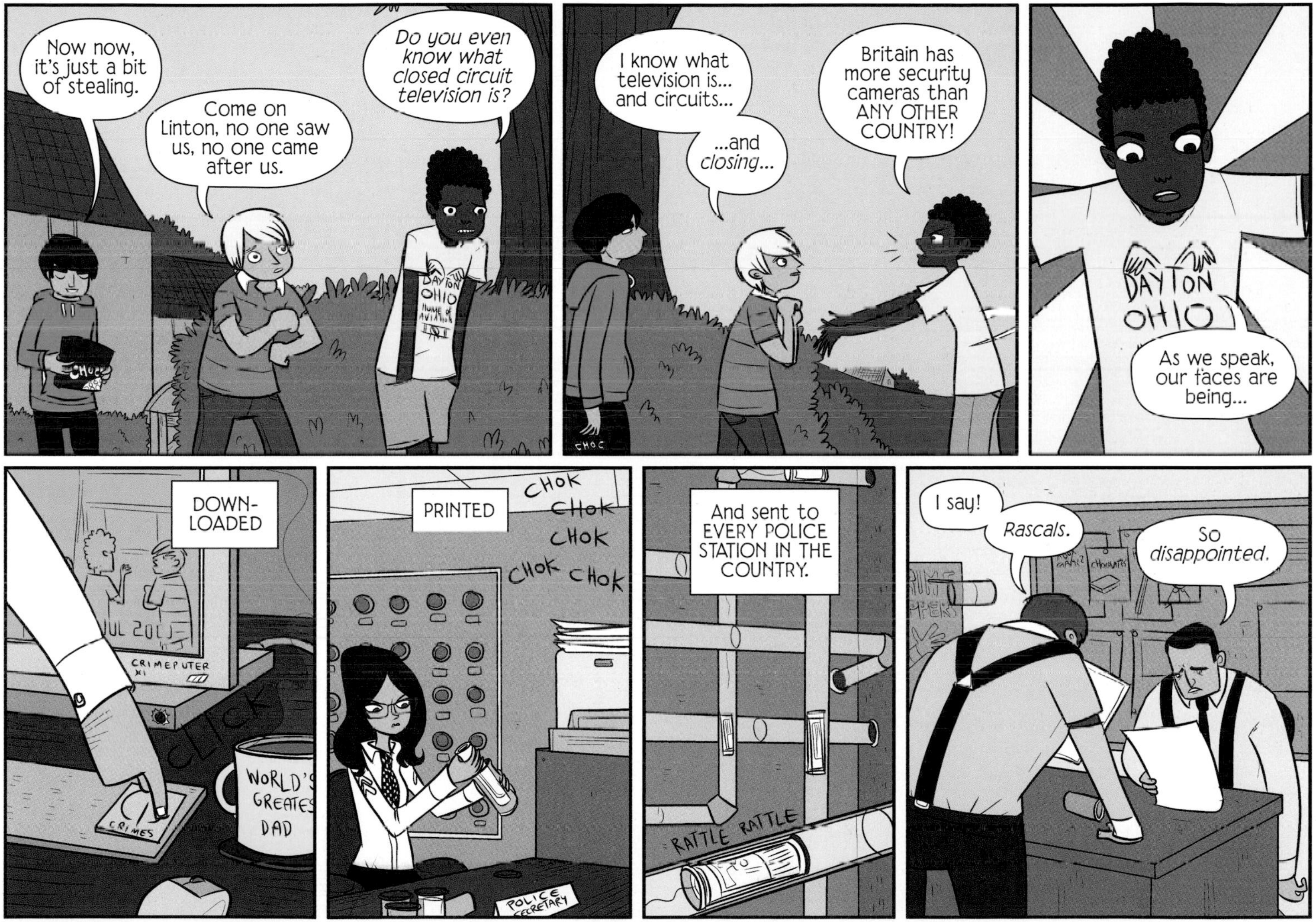

Now now, it's just a bit of stealing.
Come on Linton, no one saw us, no one came after us.
Do you even know what closed circuit television is?
DAYTON OHIO
CHOC
I know what television is... and circuits...
...and *closing*...
Britain has more security cameras than ANY OTHER COUNTRY!
CHOC
DAYTON OHIO
As we speak, our faces are being...
DOWN-LOADED
CRIMEPUTER XI
CLICK
CRIMES
WORLD'S GREATEST DAD
PRINTED
CHOK CHOK CHOK CHOK CHOK
POLICE SECRETARY
And sent to EVERY POLICE STATION IN THE COUNTRY.
RATTLE RATTLE
I say!
Rascals.
So *disappointed.*

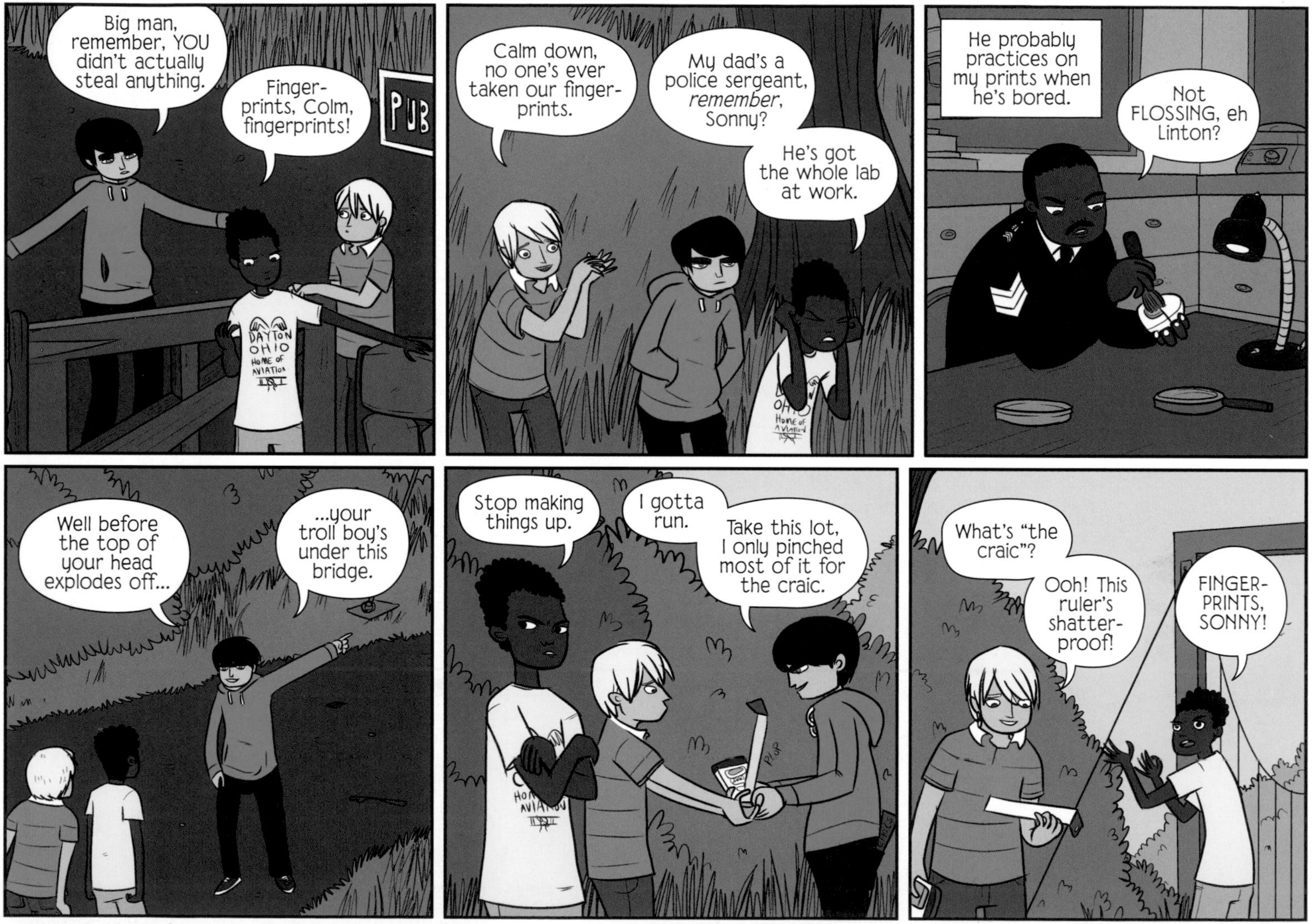
Big man, remember, YOU didn't actually steal anything.
Finger-prints, Colm, fingerprints!
PUB
DAYTON OHIO HOME OF AVIATION
Calm down, no one's ever taken our finger-prints.
My dad's a police sergeant, *remember*, Sonny?
He's got the whole lab at work.
He probably practices on my prints when he's bored.
Not FLOSSING, eh Linton?
Well before the top of your head explodes off...
...your troll boy's under this bridge.
Stop making things up.
I gotta run.
Take this lot, I only pinched most of it for the craic.
What's "the craic"?
Ooh! This ruler's shatter-proof!
FINGER-PRINTS, SONNY!

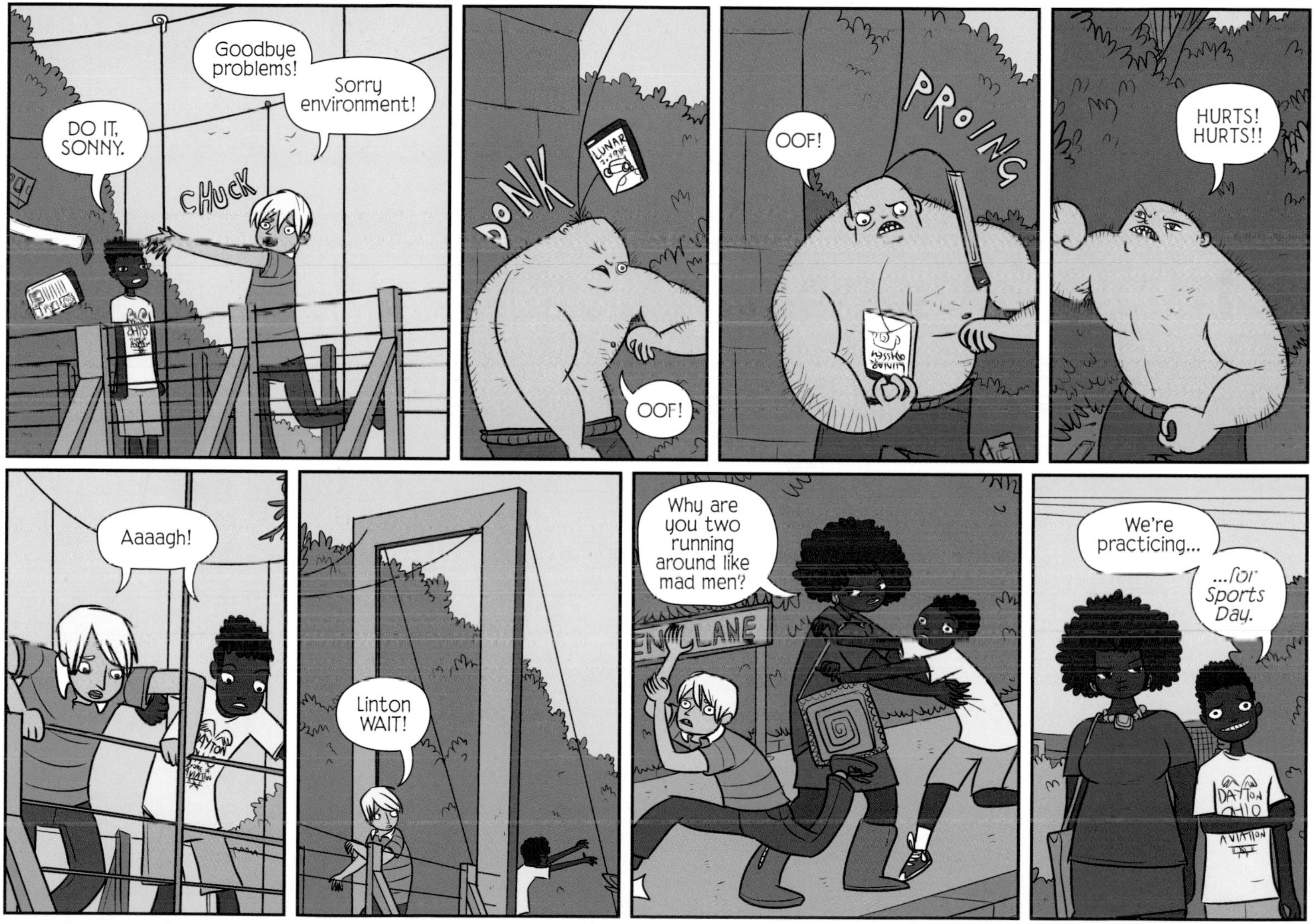
Goodbye problems!
Sorry environment!
DO IT, SONNY.
CHUCK
DONK
OOF!
OOF!
PROING
HURTS! HURTS!!
Aaaagh!
Linton WAIT!
Why are you two running around like mad men?
LANE
We're practicing...
...for Sports Day.

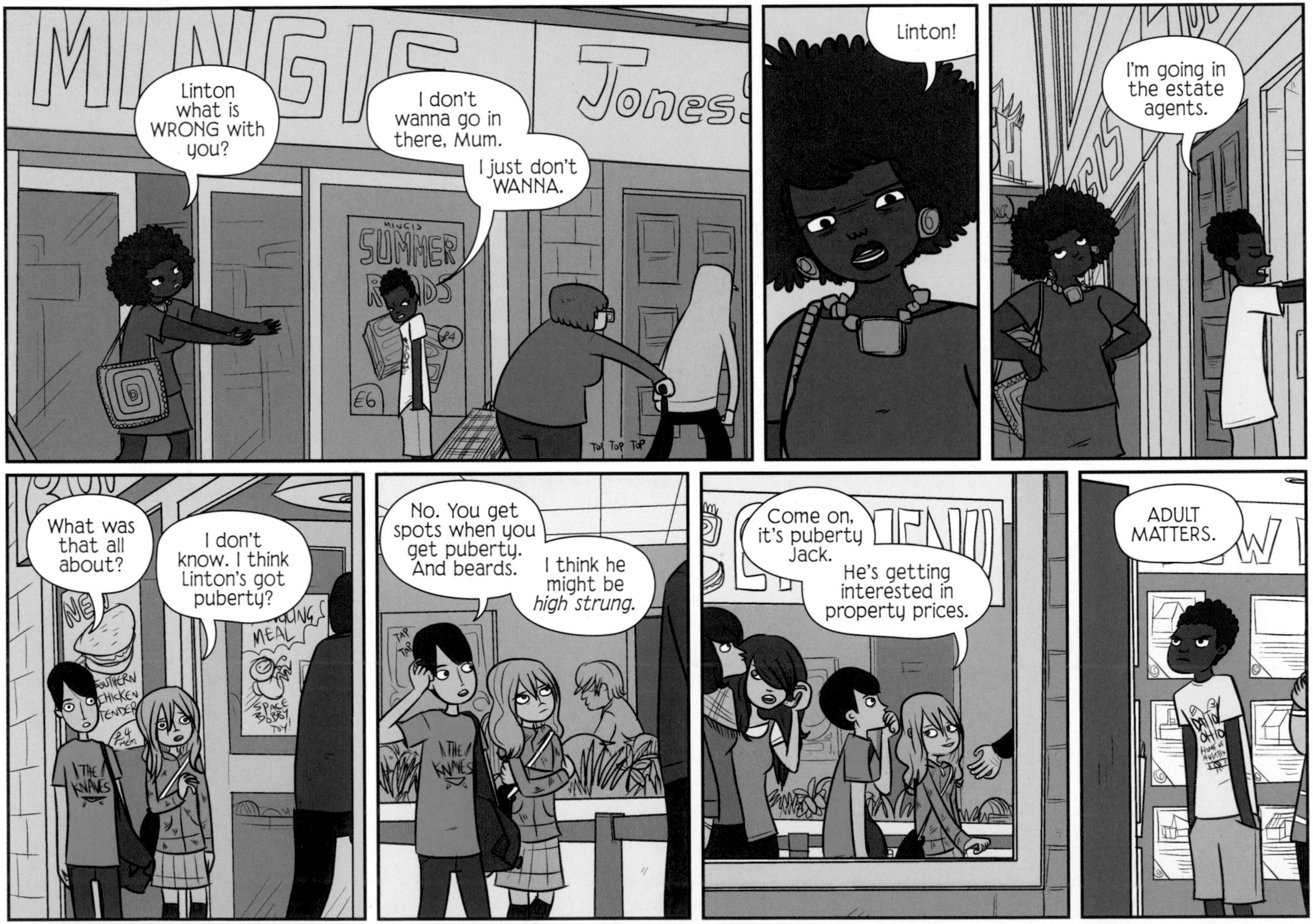
Linton what is WRONG with you?
I don't wanna go in there, Mum.
I just don't WANNA.
TOP TOP TOP
Linton!
I'm going in the estate agents.
What was that all about?
I don't know. I think Linton's got puberty?
No. You get spots when you get puberty. And beards.
I think he might be *high strung.*
Come on, it's puberty Jack.
He's getting interested in property prices.
ADULT MATTERS.

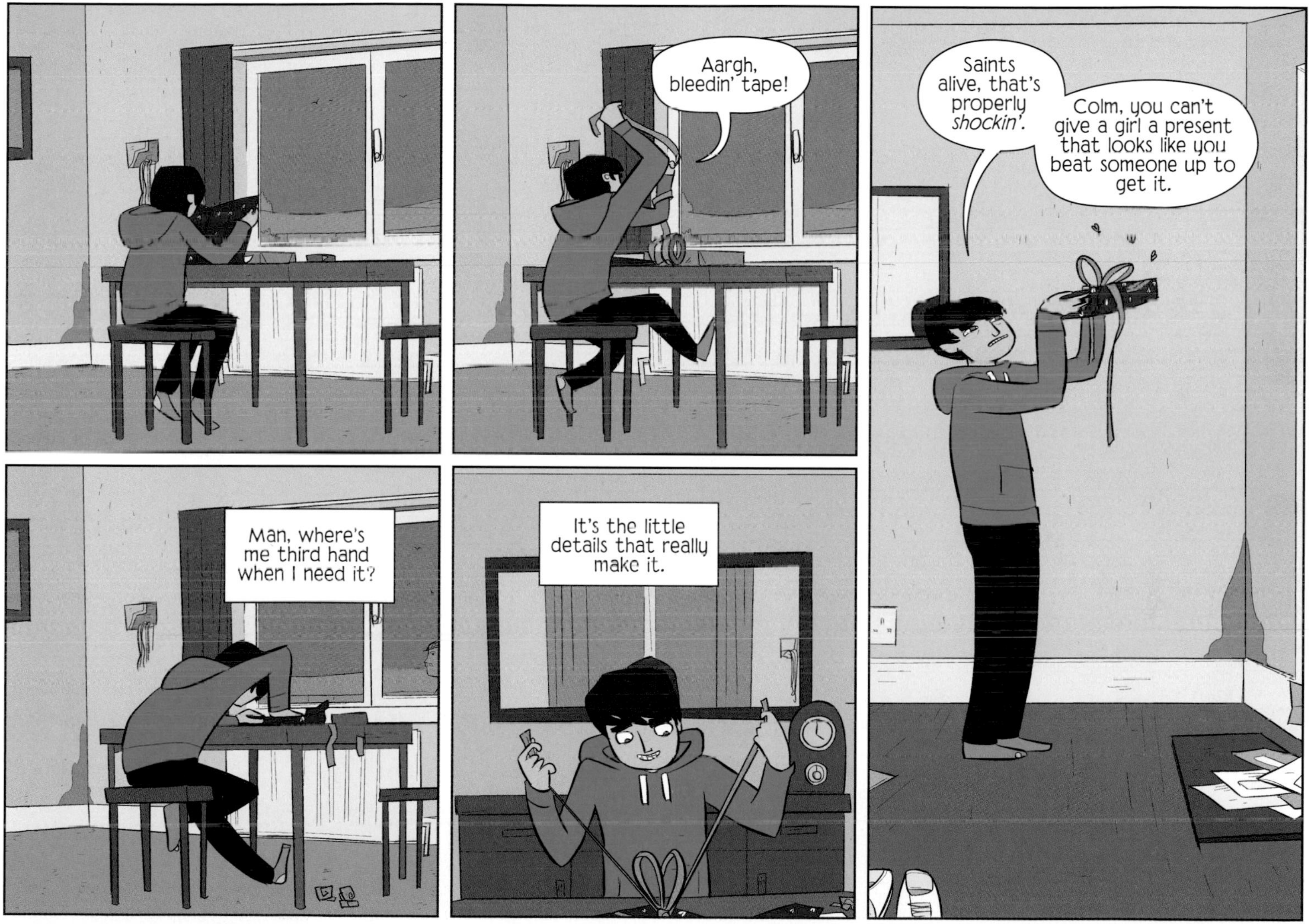
Aargh, bleedin' tape!
Man, where's me third hand when I need it?
It's the little details that really make it.
Saints alive, that's properly *shockin'*.
Colm, you can't give a girl a present that looks like you beat someone up to get it.

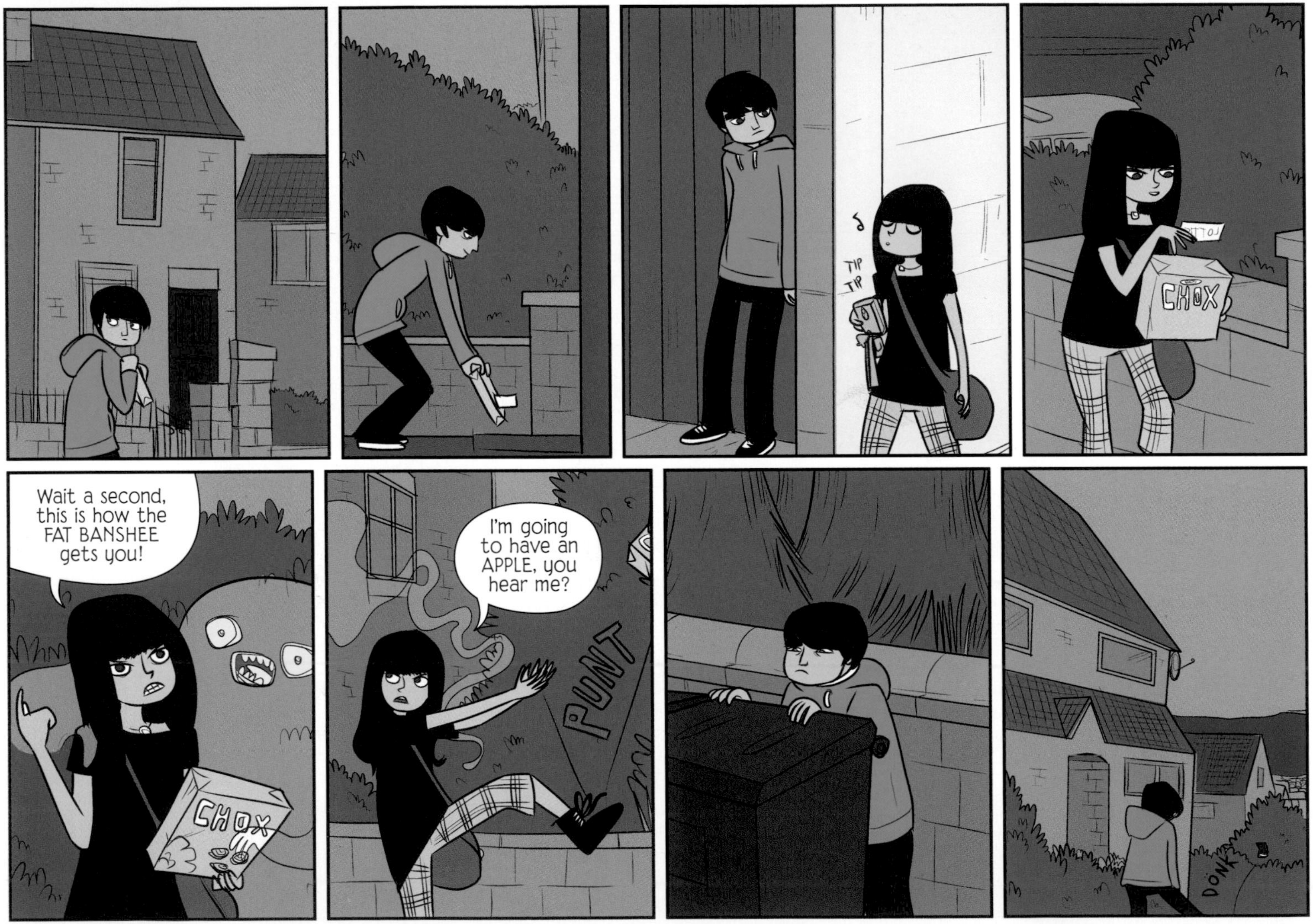
TIP
TIP
CHOX
Wait a second, this is how the FAT BANSHEE gets you!
CHOX
I'm going to have an APPLE, you hear me?
PUNT
DONK

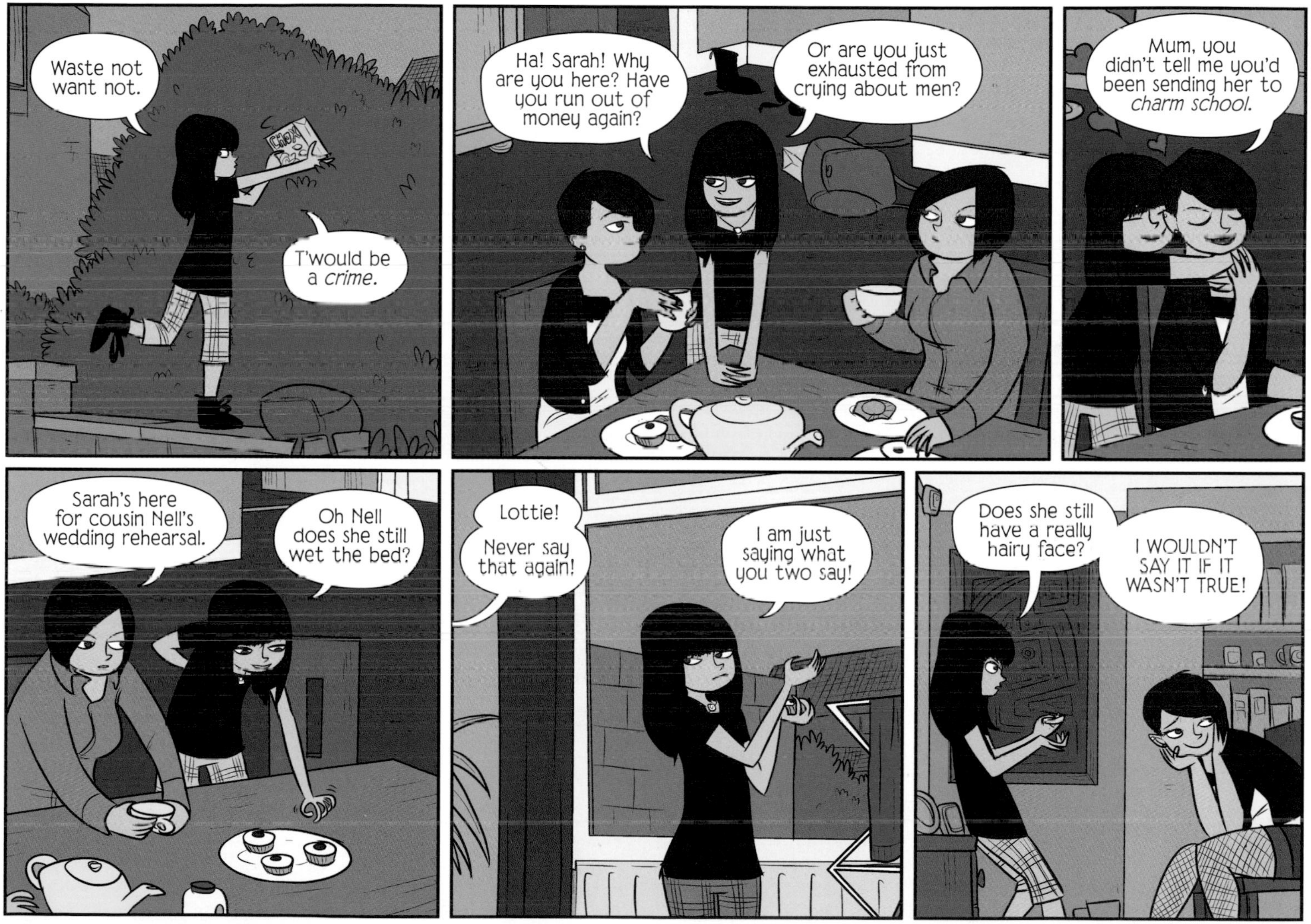
Waste not want not.
T'would be a *crime.*
Ha! Sarah! Why are you here? Have you run out of money again?
Or are you just exhausted from crying about men?
Mum, you didn't tell me you'd been sending her to *charm school.*
Sarah's here for cousin Nell's wedding rehearsal.
Oh Nell does she still wet the bed?
Lottie!
Never say that again!
I am just saying what you two say!
Does she still have a really hairy face?
I WOULDN'T SAY IT IF IT WASN'T TRUE!

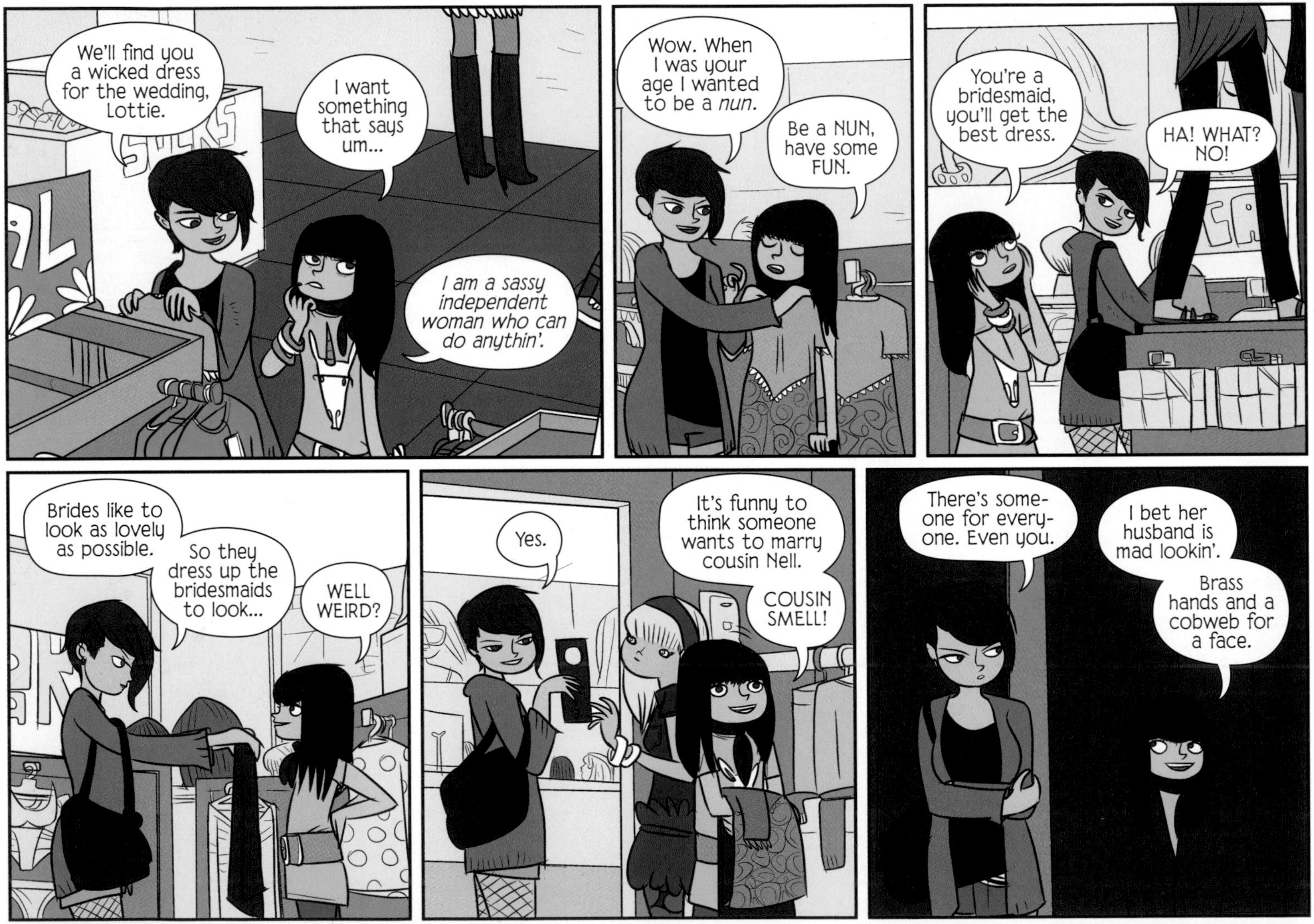

We'll find you a wicked dress for the wedding, Lottie.
I want something that says um...
I am a sassy independent woman who can do anythin'.
Wow. When I was your age I wanted to be a *nun*.
Be a NUN, have some FUN.
You're a bridesmaid, you'll get the best dress.
HA! WHAT? NO!
Brides like to look as lovely as possible.
So they dress up the bridesmaids to look...
WELL WEIRD?
Yes.
It's funny to think someone wants to marry cousin Nell.
COUSIN SMELL!
There's some-one for every-one. Even you.
I bet her husband is mad lookin'.
Brass hands and a cobweb for a face.

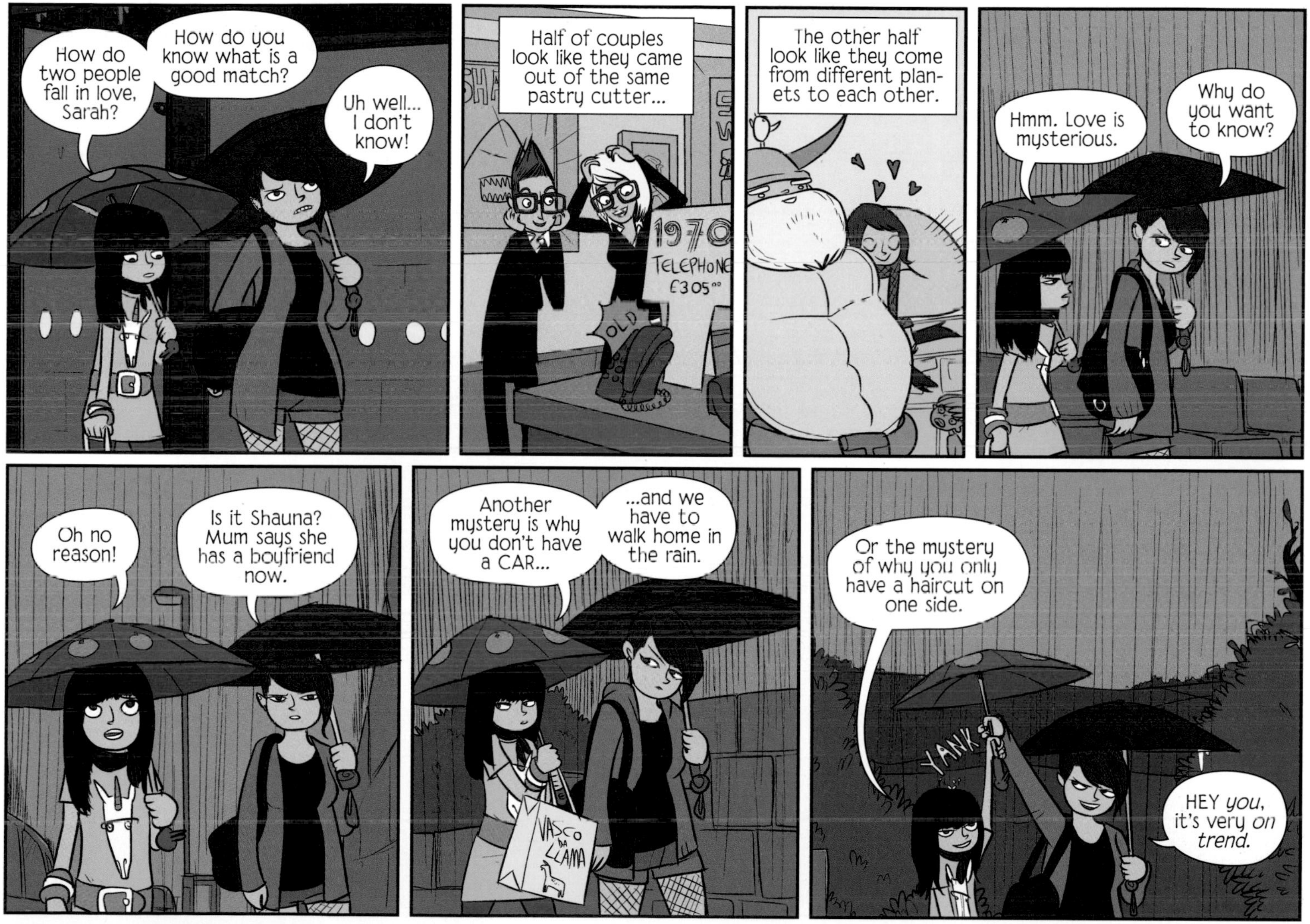

How do two people fall in love, Sarah?
How do you know what is a good match?
Uh well... I don't know!
Half of couples look like they came out of the same pastry cutter...
1970
TELEPHONE
£305.00
OLD
The other half look like they come from different plan-ets to each other.
Hmm. Love is mysterious.
Why do you want to know?
Oh no reason!
Is it Shauna? Mum says she has a boyfriend now.
Another mystery is why you don't have a CAR...
...and we have to walk home in the rain.
VASCO DA LLAMA
Or the mystery of why you only have a haircut on one side.
YANK
HEY *you*, it's very *on trend*.

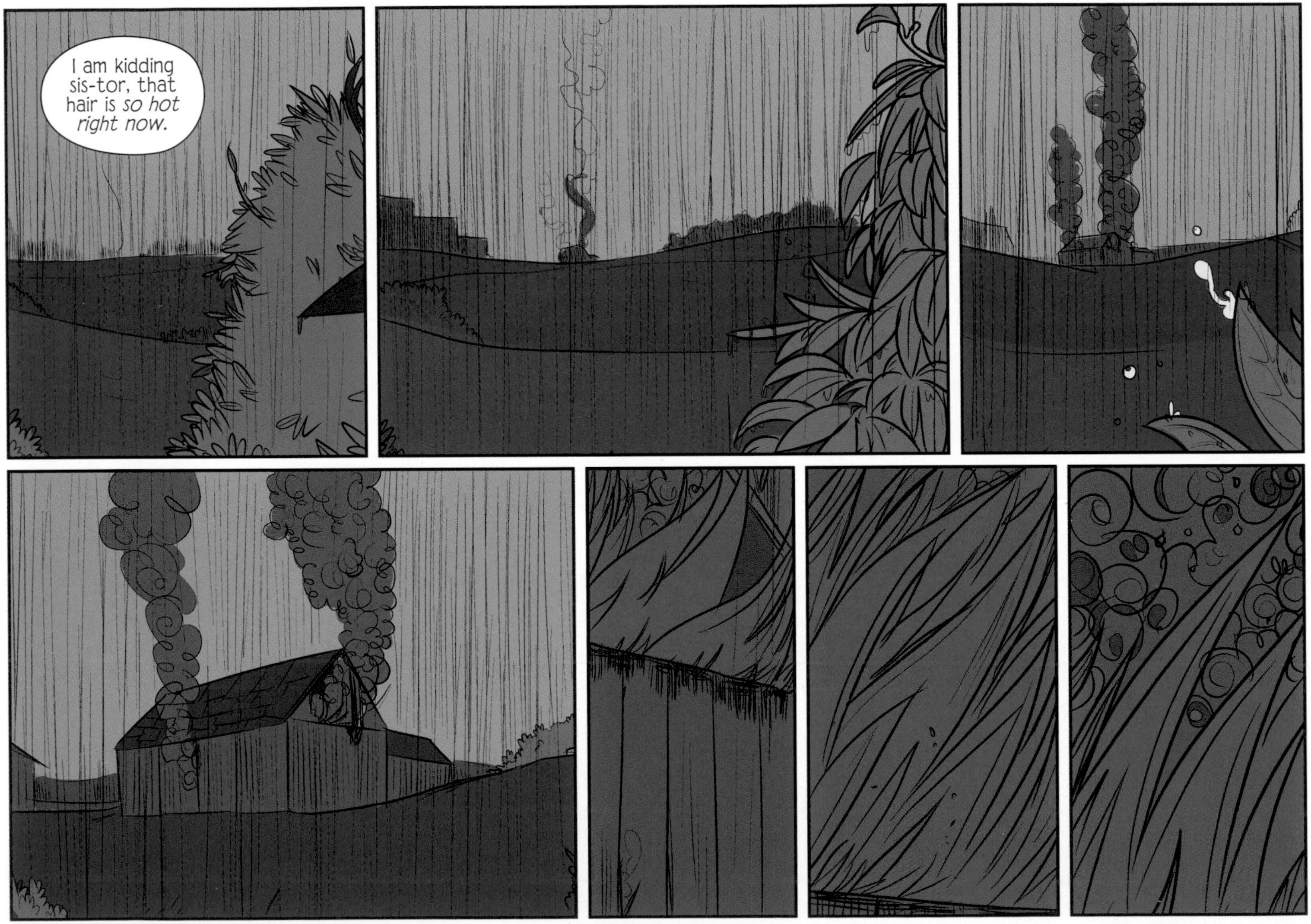
I am kidding sis-tor, that hair is *so hot right now.*

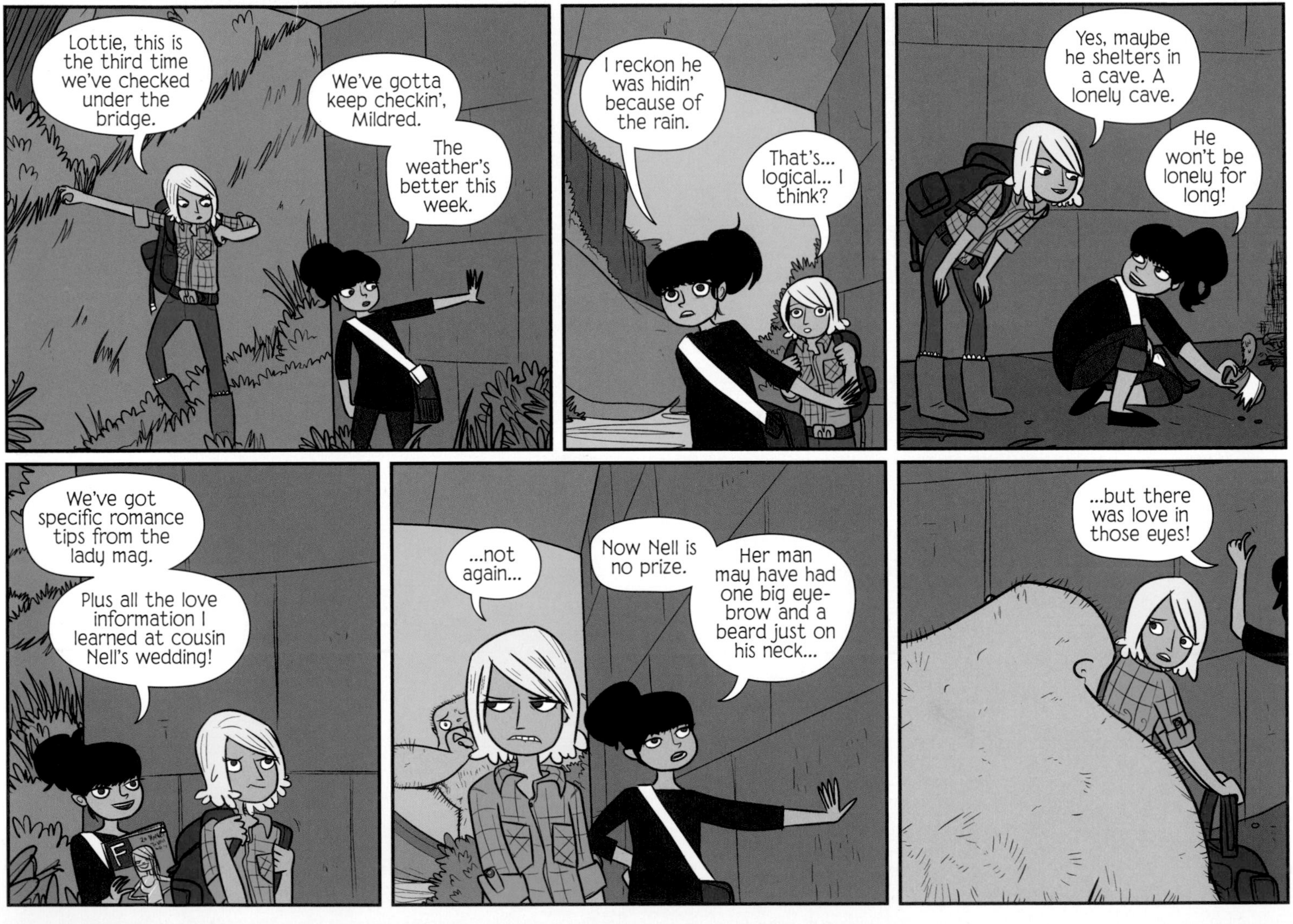

Lottie, this is the third time we've checked under the bridge.
We've gotta keep checkin', Mildred.
The weather's better this week.
I reckon he was hidin' because of the rain.
That's... logical... I think?
Yes, maybe he shelters in a cave. A lonely cave.
He won't be lonely for long!
We've got specific romance tips from the lady mag.
Plus all the love information I learned at cousin Nell's wedding!
...not again...
Now Nell is no prize.
Her man may have had one big eye-brow and a beard just on his neck...
...but there was love in those eyes!

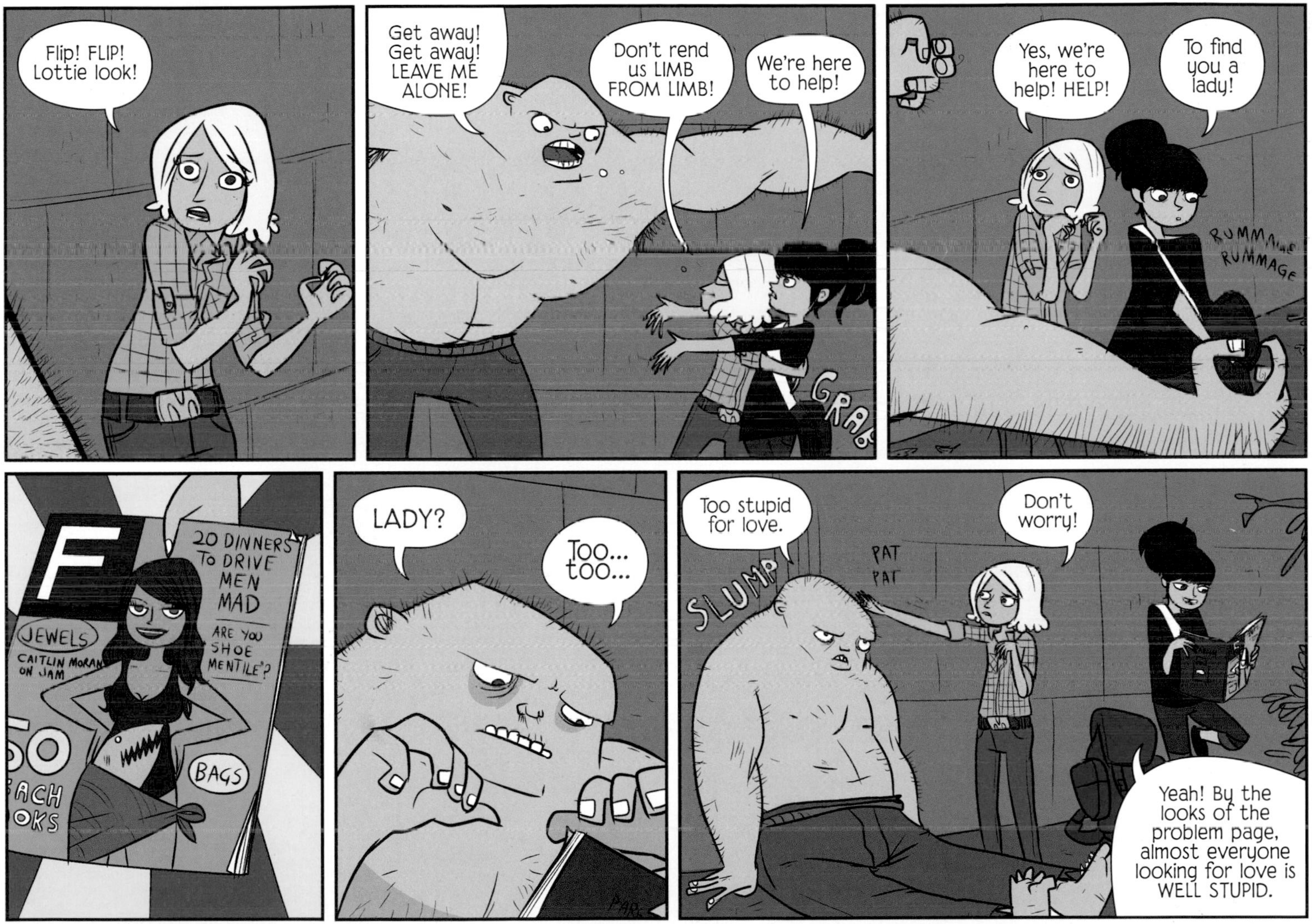
Flip! FLIP! Lottie look!
Get away! Get away! LEAVE ME ALONE!
Don't rend us LIMB FROM LIMB!
We're here to help!
GRAB
Yes, we're here to help! HELP!
To find you a lady!
RUMMAGE RUMMAGE
F
20 DINNERS TO DRIVE MEN MAD
ARE YOU SHOE MENTILE'?
JEWELS
CAITLIN MORAN ON JAM
BAGS
LADY?
Too... too...
Too stupid for love.
SLUMP
PAT PAT
Don't worry!
Yeah! By the looks of the problem page, almost everyone looking for love is WELL STUPID.

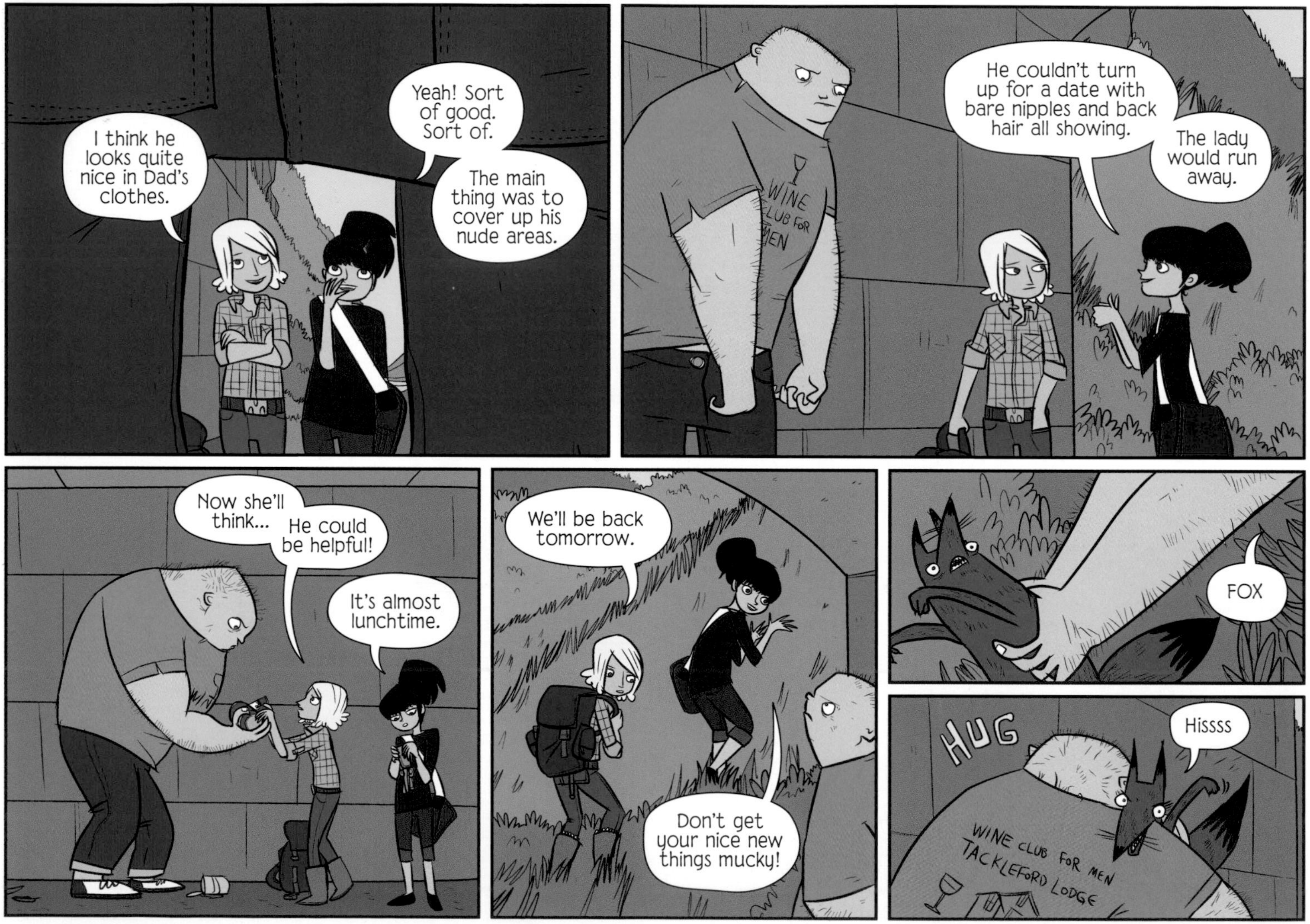
I think he looks quite nice in Dad's clothes.
Yeah! Sort of good. Sort of.
The main thing was to cover up his nude areas.
He couldn't turn up for a date with bare nipples and back hair all showing.
The lady would run away.
WINE CLUB FOR MEN
Now she'll think...
He could be helpful!
It's almost lunchtime.
We'll be back tomorrow.
Don't get your nice new things mucky!
FOX
HUG
Hissss
WINE CLUB FOR MEN
TACKLEFORD LODGE

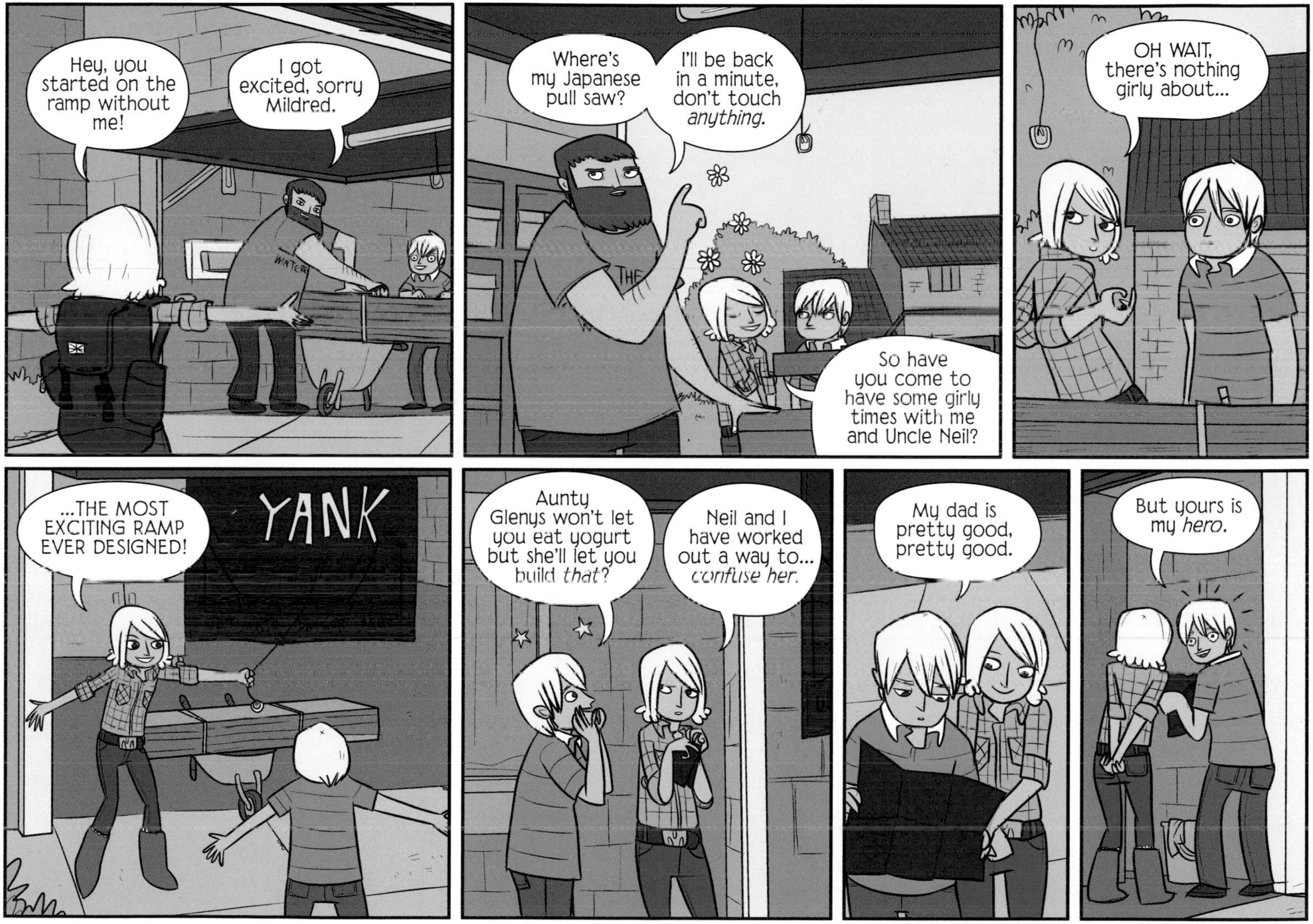

Hey, you started on the ramp without me!
I got excited, sorry Mildred.
Where's my Japanese pull saw?
I'll be back in a minute, don't touch *anything.*
So have you come to have some girly times with me and Uncle Neil?
OH WAIT, there's nothing girly about...
...THE MOST EXCITING RAMP EVER DESIGNED!
YANK
Aunty Glenys won't let you eat yogurt but she'll let you build *that*?
Neil and I have worked out a way to... *confuse her.*
My dad is pretty good, pretty good.
But yours is my *hero.*

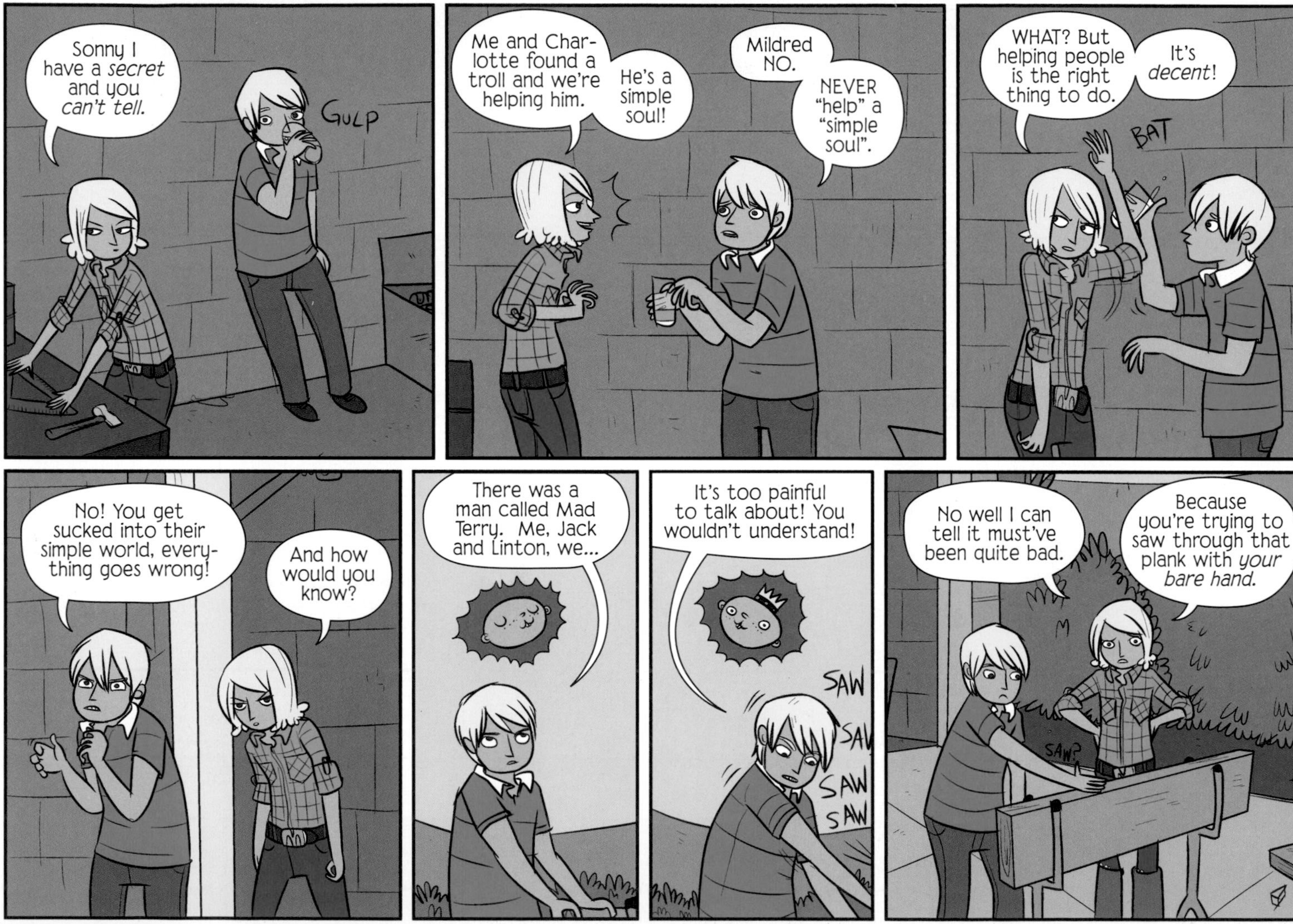
Sonny I have a *secret* and you *can't tell.*
GULP
Me and Charlotte found a troll and we're helping him.
He's a simple soul!
Mildred NO.
NEVER "help" a "simple soul".
WHAT? But helping people is the right thing to do.
It's *decent*!
BAT
No! You get sucked into their simple world, everything goes wrong!
And how would you know?
There was a man called Mad Terry. Me, Jack and Linton, we...
It's too painful to talk about! You wouldn't understand!
SAW
SAW
SAW
SAW
No well I can tell it must've been quite bad.
Because you're trying to saw through that plank with *your bare hand.*
SAW?

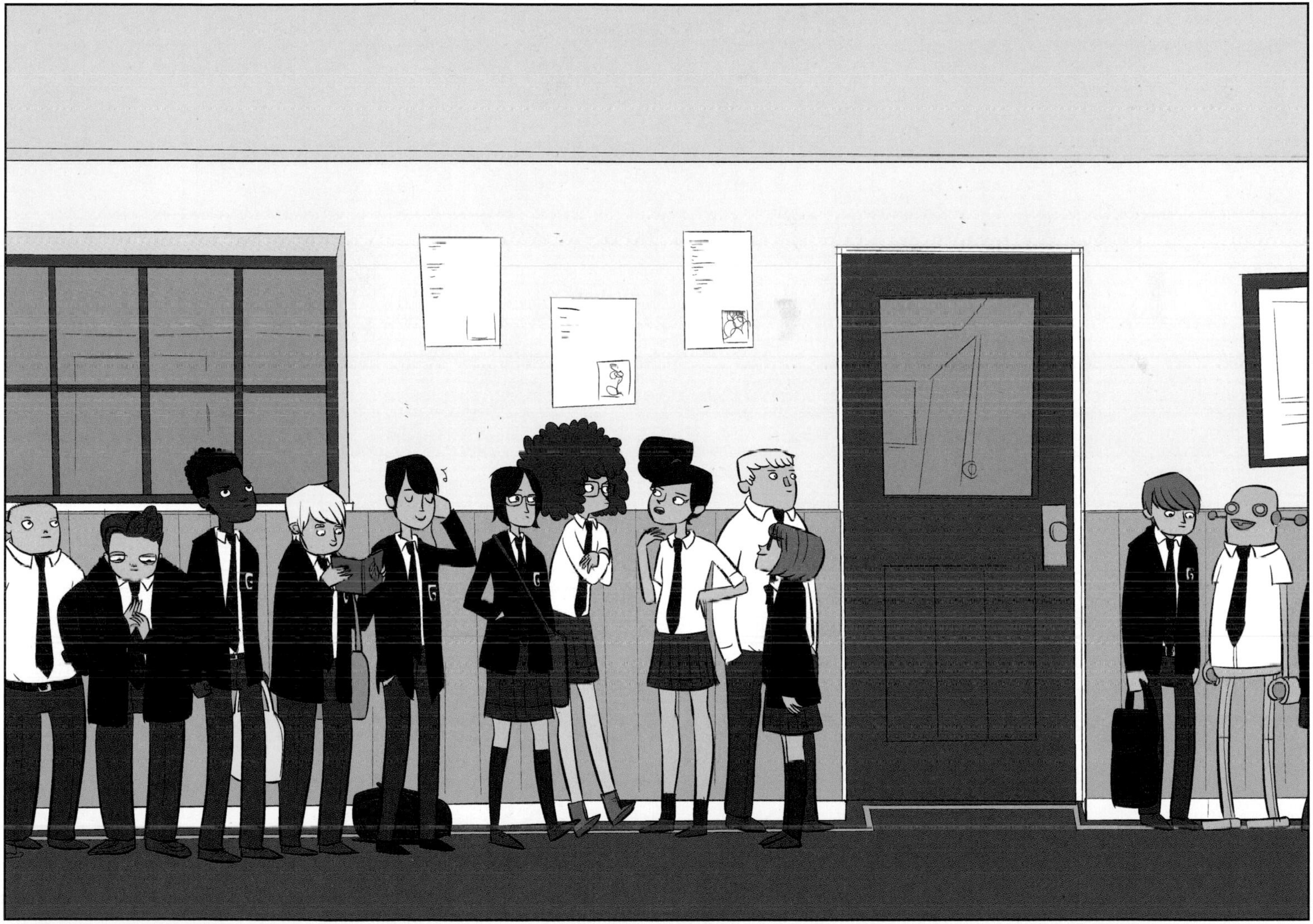

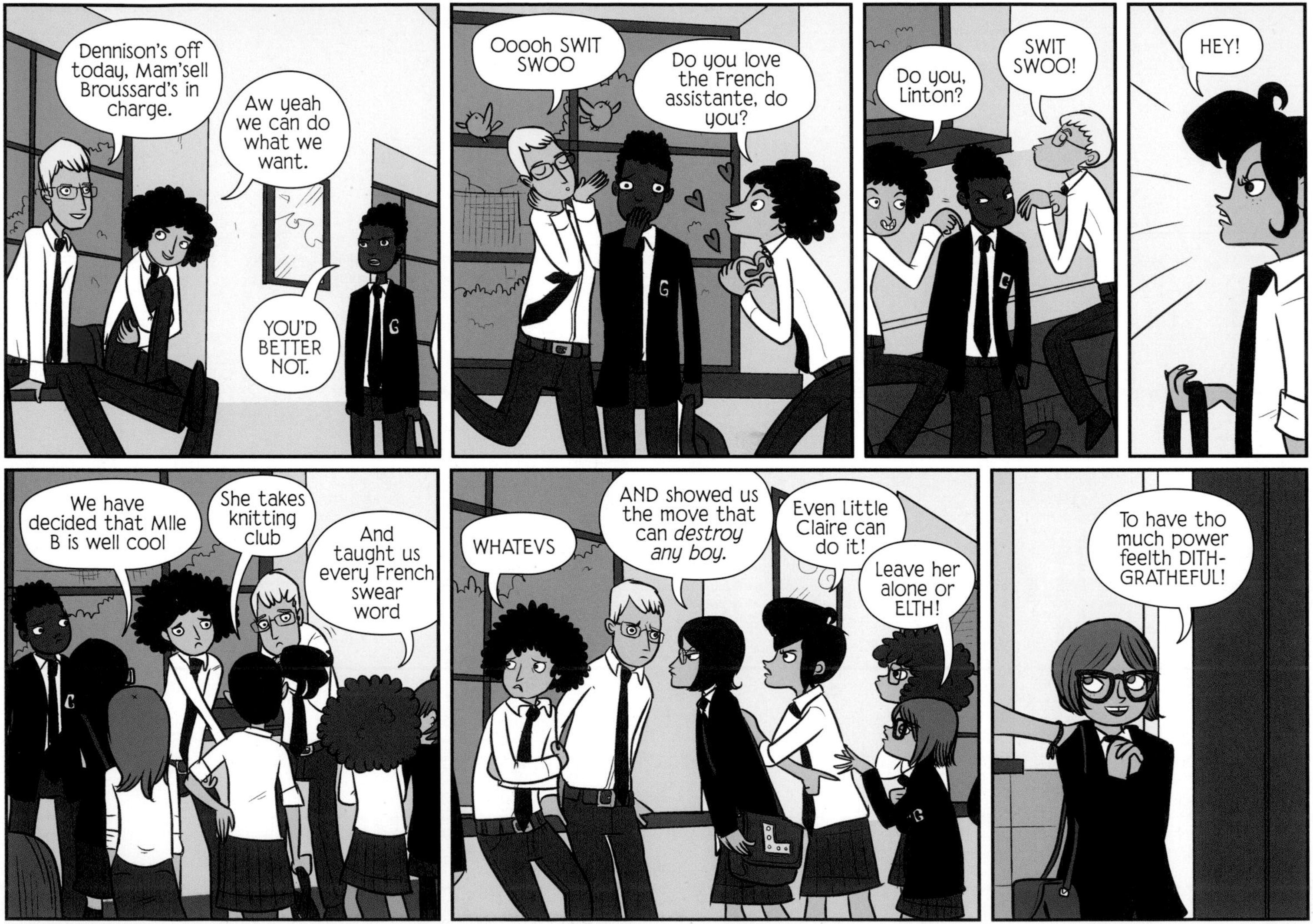
Dennison's off today, Mam'sell Broussard's in charge.
Aw yeah we can do what we want.
YOU'D BETTER NOT.
Ooooh SWIT SWOO
Do you love the French assistante, do you?
Do you, Linton?
SWIT SWOO!
HEY!
We have decided that Mlle B is well cool
She takes knitting club
And taught us every French swear word
WHATEVS
AND showed us the move that can *destroy any boy*.
Even Little Claire can do it!
Leave her alone or ELTH!
To have tho much power feelth DITH-GRATHEFUL!

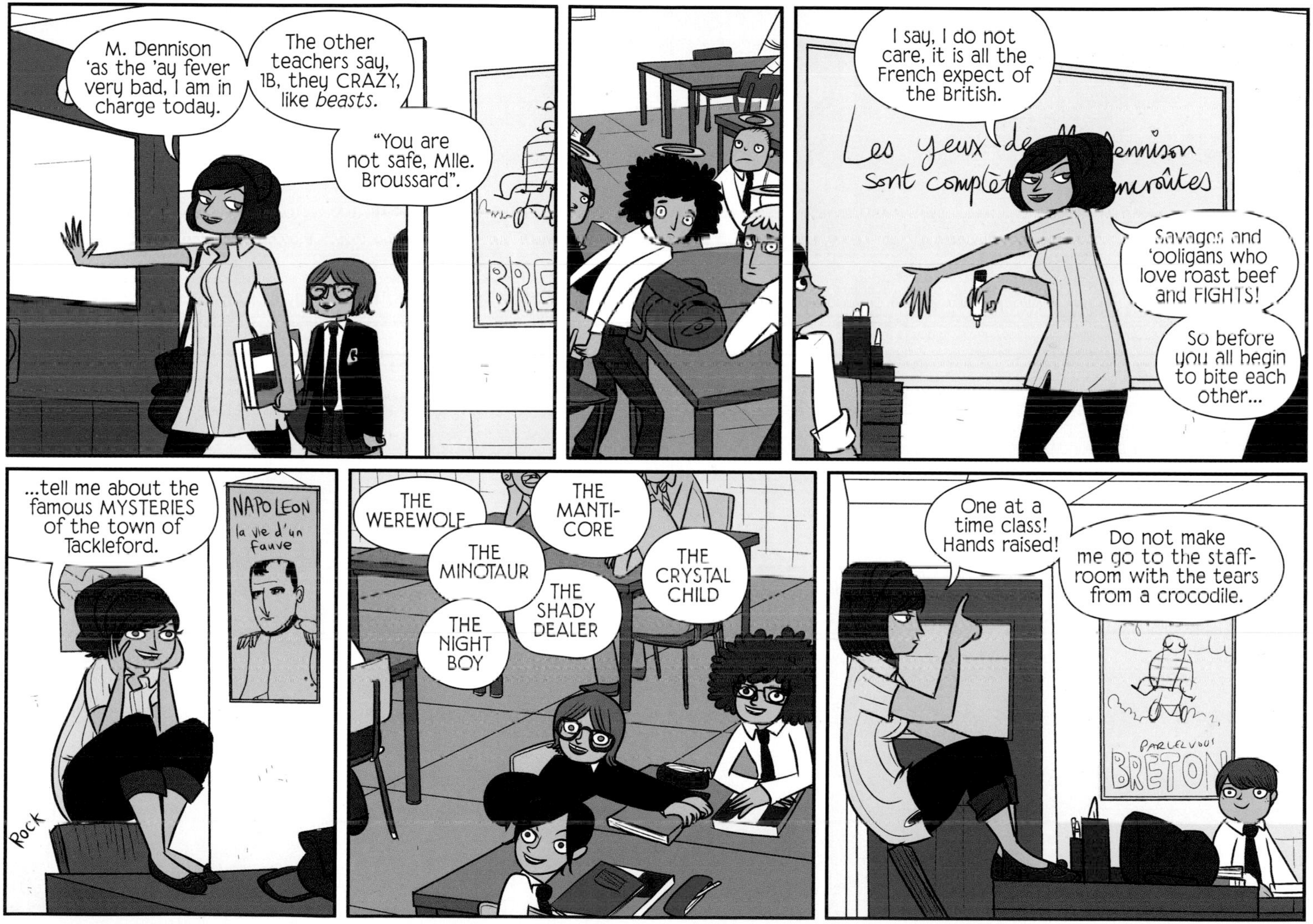
M. Dennison 'as the 'ay fever very bad, I am in charge today.
The other teachers say, 1B, they CRAZY, like *beasts*.
"You are not safe, Mlle. Broussard".
I say, I do not care, it is all the French expect of the British.
Savages and 'ooligans who love roast beef and FIGHTS!
So before you all begin to bite each other...
...tell me about the famous MYSTERIES of the town of Tackleford.
NAPOLEON
la vie d'un fauve
ROCK
THE WEREWOLF
THE MINOTAUR
THE MANTI-CORE
THE SHADY DEALER
THE CRYSTAL CHILD
THE NIGHT BOY
One at a time class! Hands raised!
Do not make me go to the staff-room with the tears from a crocodile.
PARLEZ VOUS
BRETON

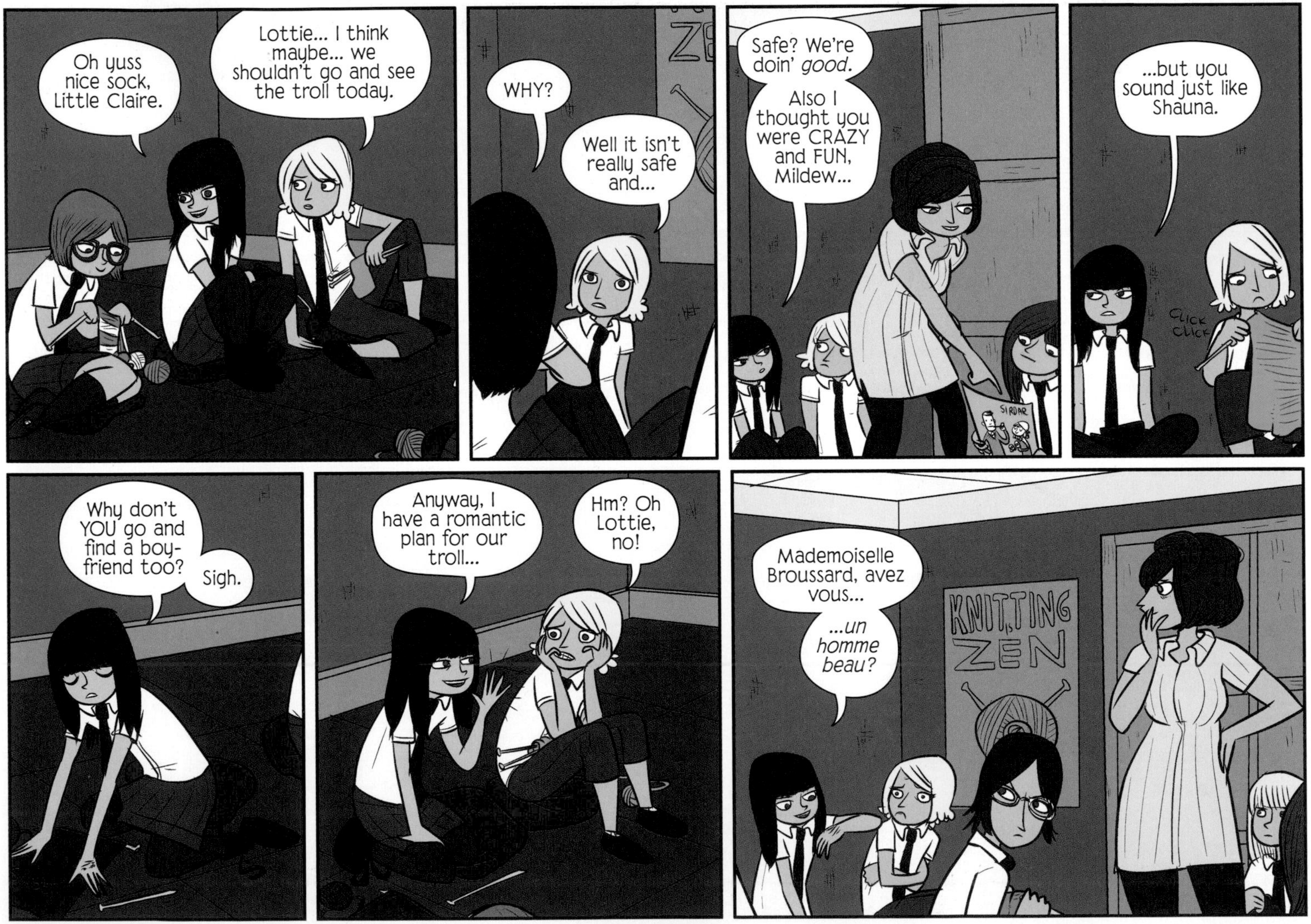
Oh yuss nice sock, Little Claire.
Lottie... I think maybe... we shouldn't go and see the troll today.
WHY?
Well it isn't really safe and...
Safe? We're doin' *good.*
Also I thought you were CRAZY and FUN, Mildew...
SIRDAR
...but you sound just like Shauna.
CLICK CLICK
Why don't YOU go and find a boy-friend too?
Sigh.
Anyway, I have a romantic plan for our troll...
Hm? Oh Lottie, no!
Mademoiselle Broussard, avez vous...
...*un homme beau?*
KNITTING
ZEN

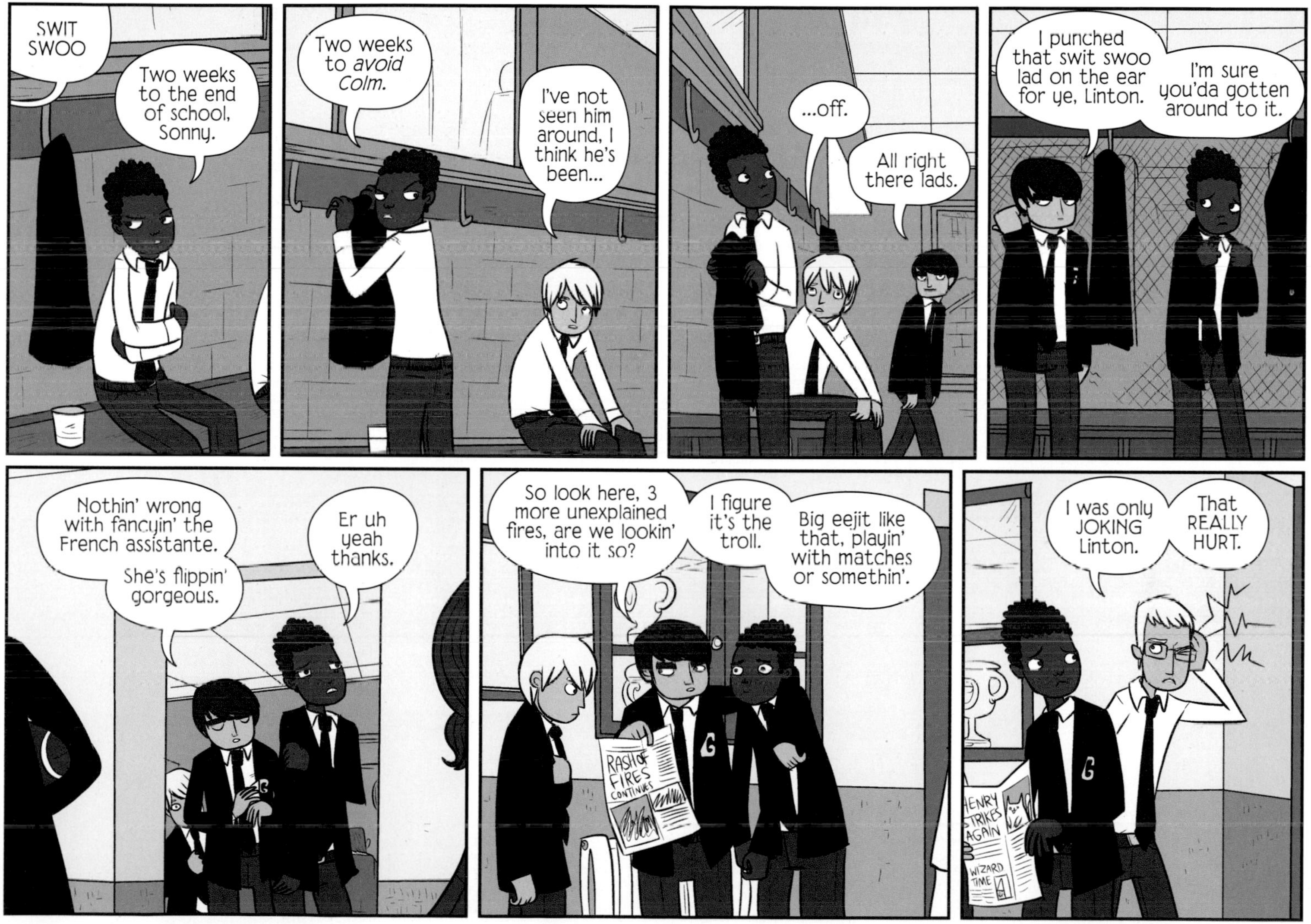
SWIT SWOO
Two weeks to the end of school, Sonny.
Two weeks to *avoid Colm.*
I've not seen him around, I think he's been...
...off.
All right there lads.
I punched that swit swoo lad on the ear for ye, Linton.
I'm sure you'da gotten around to it.
Nothin' wrong with fancyin' the French assistante.
She's flippin' gorgeous.
Er uh yeah thanks.
So look here, 3 more unexplained fires, are we lookin' into it so?
RASH OF FIRES CONTINUES
I figure it's the troll.
Big eejit like that, playin' with matches or somethin'.
I was only JOKING Linton.
That REALLY HURT.
HENRY STRIKES AGAIN
WIZARD TIME

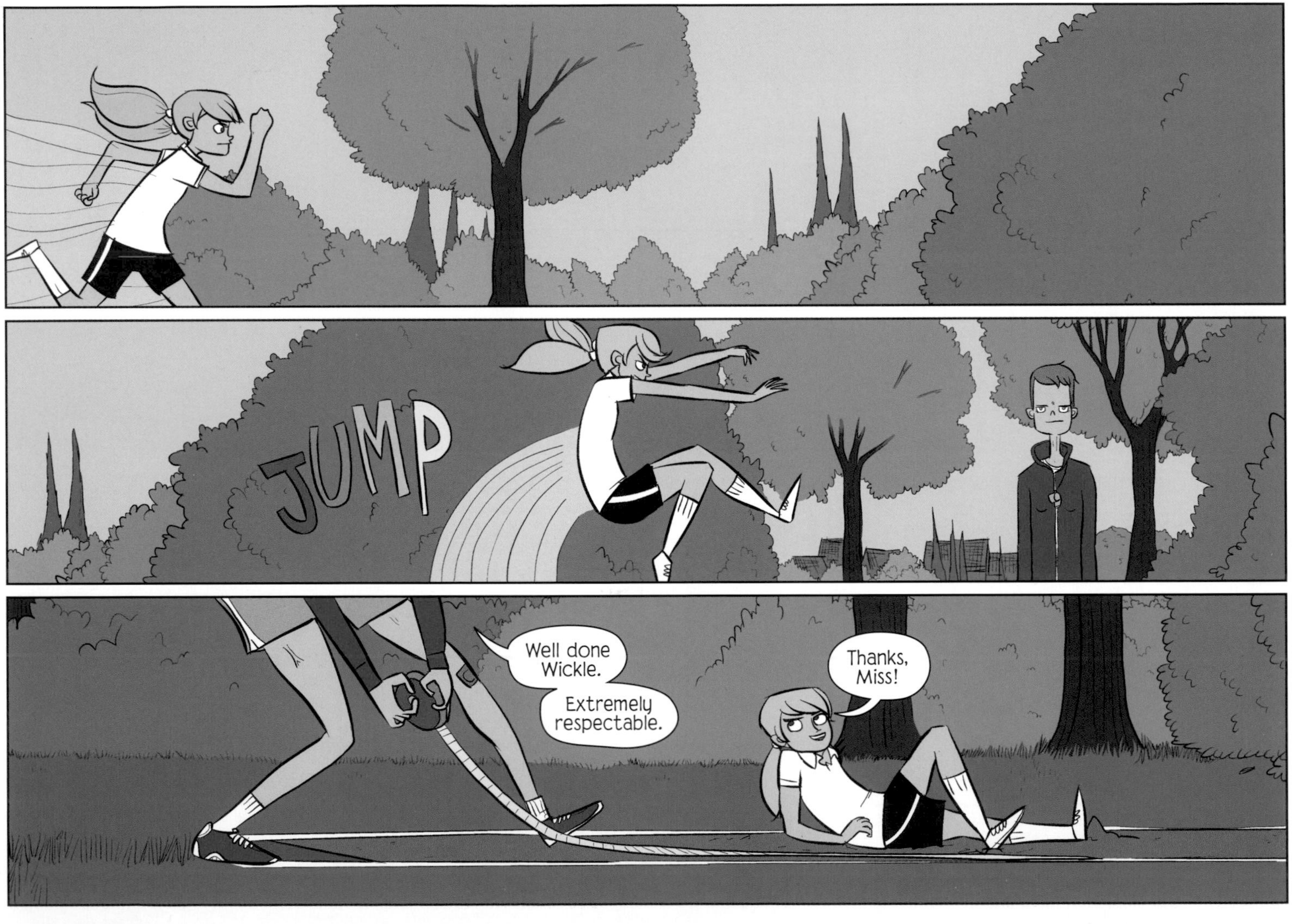

JUMP
Well done Wickle.
Extremely respectable.
Thanks, Miss!

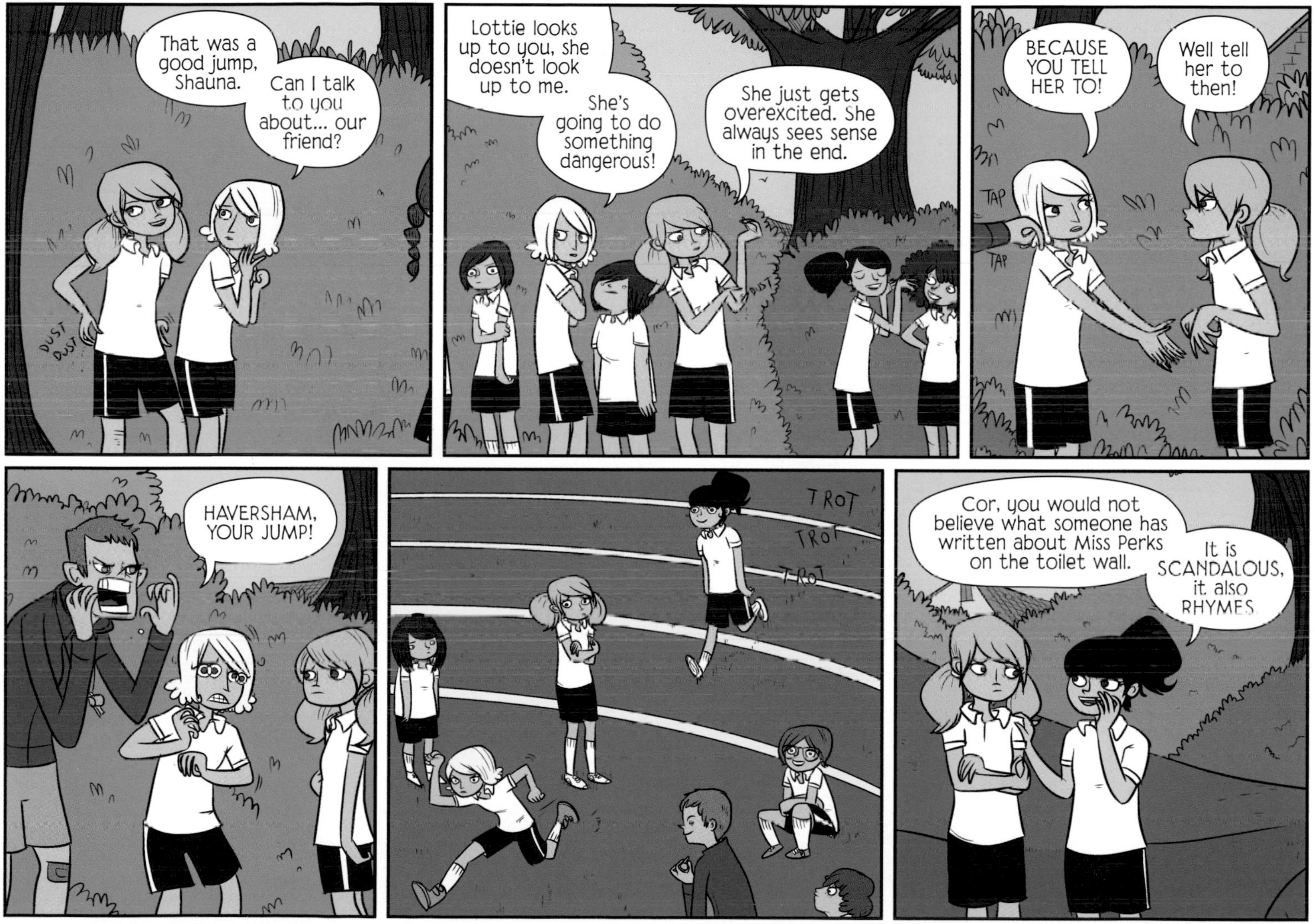
That was a good jump, Shauna.
Can I talk to you about... our friend?
DUST DUST
Lottie looks up to you, she doesn't look up to me.
She's going to do something dangerous!
She just gets overexcited. She always sees sense in the end.
DUST
TAP
TAP
BECAUSE YOU TELL HER TO!
Well tell her to then!
HAVERSHAM, YOUR JUMP!
TROT
TROT
TROT
Cor, you would not believe what someone has written about Miss Perks on the toilet wall.
It is SCANDALOUS, it also RHYMES.

Bad Machinery, Volume Three

The Case of the Simple Soul

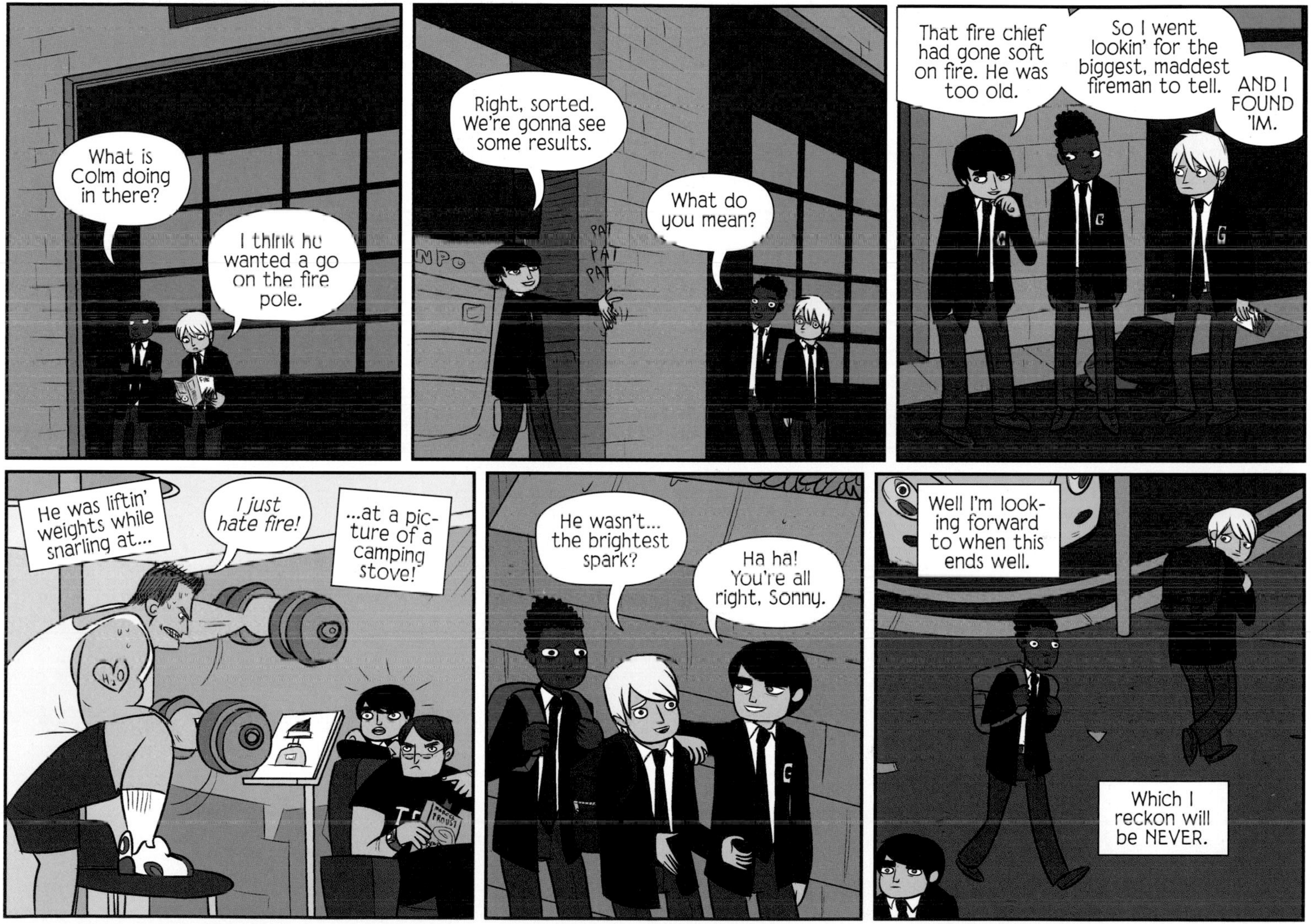
What is Colm doing in there?
I think he wanted a go on the fire pole.
Right, sorted. We're gonna see some results.
PAT PAT PAT
What do you mean?
That fire chief had gone soft on fire. He was too old.
So I went lookin' for the biggest, maddest fireman to tell.
AND I FOUND 'IM.
He was liftin' weights while snarling at...
I just hate fire!
...at a picture of a camping stove!
He wasn't... the brightest spark?
Ha ha! You're all right, Sonny.
Well I'm looking forward to when this ends well.
Which I reckon will be NEVER.

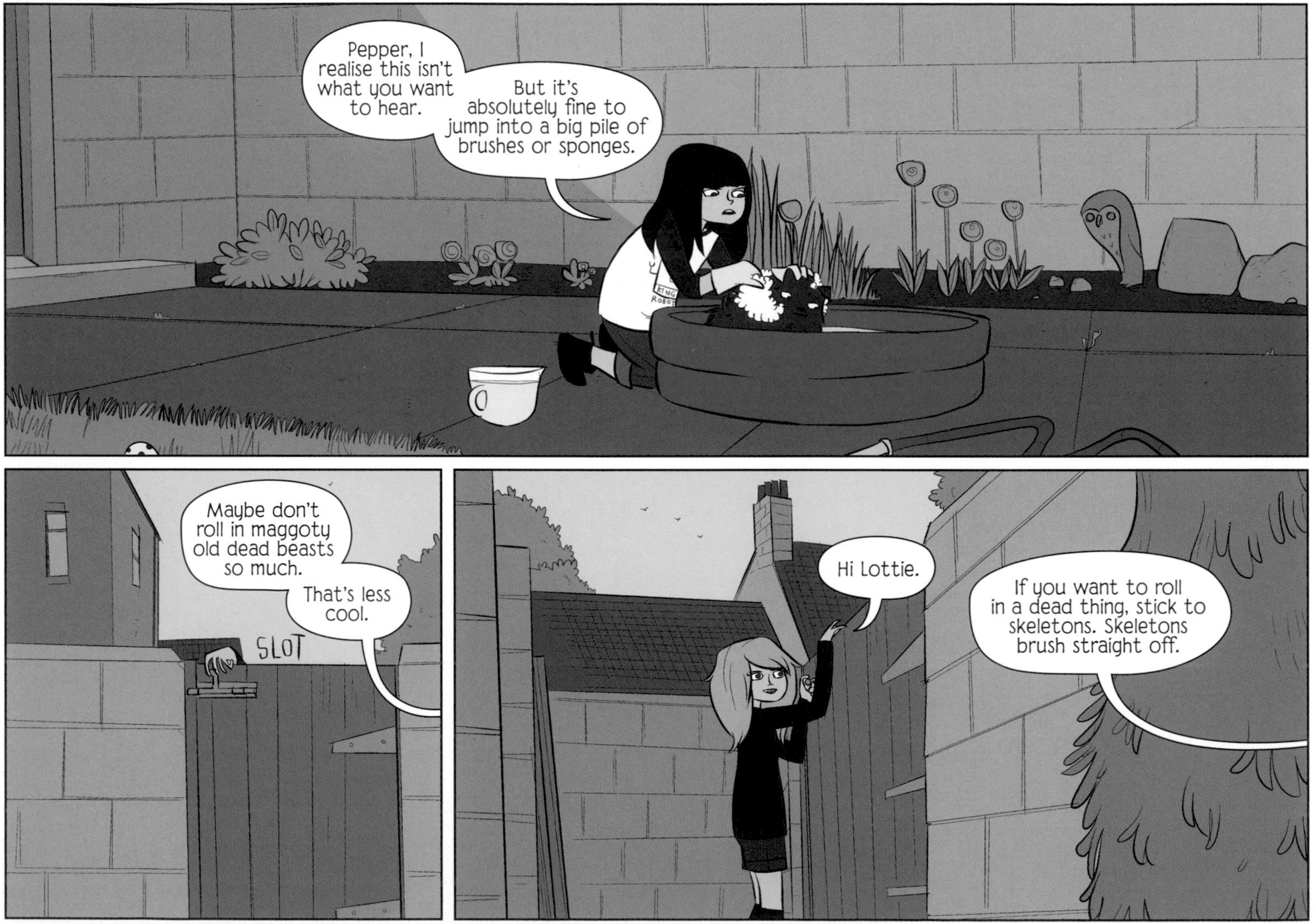
Pepper, I realise this isn't what you want to hear.
But it's absolutely fine to jump into a big pile of brushes or sponges.
Maybe don't roll in maggoty old dead beasts so much.
That's less cool.
SLOT
Hi Lottie.
If you want to roll in a dead thing, stick to skeletons. Skeletons brush straight off.

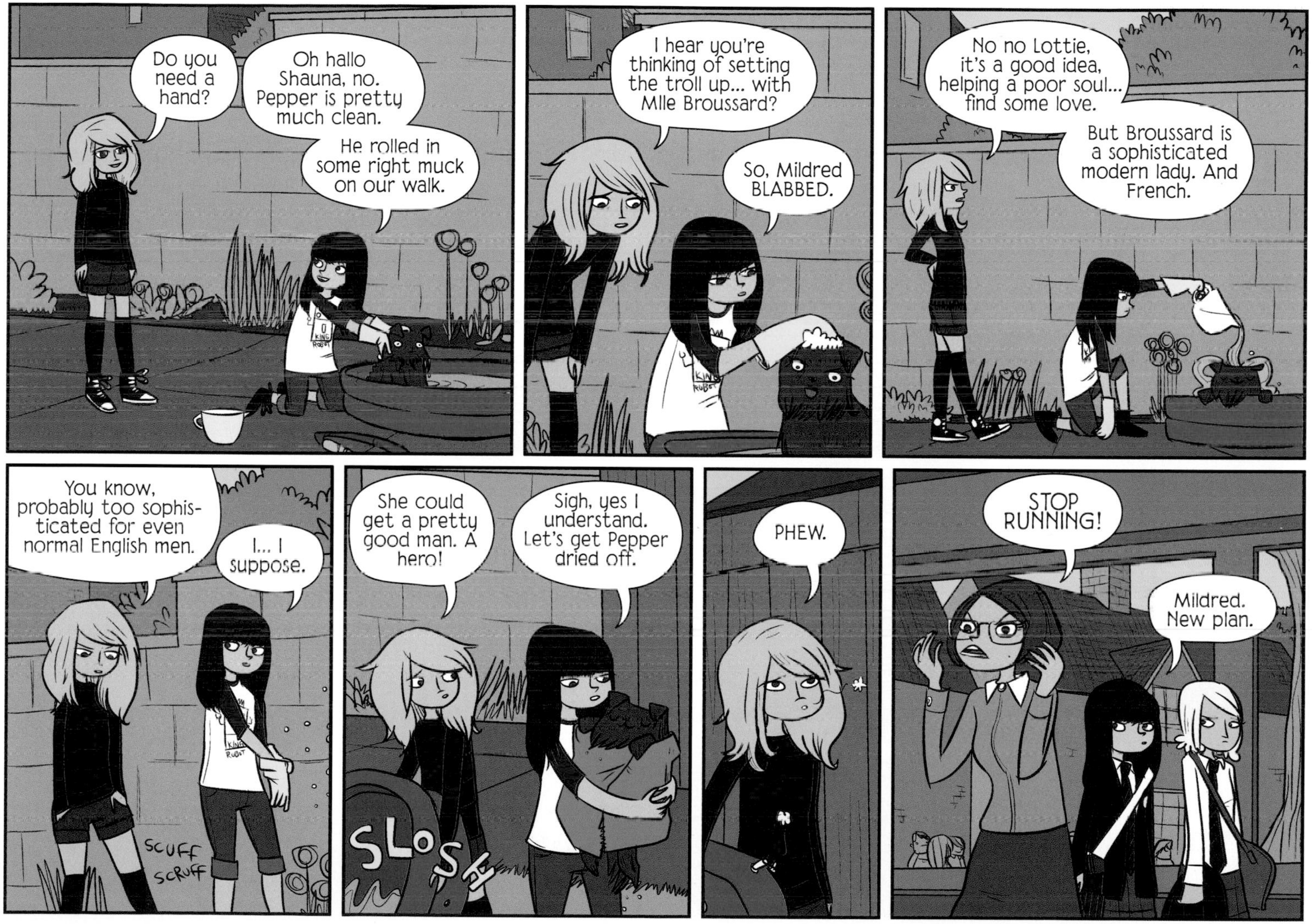

Do you need a hand?
Oh hallo Shauna, no. Pepper is pretty much clean.
He rolled in some right muck on our walk.
I hear you're thinking of setting the troll up... with Mlle Broussard?
So, Mildred BLABBED.
No no Lottie, it's a good idea, helping a poor soul... find some love.
But Broussard is a sophisticated modern lady. And French.
You know, probably too sophisticated for even normal English men.
I... I suppose.
SCUFF
SCRUFF
She could get a pretty good man. A hero!
Sigh, yes I understand. Let's get Pepper dried off.
SLOSH
PHEW.
STOP RUNNING!
Mildred. New plan.

Bad Machinery, Volume Three

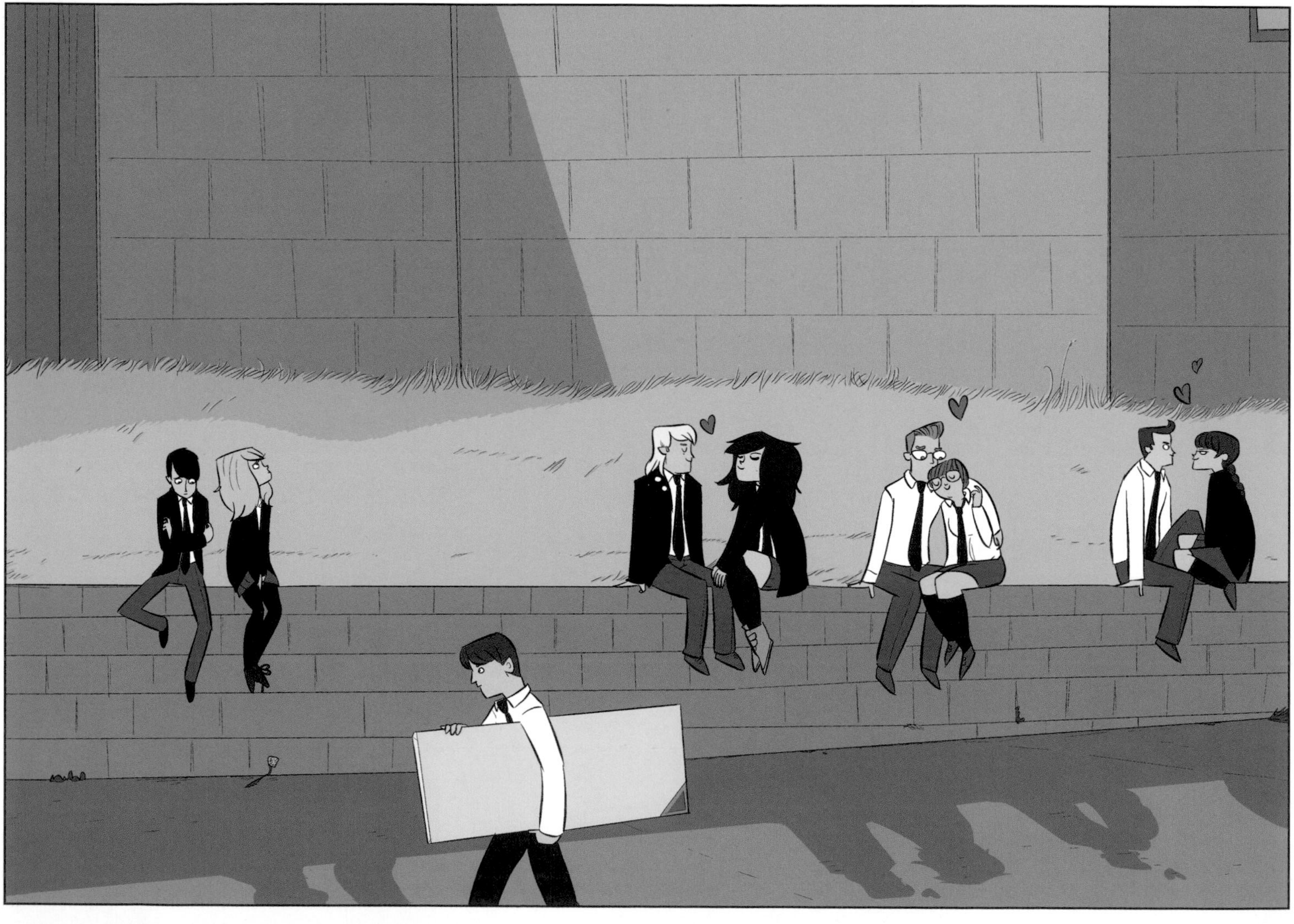

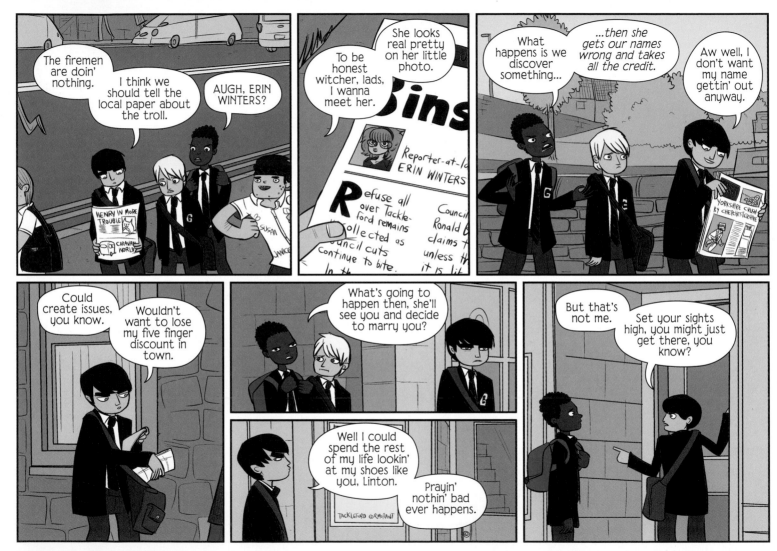

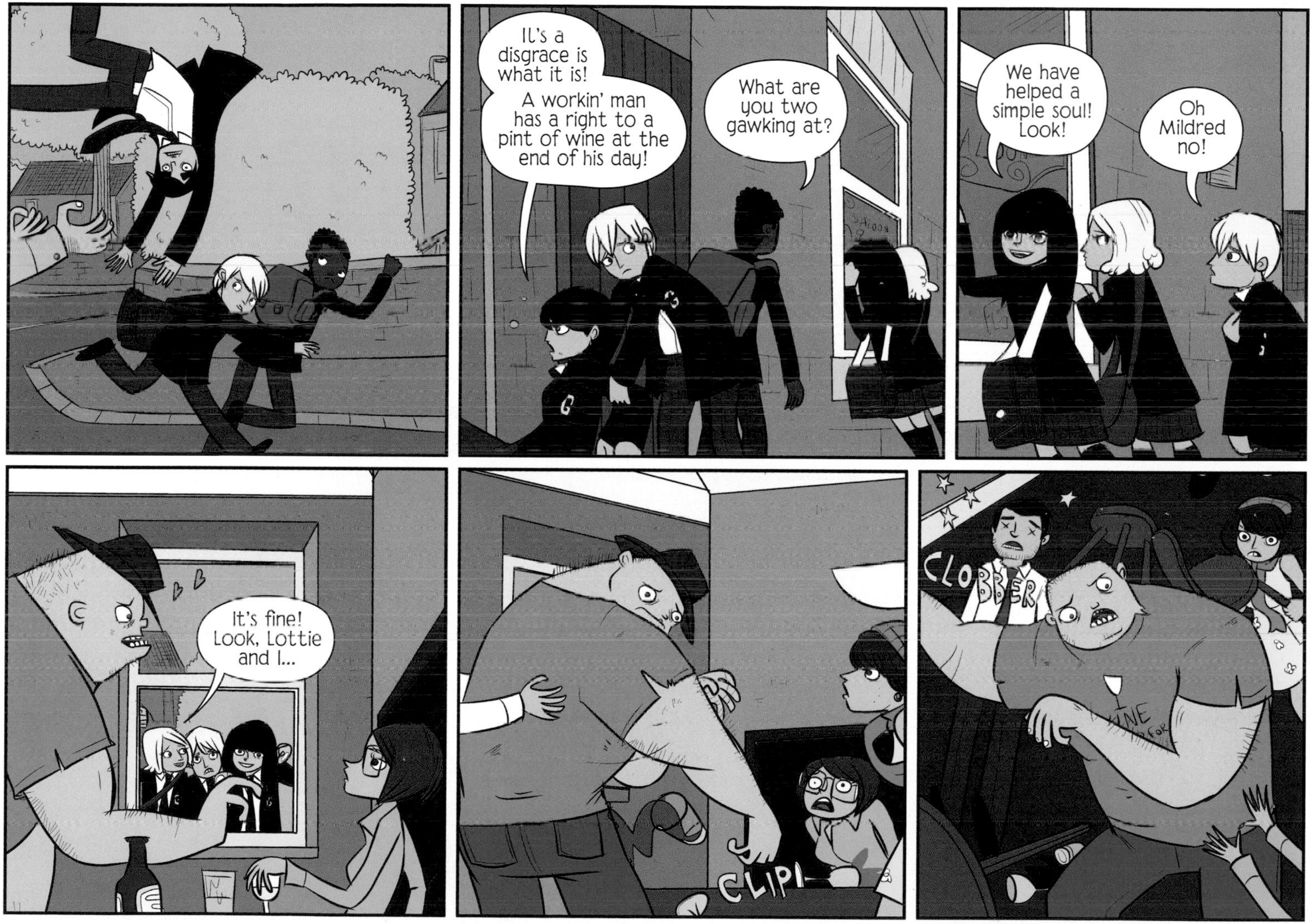
It's a disgrace is what it is!
A workin' man has a right to a pint of wine at the end of his day!
What are you two gawking at?
We have helped a simple soul! Look!
Oh Mildred no!
It's fine! Look, Lottie and I...
CLIP!
CLOBBER

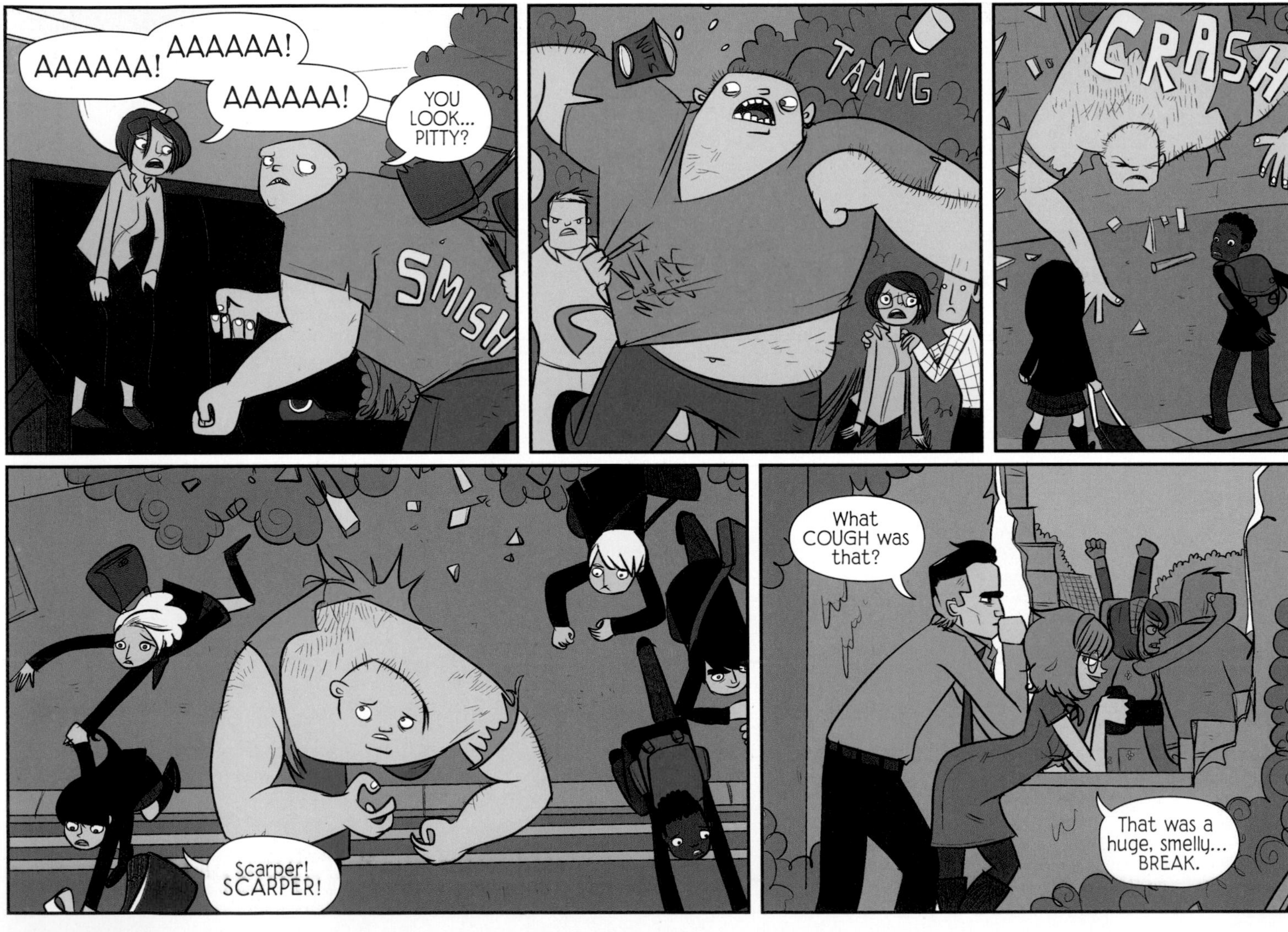
AAAAAA!
AAAAAA!
AAAAAA!
YOU LOOK... PITTY?
SMISH
TAANG
NUTS
CRASH
Scarper! SCARPER!
What COUGH was that?
That was a huge, smelly... BREAK.

The Case of the Simple Soul

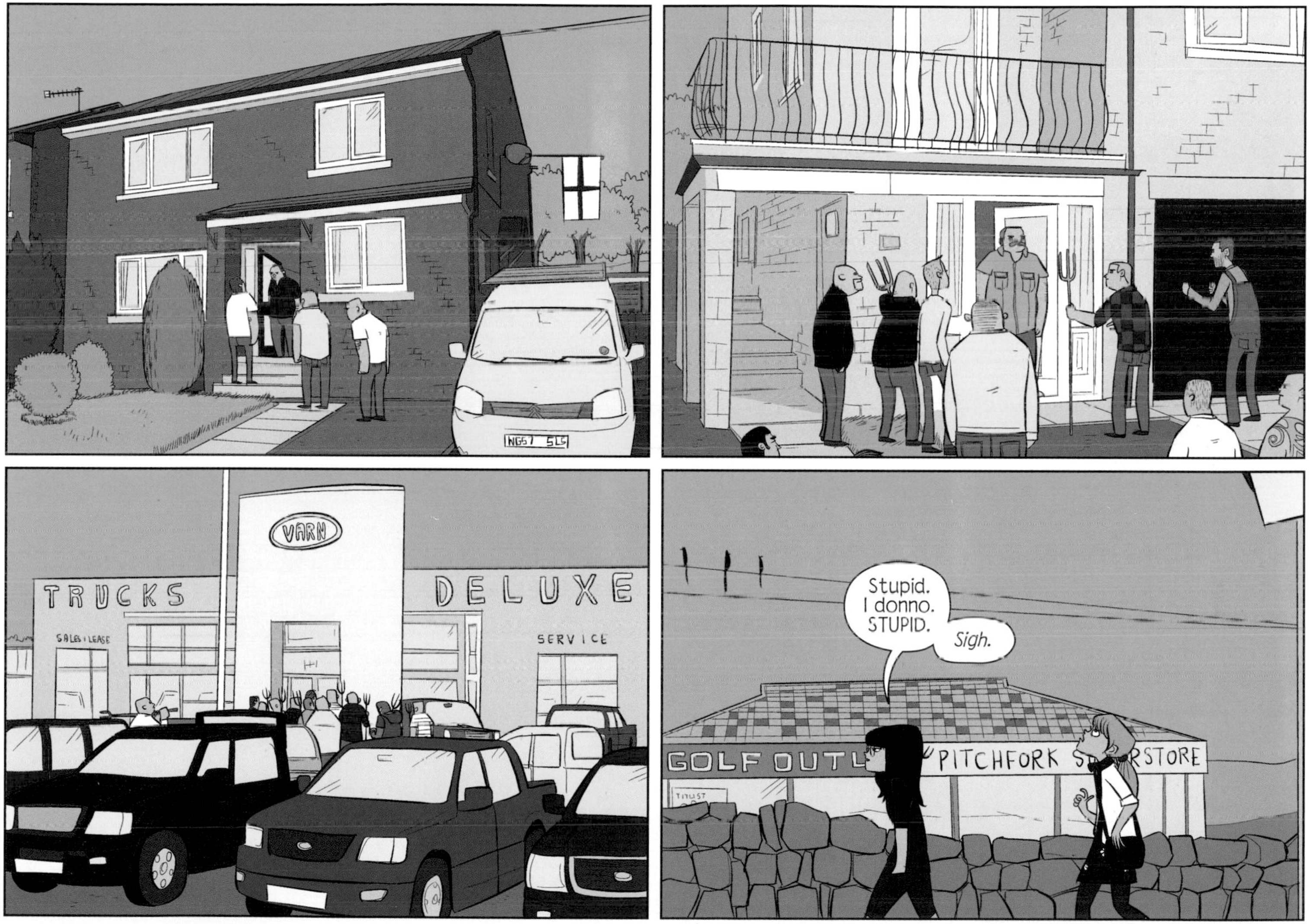
VARN
TRUCKS
DELUXE
SALES/LEASE
SERVICE
Stupid.
I donno.
STUPID.
Sigh.

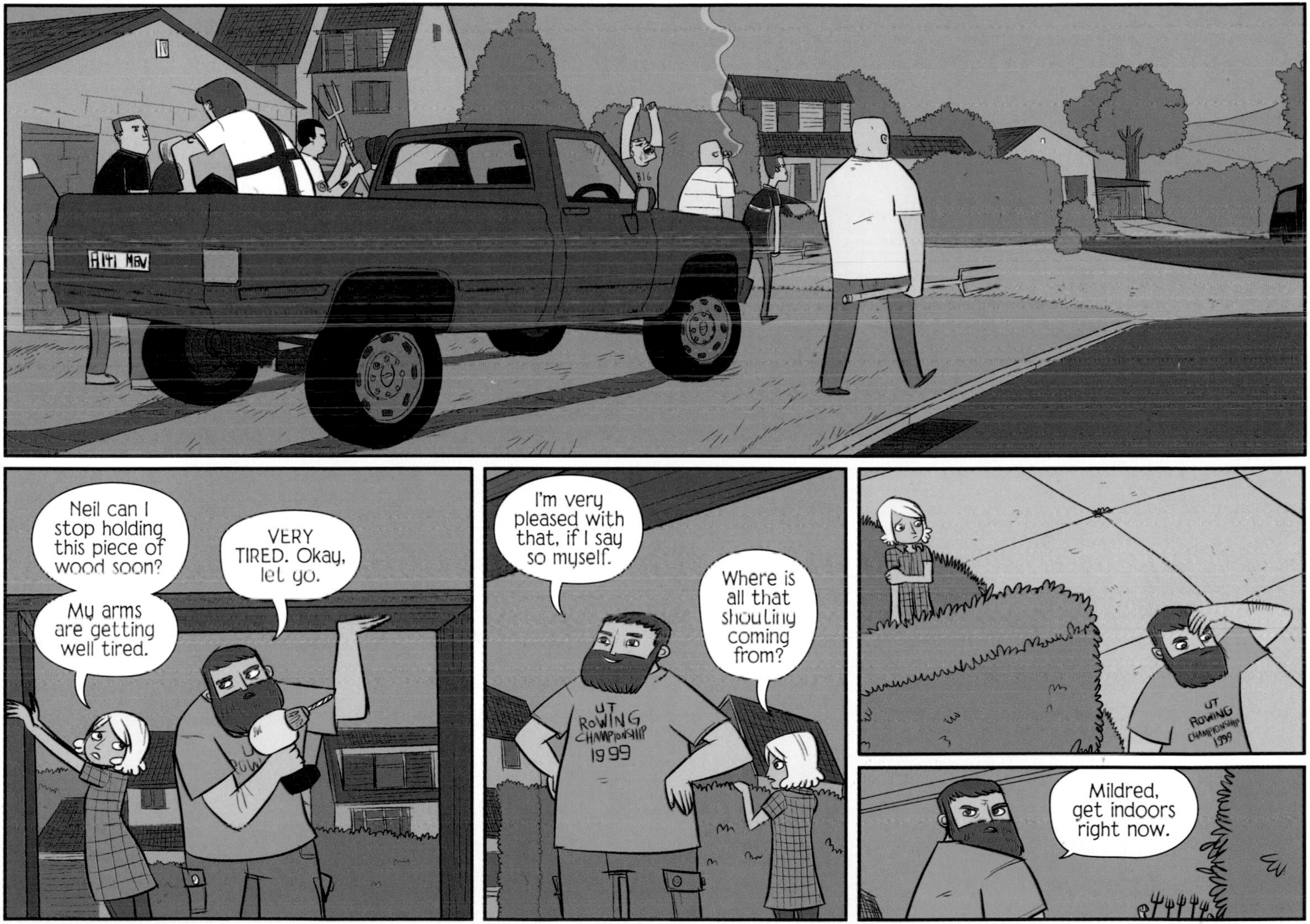
Neil can I stop holding this piece of wood soon?
My arms are getting well tired.
VERY TIRED. Okay, let go.
I'm very pleased with that, if I say so myself.
UT ROWING CHAMPIONSHIP 1999
Where is all that shouting coming from?
Mildred, get indoors right now.

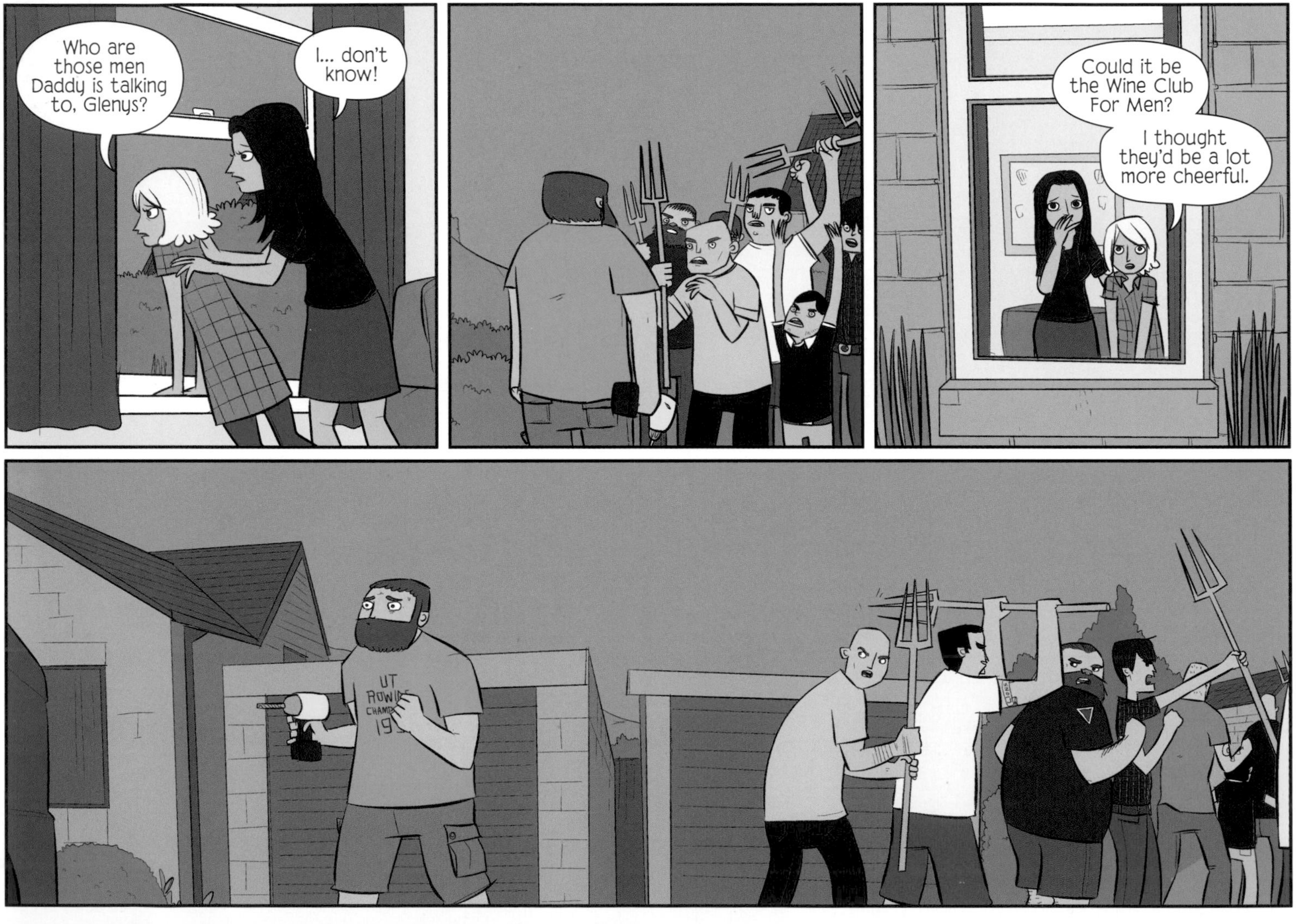
Who are those men Daddy is talking to, Glenys?
I... don't know!
Could it be the Wine Club For Men?
I thought they'd be a lot more cheerful.

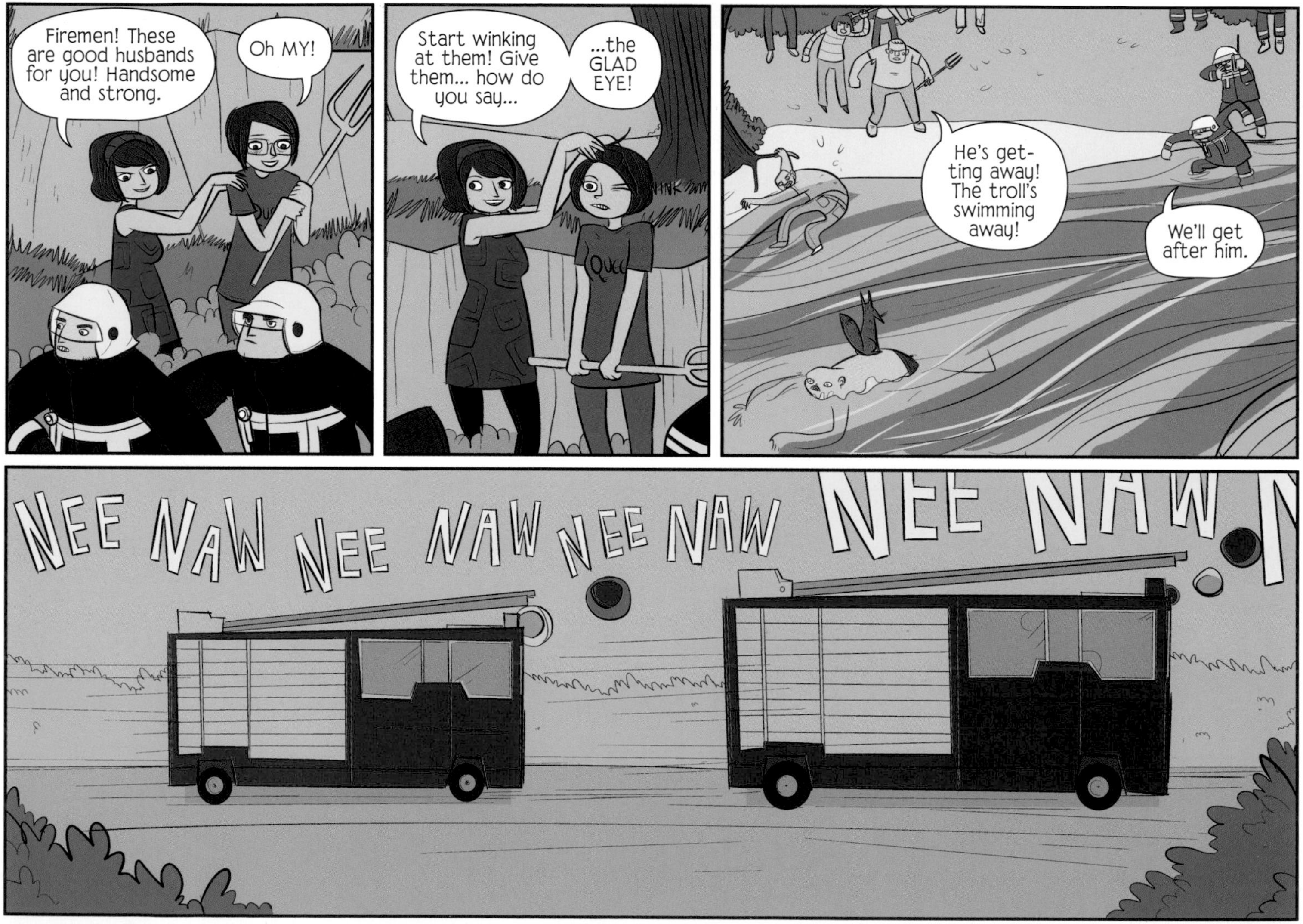
Firemen! These are good husbands for you! Handsome and strong.
Oh MY!
Start winking at them! Give them... how do you say...
...the GLAD EYE!
WINK
He's get-ting away! The troll's swimming away!
We'll get after him.
NEE NAW NEE NAW NEE NAW NEE NAW N

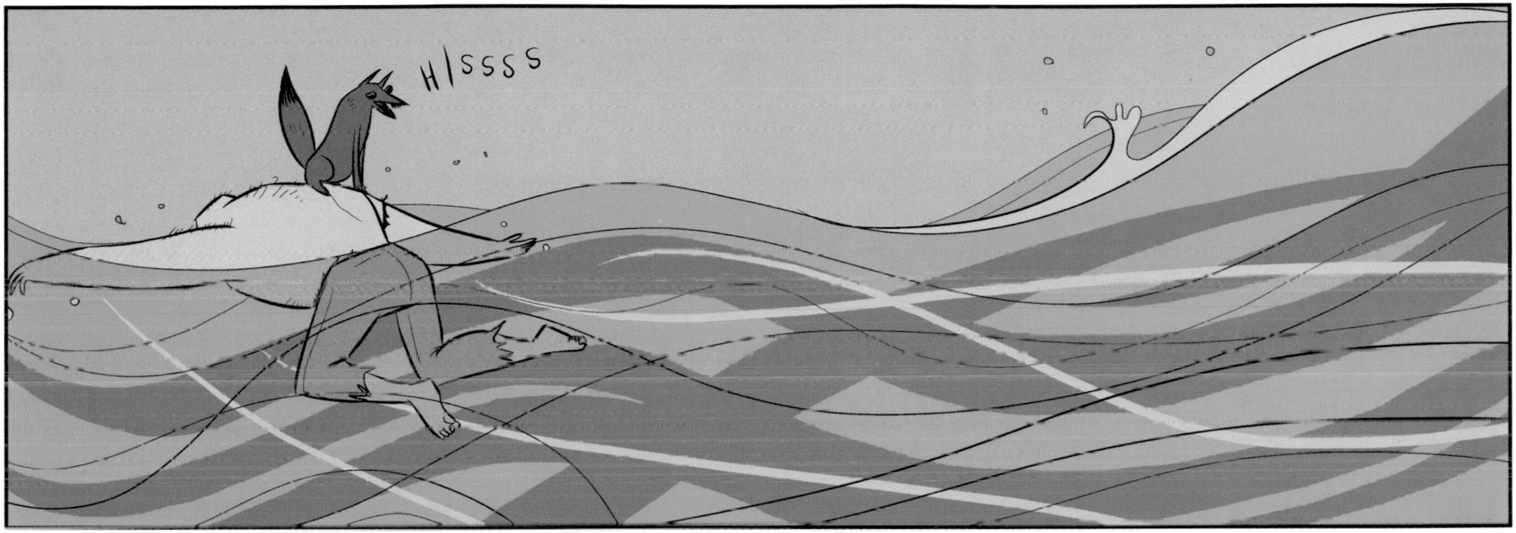
HISSSS

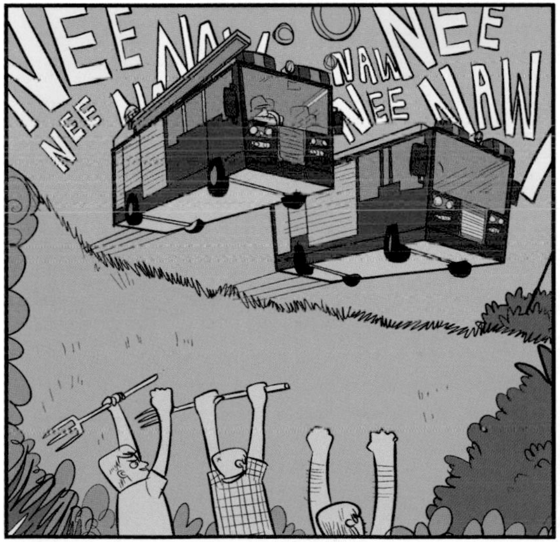
NEE NAW NEE NAW NEE NAW NEE NAW

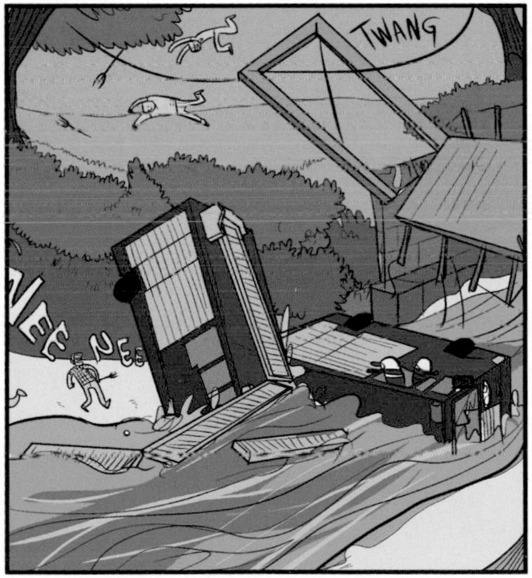
TWANG
NEE NEE

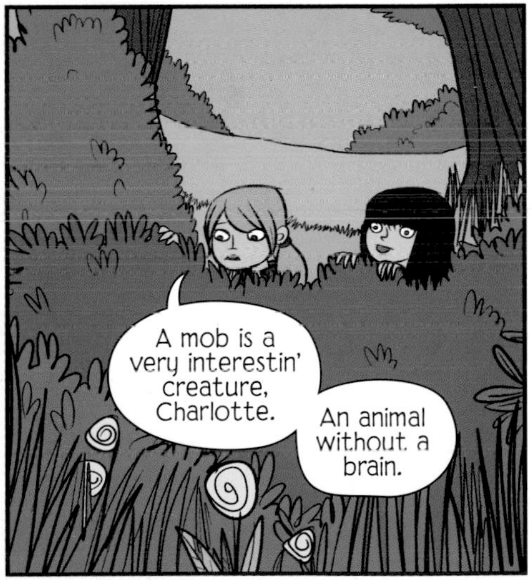
A mob is a very interestin' creature, Charlotte.
An animal without a brain.

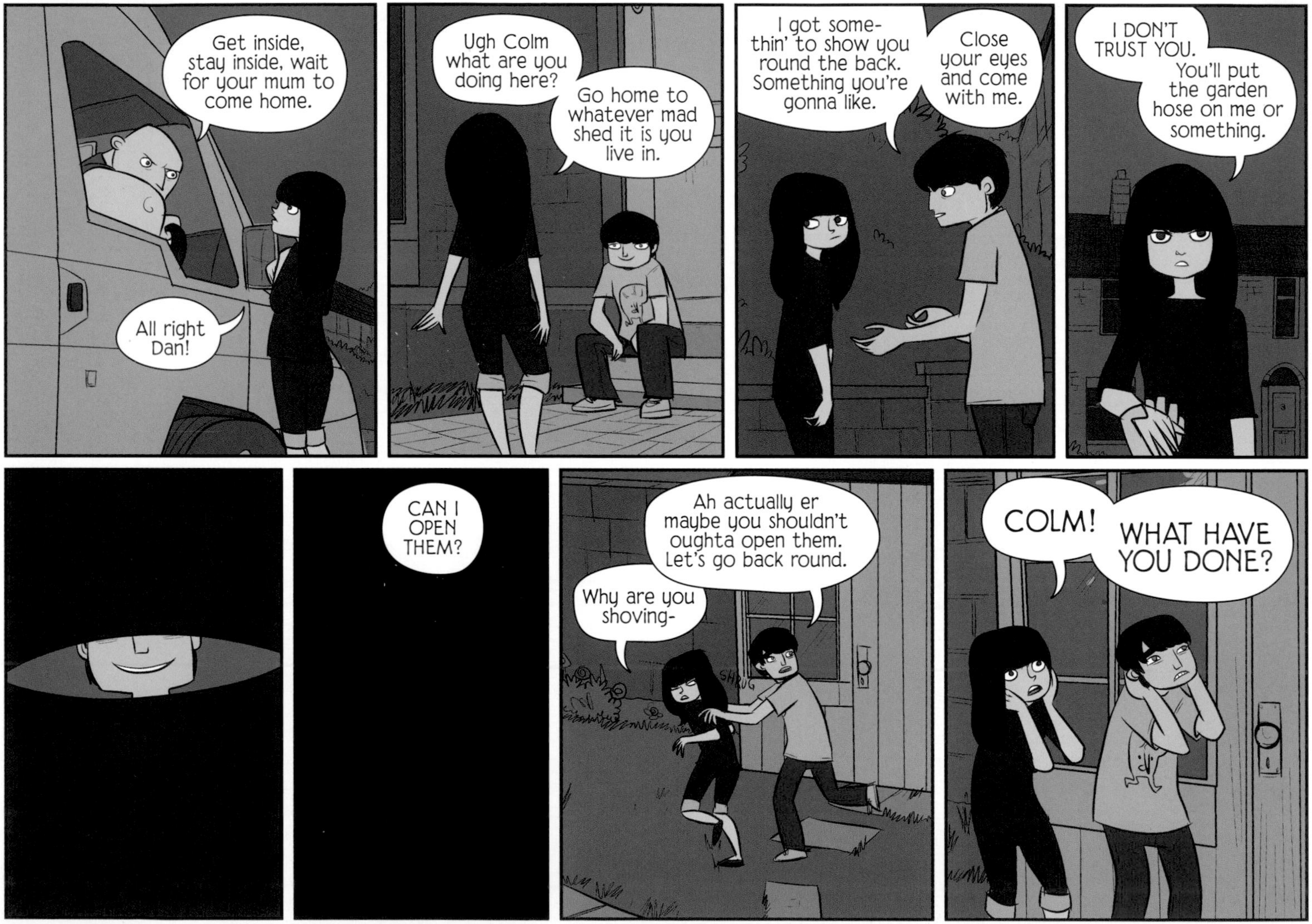
Get inside, stay inside, wait for your mum to come home.
All right Dan!
Ugh Colm what are you doing here?
Go home to whatever mad shed it is you live in.
I got somethin' to show you round the back. Something you're gonna like.
Close your eyes and come with me.
I DON'T TRUST YOU.
You'll put the garden hose on me or something.
CAN I OPEN THEM?
Ah actually er maybe you shouldn't oughta open them. Let's go back round.
Why are you shoving-
SHRUG
COLM!
WHAT HAVE YOU DONE?

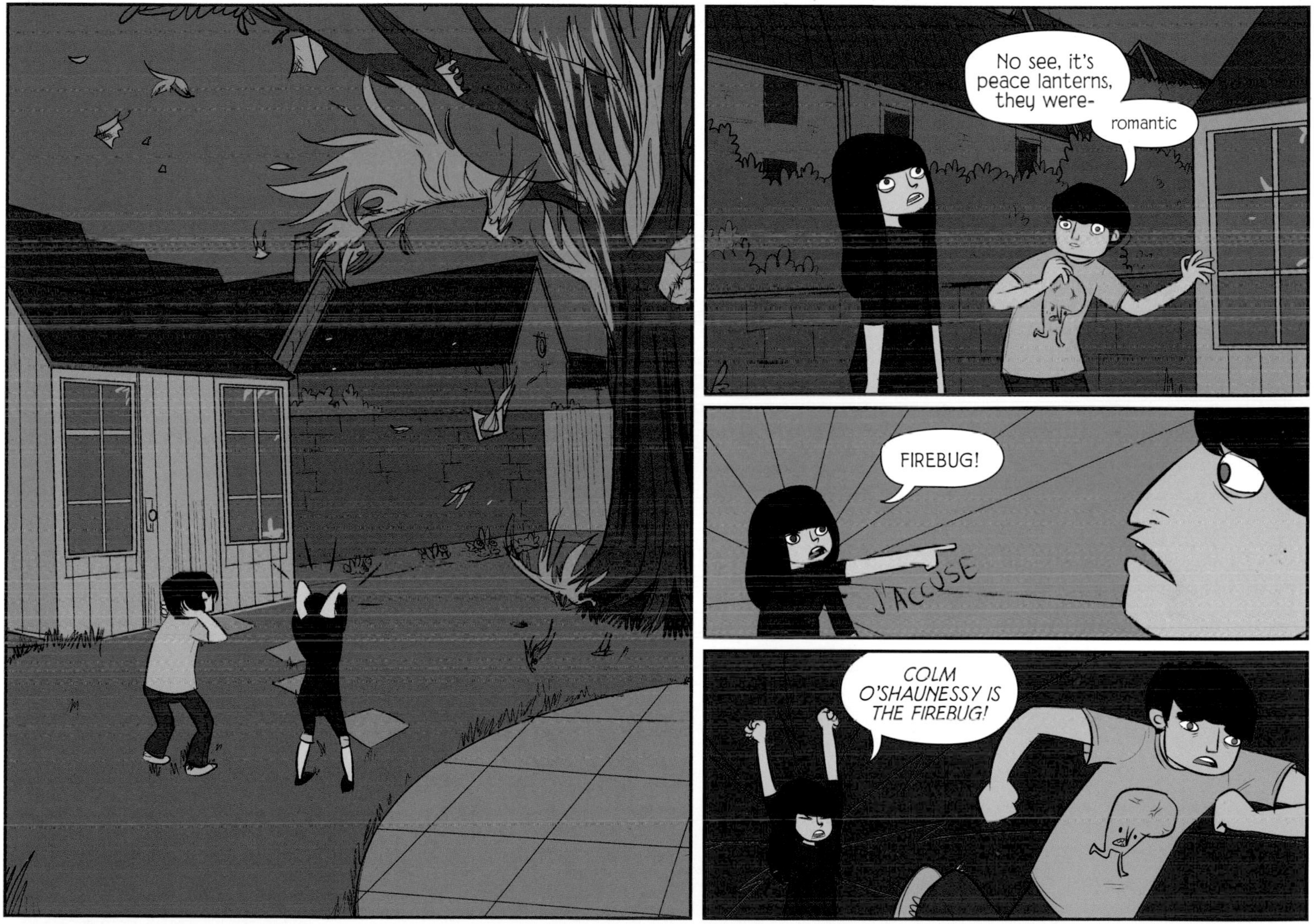
No see, it's peace lanterns, they were-
romantic
FIREBUG!
J'ACCUSE
COLM O'SHAUNESSY IS THE FIREBUG!

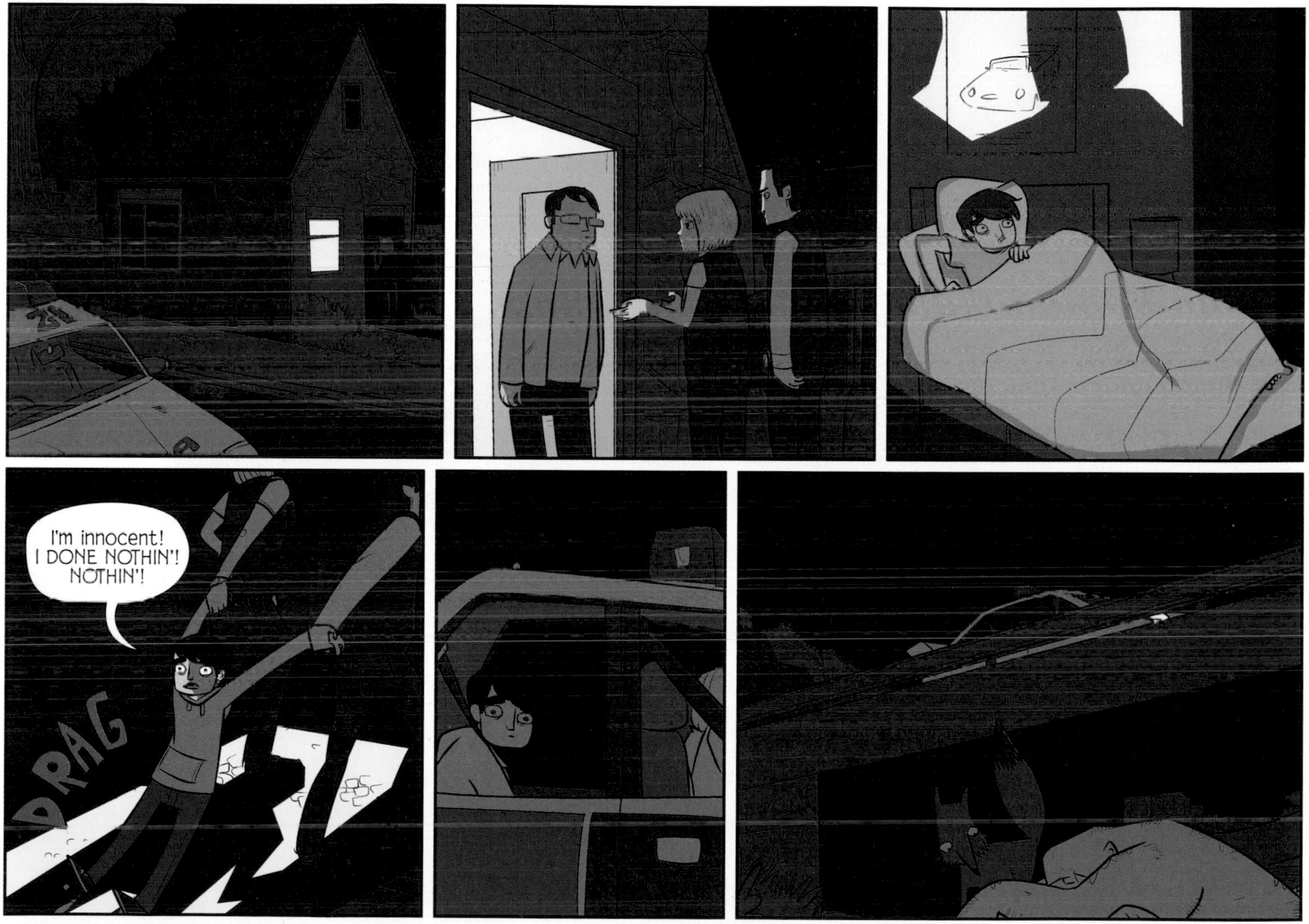
I'm innocent! I DONE NOTHIN'! NOTHIN'!
DRAG

The Case of the Simple Soul

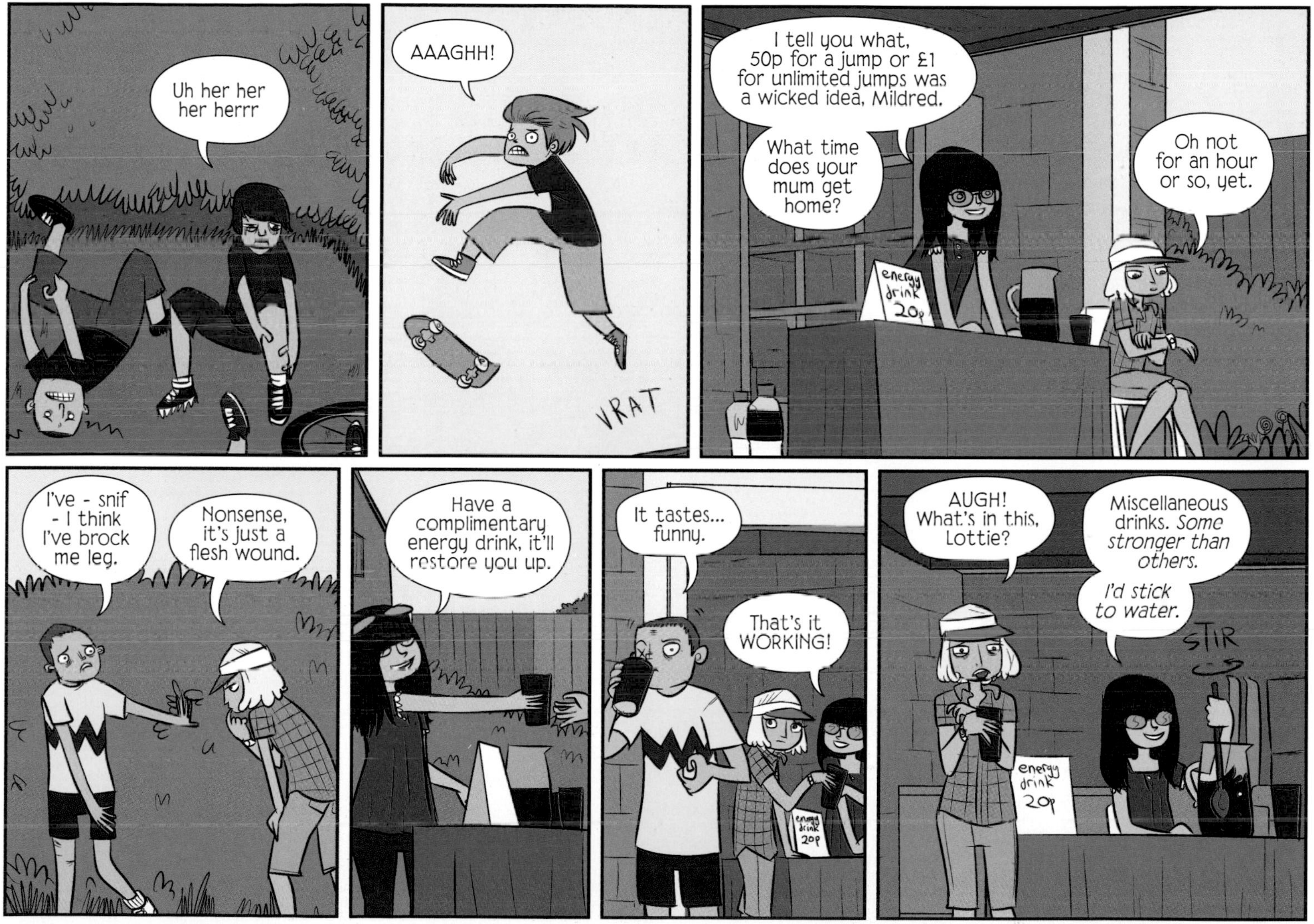

Uh her her
her herrr
AAAGHH!
VRAT
I tell you what, 50p for a jump or £1 for unlimited jumps was a wicked idea, Mildred.
What time does your mum get home?
Oh not for an hour or so, yet.
energy drink 20p
I've - snif - I think I've brock me leg.
Nonsense, it's just a flesh wound.
Have a complimentary energy drink, it'll restore you up.
It tastes... funny.
That's it WORKING!
energy drink 20p
AUGH! What's in this, Lottie?
Miscellaneous drinks. *Some stronger than others.*
I'd stick to water.
STIR
energy drink 20p

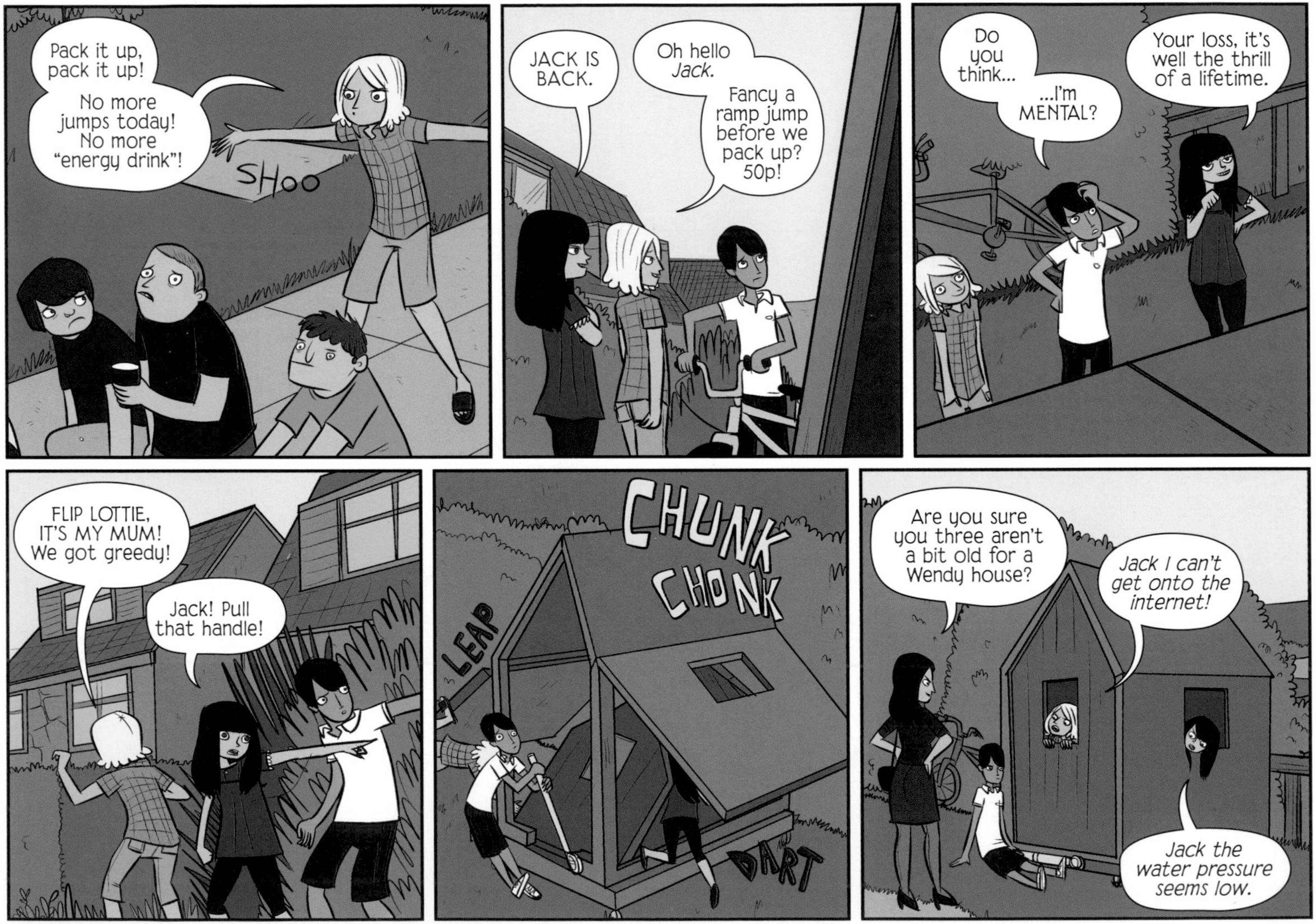
Pack it up, pack it up!
No more jumps today! No more "energy drink"!
SHOO
JACK IS BACK.
Oh hello *Jack.*
Fancy a ramp jump before we pack up? 50p!
Do you think...
...I'm MENTAL?
Your loss, it's well the thrill of a lifetime.
FLIP LOTTIE, IT'S MY MUM! We got greedy!
Jack! Pull that handle!
LEAP
CHUNK
CHONK
DART
Are you sure you three aren't a bit old for a Wendy house?
Jack I can't get onto the internet!
Jack the water pressure seems low.

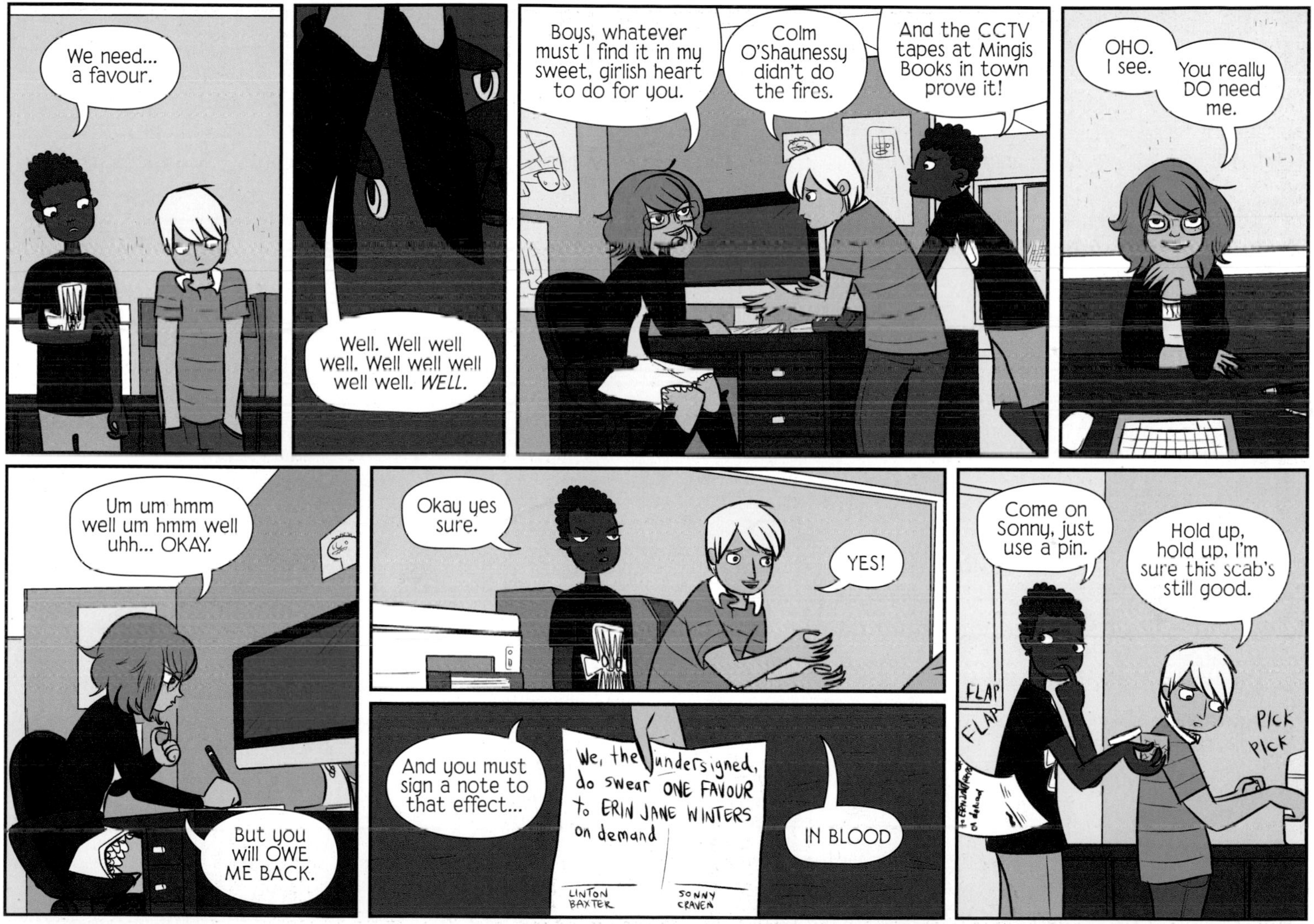

We need... a favour.
Well. Well well well. Well well well well well. *WELL.*
Boys, whatever must I find it in my sweet, girlish heart to do for you.
Colm O'Shaunessy didn't do the fires.
And the CCTV tapes at Mingis Books in town prove it!
OHO. I see.
You really DO need me.
Um um hmm well um hmm well uhh... OKAY.
But you will OWE ME BACK.
Okay yes sure.
YES!
And you must sign a note to that effect...
We, the undersigned, do swear ONE FAVOUR to ERIN JANE WINTERS on demand
LINTON BAXTER
SONNY CRAVEN
IN BLOOD
Come on Sonny, just use a pin.
Hold up, hold up, I'm sure this scab's still good.
FLAP
FLAP
PICK
PICK

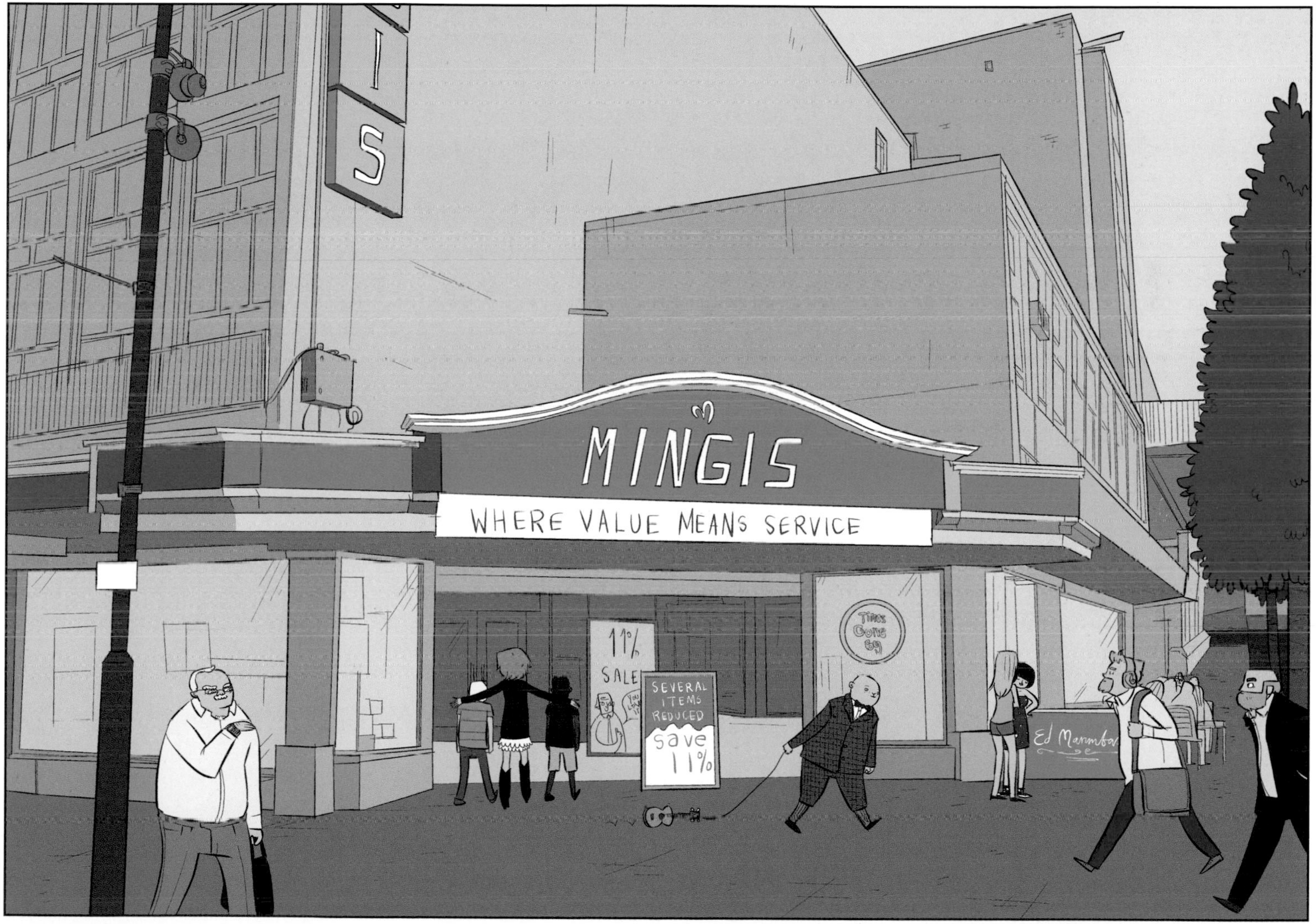
MINGIS
WHERE VALUE MEANS SERVICE
11% SALE
SEVERAL ITEMS REDUCED
save 11%
Times Gone By

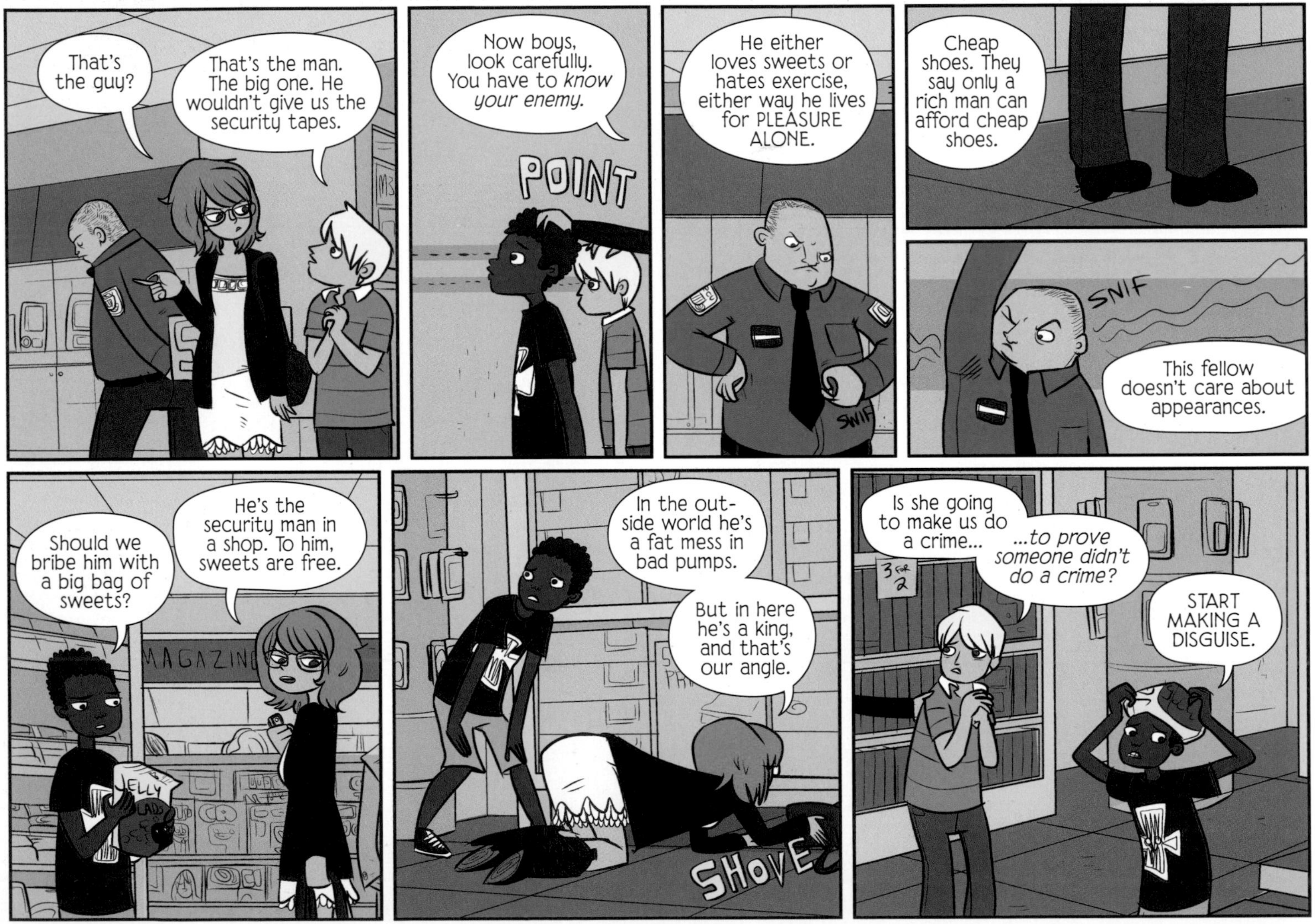
That's the guy?
That's the man. The big one. He wouldn't give us the security tapes.
Now boys, look carefully. You have to *know your enemy*.
POINT
He either loves sweets or hates exercise, either way he lives for PLEASURE ALONE.
SNIF
Cheap shoes. They say only a rich man can afford cheap shoes.
SNIF
This fellow doesn't care about appearances.
Should we bribe him with a big bag of sweets?
He's the security man in a shop. To him, sweets are free.
MAGAZINE
In the out-side world he's a fat mess in bad pumps.
But in here he's a king, and that's our angle.
SHOVE
Is she going to make us do a crime...
...to prove someone didn't do a crime?
3 for 2
START MAKING A DISGUISE.

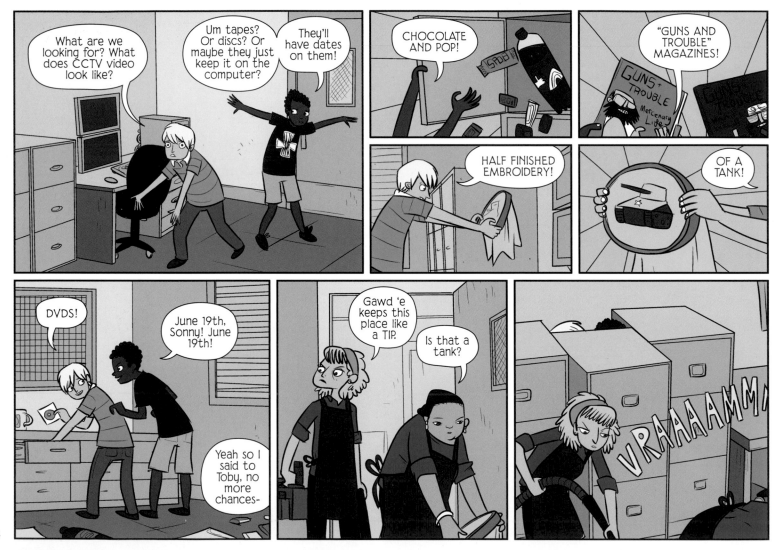

The Case of the Simple Soul

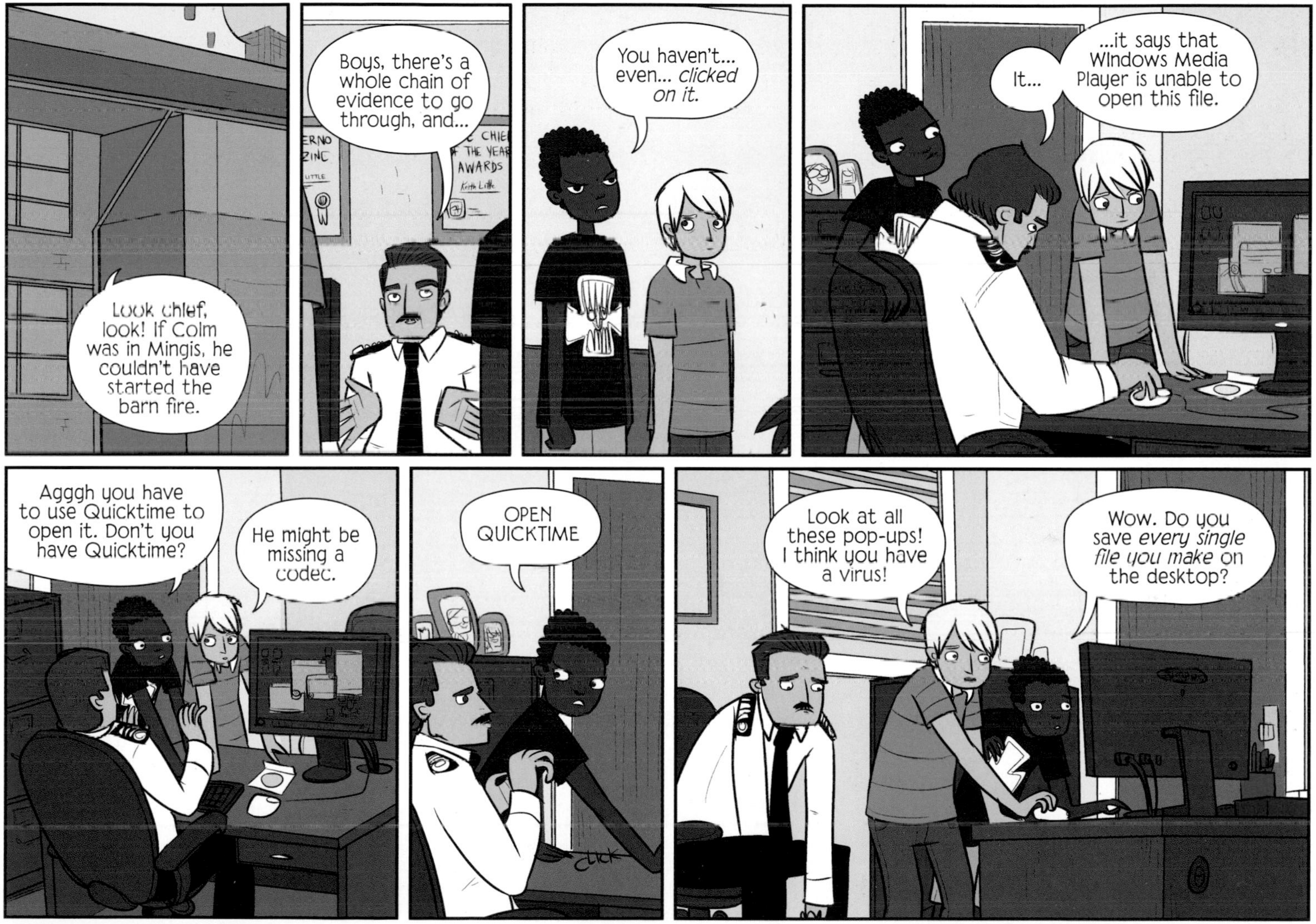
Look chief, look! If Colm was in Mingis, he couldn't have started the barn fire.
Boys, there's a whole chain of evidence to go through, and...
You haven't... even... *clicked on it.*
It...
...it says that Windows Media Player is unable to open this file.
Agggh you have to use Quicktime to open it. Don't you have Quicktime?
He might be missing a codec.
OPEN QUICKTIME
CLICK
Look at all these pop-ups! I think you have a virus!
Wow. Do you save *every single file you make* on the desktop?

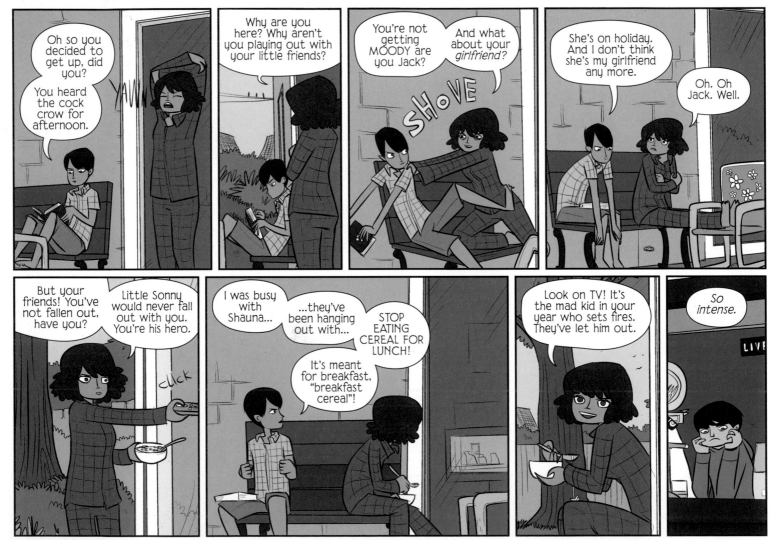

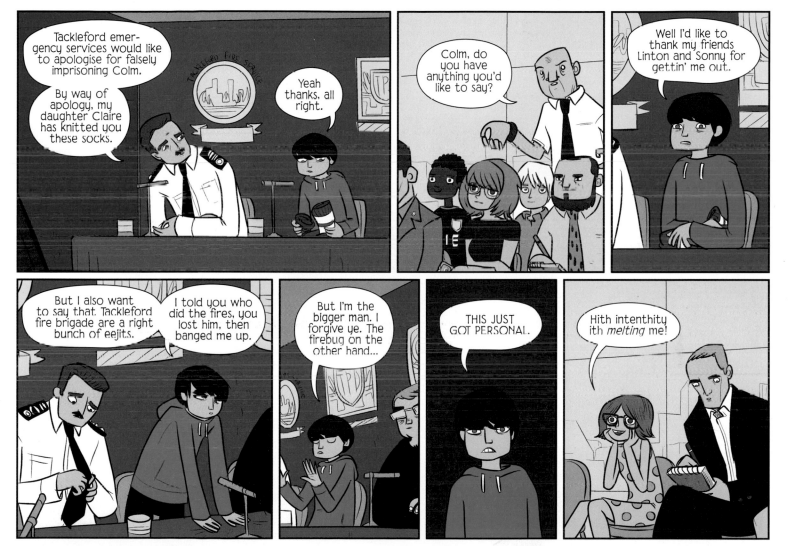

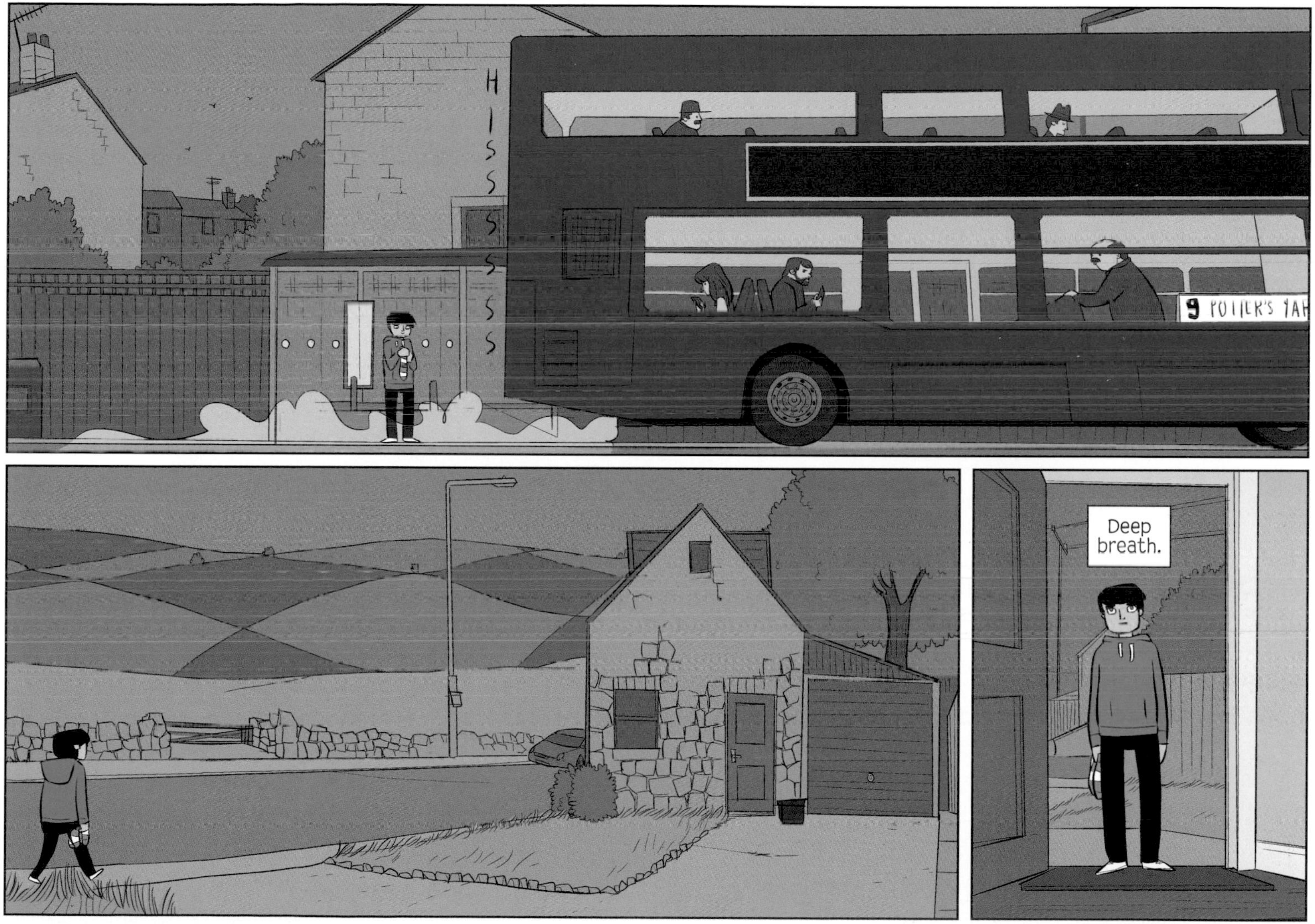
HISSSSSS
Deep breath.

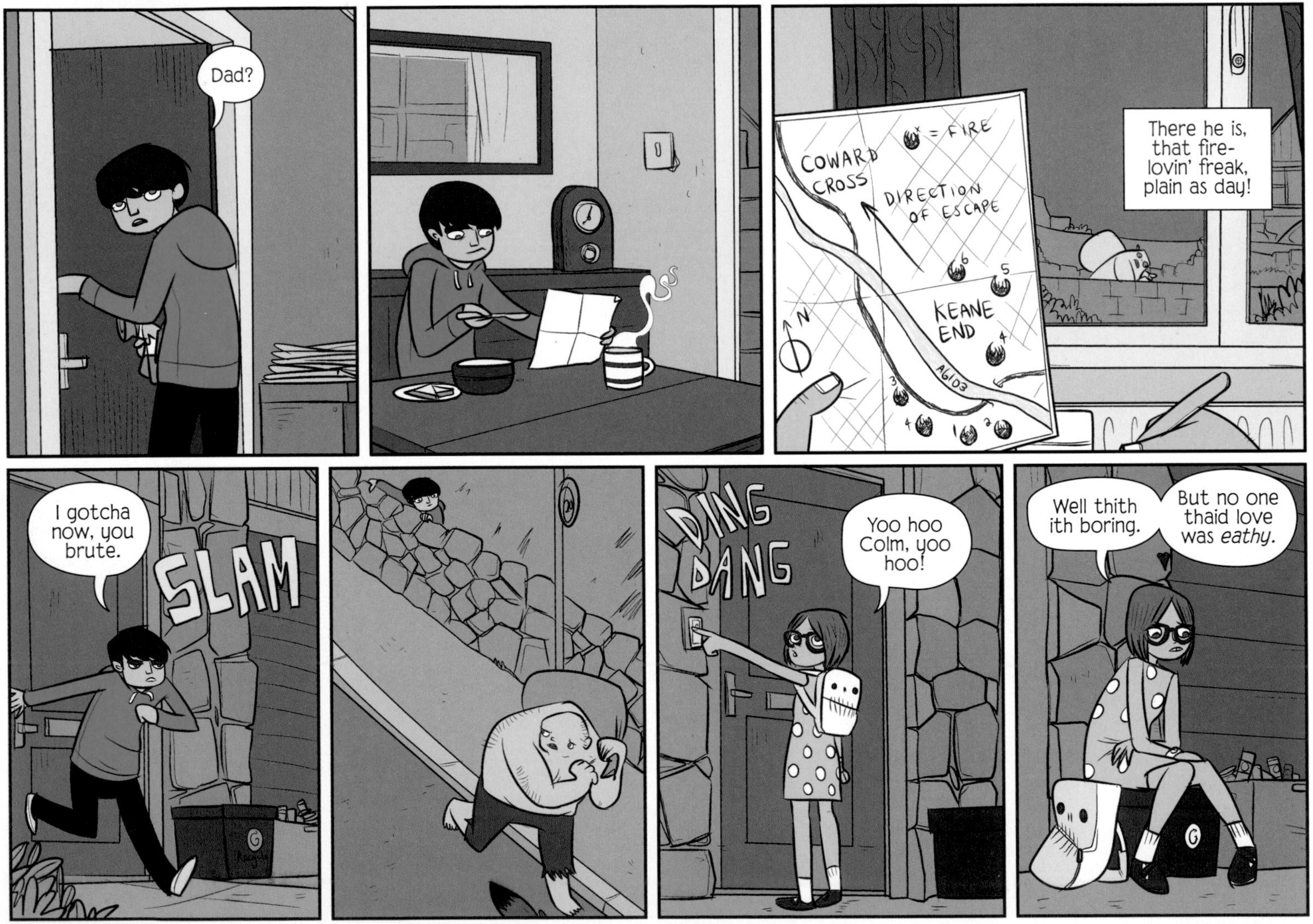

Dad?
COWARD CROSS
= FIRE
DIRECTION OF ESCAPE
N
KEANE END
A6103
There he is, that fire-lovin' freak, plain as day!
I gotcha now, you brute.
SLAM
DING DANG
Yoo hoo Colm, yoo hoo!
Well thith ith boring.
But no one thaid love was *eathy*.

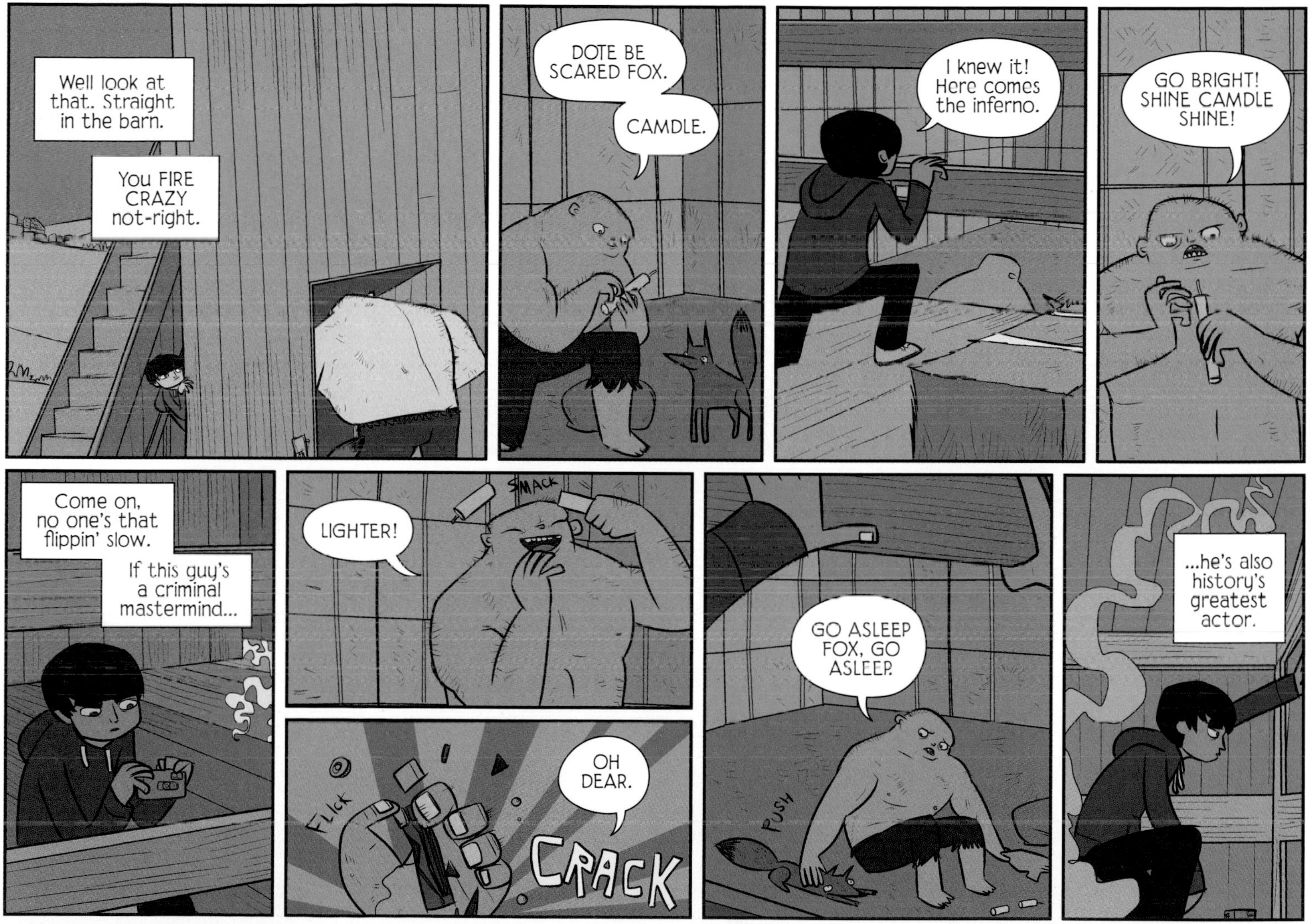
Well look at that.. Straight in the barn.
You FIRE CRAZY not-right.
DOTE BE SCARED FOX.
CAMDLE.
I knew it! Here comes the inferno.
GO BRIGHT! SHINE CAMDLE SHINE!
Come on, no one's that flippin' slow.
If this guy's a criminal mastermind...
SMACK
LIGHTER!
FLICK
OH DEAR.
CRACK
PUSH
GO ASLEEP FOX, GO ASLEEP.
...he's also history's greatest actor.

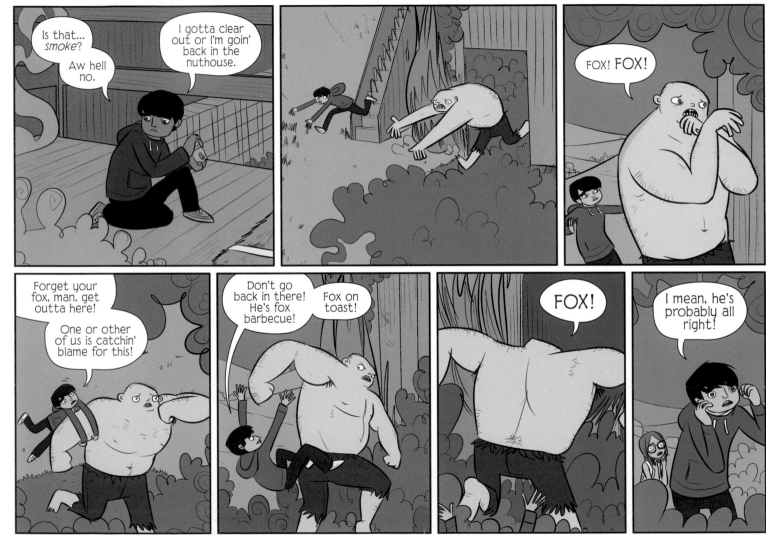

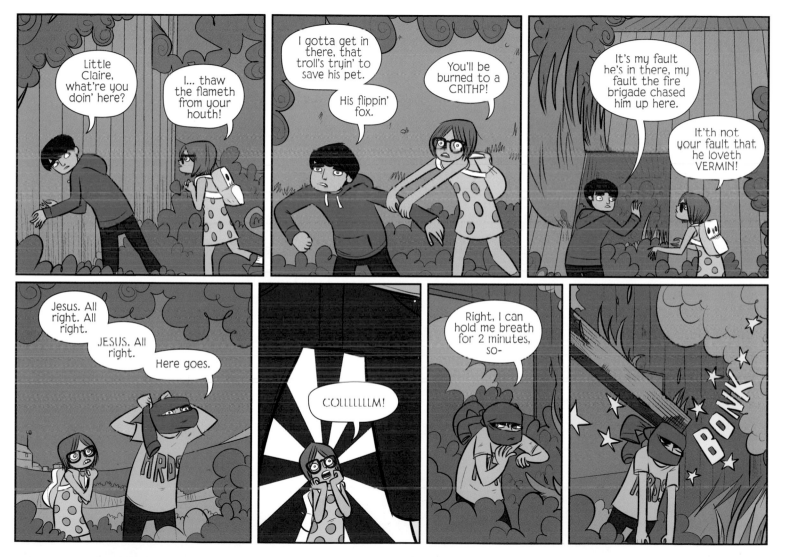

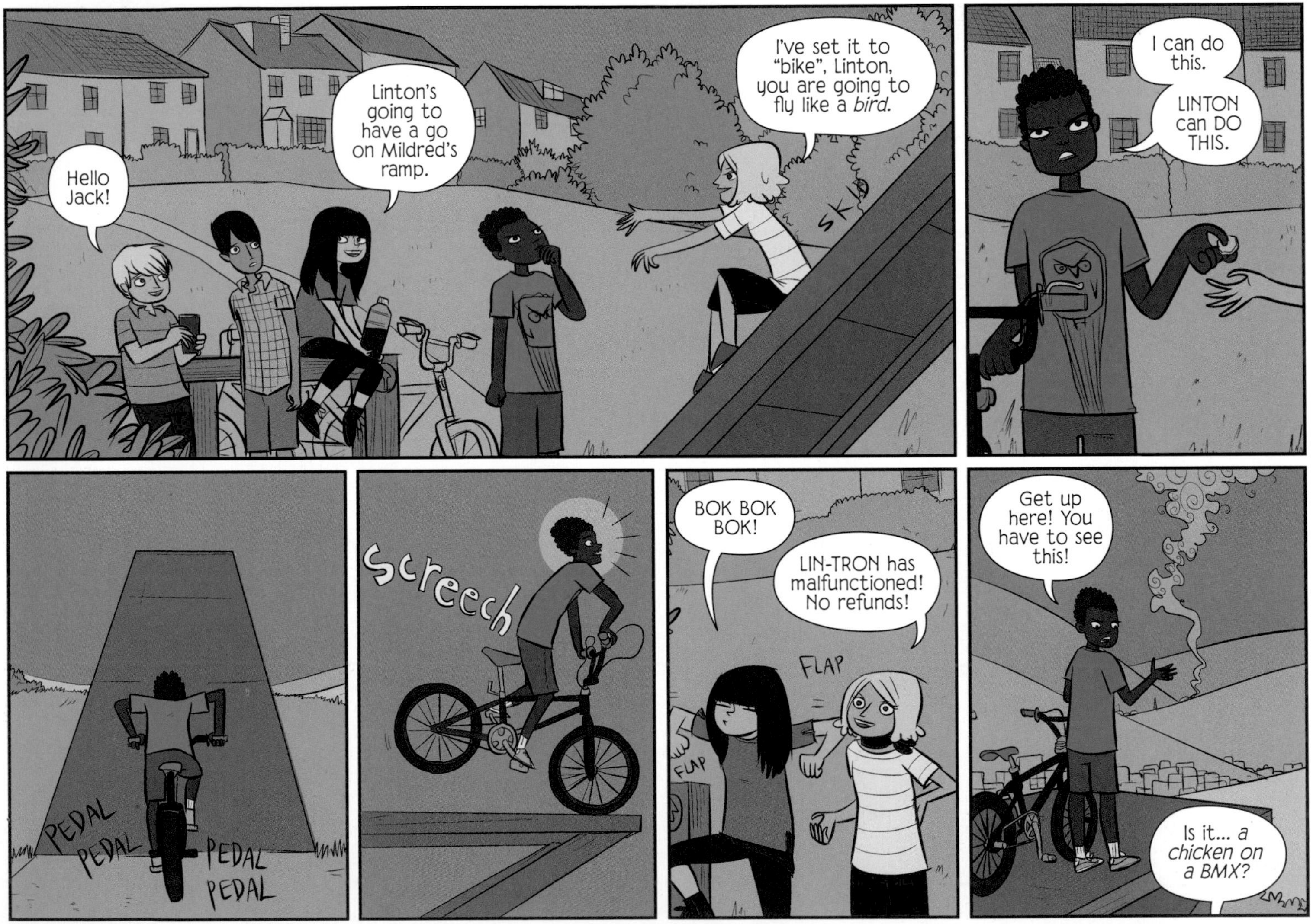
Hello Jack!
Linton's going to have a go on Mildred's ramp.
I've set it to "bike", Linton, you are going to fly like a *bird.*
I can do this.
LINTON can DO THIS.
PEDAL PEDAL PEDAL PEDAL
Screech
BOK BOK BOK!
LIN-TRON has malfunctioned! No refunds!
FLAP
FLAP
Get up here! You have to see this!
Is it... *a chicken on a BMX?*

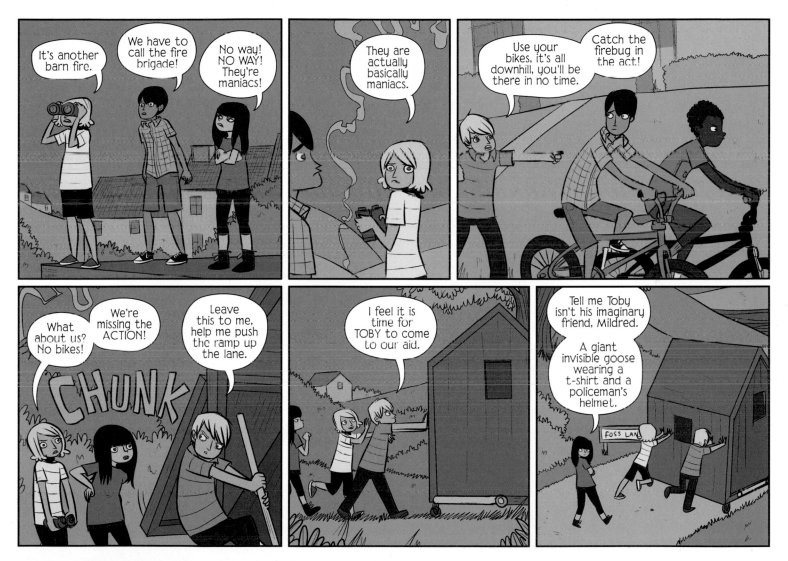

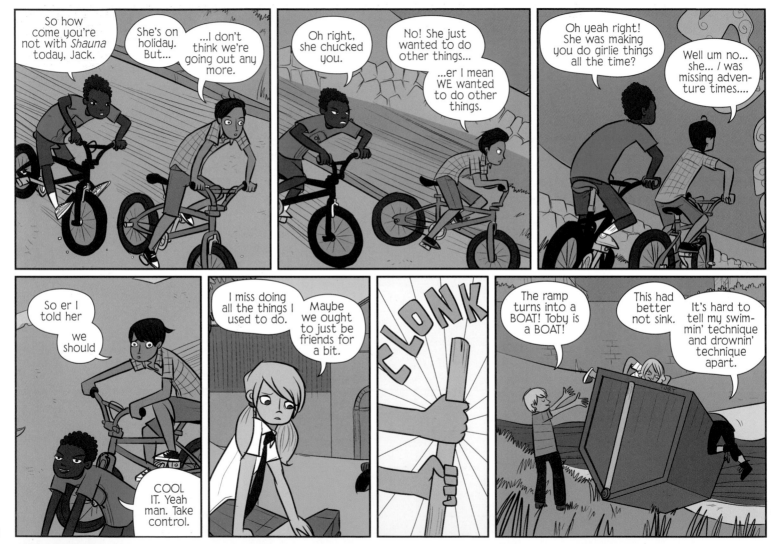

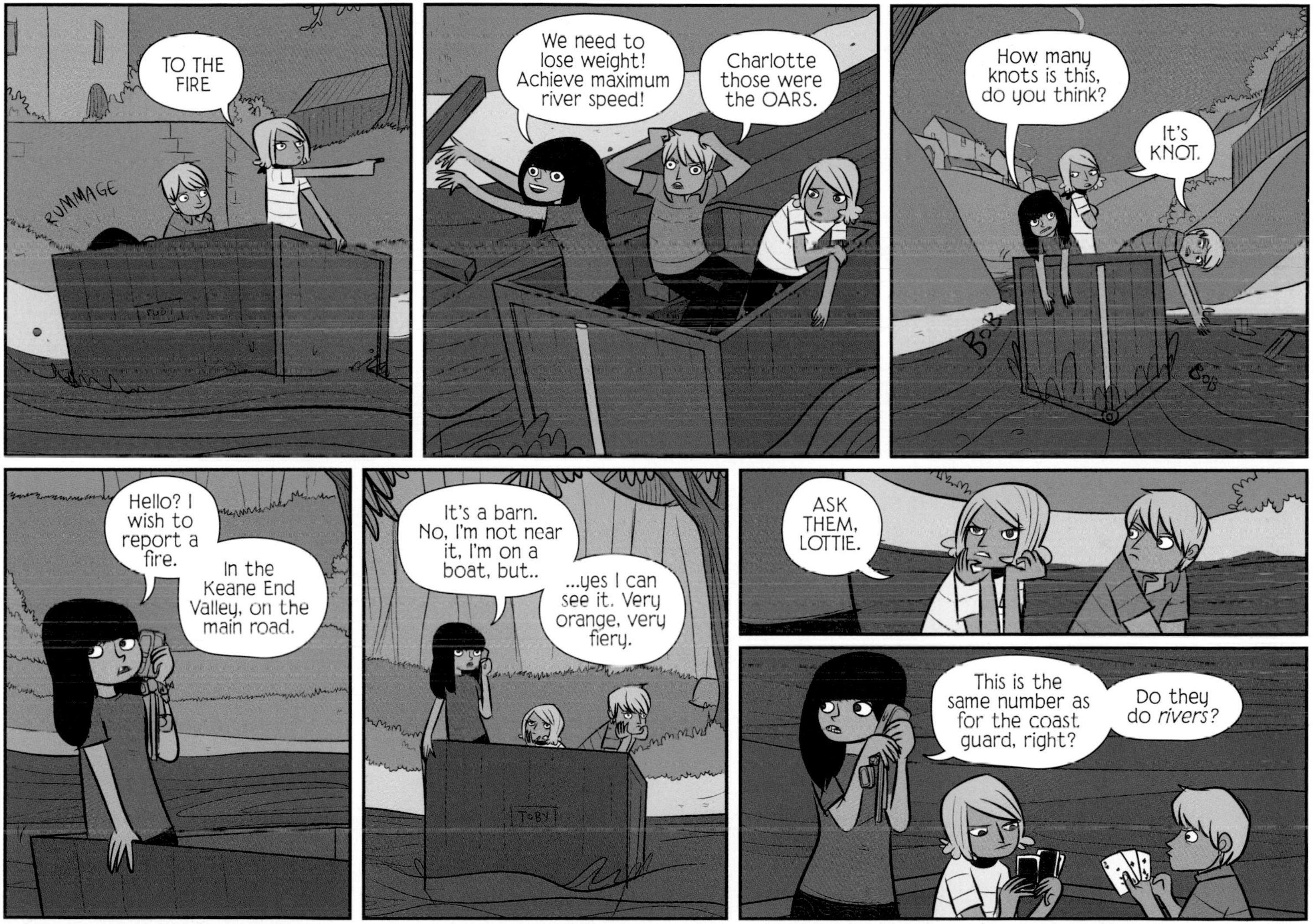

TO THE FIRE
RUMMAGE
We need to lose weight! Achieve maximum river speed!
Charlotte those were the OARS.
How many knots is this, do you think?
It's KNOT.
Bob
Bob
Hello? I wish to report a fire.
In the Keane End Valley, on the main road.
It's a barn. No, I'm not near it, I'm on a boat, but..
...yes I can see it. Very orange, very fiery.
TOBY
ASK THEM, LOTTIE.
This is the same number as for the coast guard, right?
Do they do *rivers*?

The Case of the Simple Soul

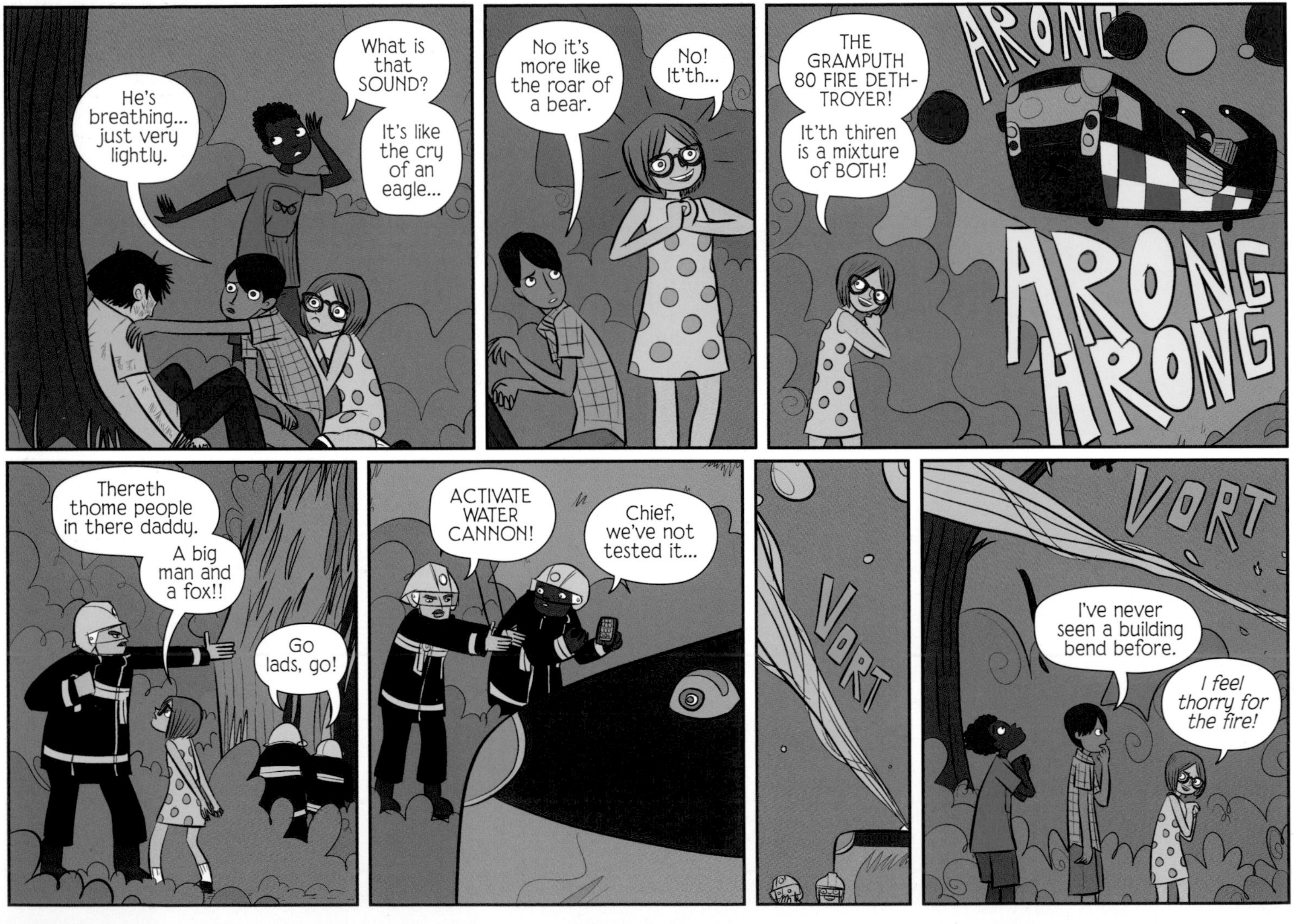
He's breathing... just very lightly.
What is that SOUND?
It's like the cry of an eagle...
No it's more like the roar of a bear.
No! It'th...
THE GRAMPUTH 80 FIRE DETH-TROYER!
It'th thiren is a mixture of BOTH!
ARONG
ARONG HRONG
Thereth thome people in there daddy.
A big man and a fox!!
Go lads, go!
ACTIVATE WATER CANNON!
Chief, we've not tested it...
VORT
VORT
I've never seen a building bend before.
I feel thorry for the fire!

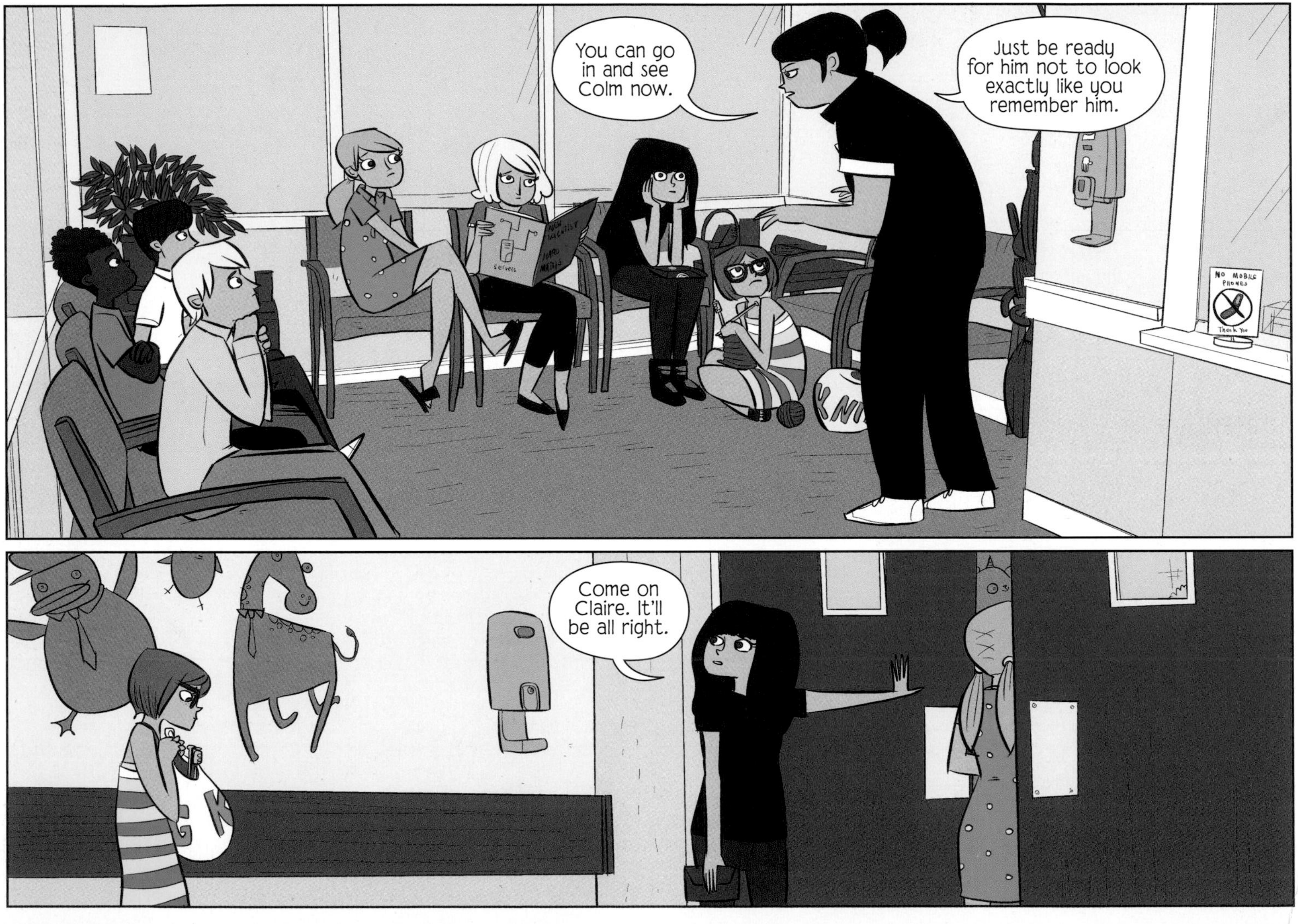
You can go in and see Colm now.
Just be ready for him not to look exactly like you remember him.
NO MOBILE PHONES
Come on Claire. It'll be all right.

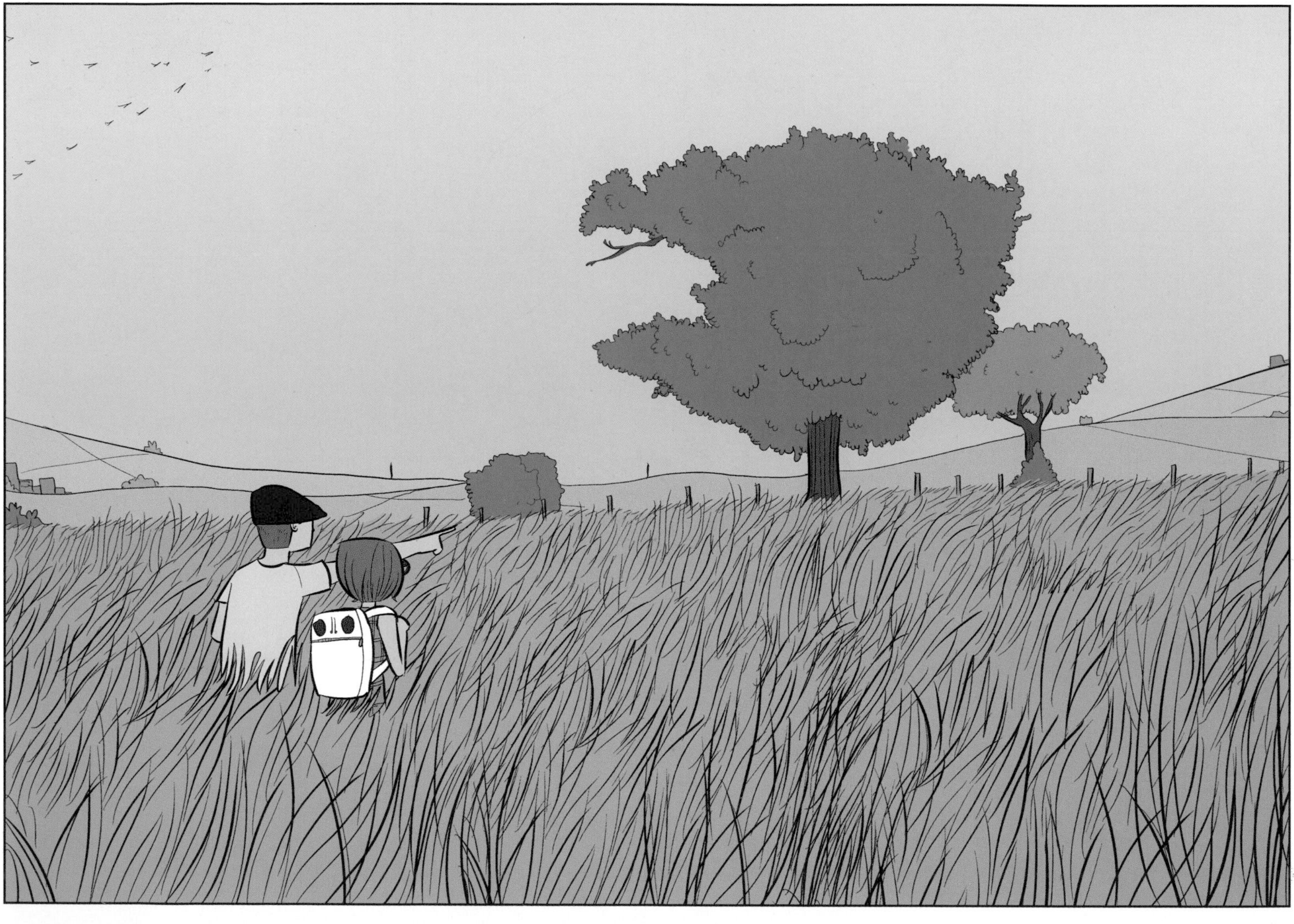

The Case of the Simple Soul

GLOSSARY

Great Britain is a comprised of four countries: England, Scotland, Wales, and Northern Ireland. Then there is Cornwall what has its own flag and language but is too obsessed with surfing to really be a country. They don't have a government but they do have "Surfers Against Sewage" which deals with probably 75% of their concerns as a nation. This mixture of people has created a lot of interesting phrases that you may wish to add to your international dictionary.

LOVE,
Charlotte
XXX

Mental: This is when your brainbox does not work quite right. Not to be confused with "The Mentalist" who is a man whose brain works maybe too well?

Parson: A holy man, a cleric. When picturing a parson as the people of Britane might think of him, imagine a priest in a cassock who has gone bright red because a lady in a short skirt just walked in. Maybe there is the sound of a swannee whistle at the same time.

Telly: Television. Please note, belly is not an abbreviation of "bellyvision" which is well a nightmare scenario.

Potty: See "mental". I resent the implication that I do not have a fully working mind. I think eventually Potty Grote will be replaced by "Hottie Grote" or, among less shallow members of the school, "Polyglotty Grote", because of my great mastery of the Fronch long-uage.

FIG 1: NON-POTTY HOBBIES

Dinner lady: In America, "lunch lady". Any meal served by the school at lunchtime is referred to as "school dinner". School dinners are a Controversial Area because in the past schools were always trying to feed you meat they found at the town dump and childers liked that bad meat because the government had made it into a fun shape and put breadcrumbs on it. Then Jamie Oliver got involved.

They all use their knife and fork wrong: Cutlery skills are very important in the UK because for many years the food was not worth eating so you had to concentrate on something else.

The craic: Something Irish people say. Maybe it means "a good time", but that could be too simple, it can also mean gossip, fine entertainment or just some red hot chat. It is a catch-all term for anything that floats the Irish boat I reckon.

Sports Day: Day on which the whole school competes with each other in a load of track and field events. Well, most do. The kids with kind parents get notes written and enjoy pulling buttercups and daisies out of the living earth in the summer sun while watching Sonia Williams from 4B throw a "shot put".

SONIA WILLIAMS: ASTOUNDING PHYSICAL POWER

Wendlefield: Tackleford's main enemy town. As soon as you go under the bridge to Wendlefield, there are no colours, milk goes sour, and a lad scratches your car with a coin while you're in the supermarket.

Property prices: If you listen carefully on any bus or train in our fine nation, this is what the adult humans are talking about.

TWITCH   TWITCH

The glad eye: When a lady has taken a shine to a man, she bestows upon him a loving and sen-sual gaze and that is the glad eye. See also: the skunk eye, the dead eye, the kill eye.

Bare nipples and back hair all showing: As soon as the sun is out, certain men head to the downtown zone with this look. The sun has confused them about how much we want to see their bare top halves. It is a national disgrace hem hem.

The nuthouse, nutters: It is important to be very respeckful of people who have mind problems, as it is not their fault. Sadly most boys have about as much respect for the feelings of the unwell as they do for an atmosphere untroubled by farts.

Wendy house: A little play house. The day you no longer fit in a Wendy house is the day you take on the cares and concerns of the adult world. Or, well, the concerns of the older than seven world. You will never own a house again (see "property prices").

Tip: The town dump (*repository for old mattresses and future school dinner meats pre-breadcrumbing*).

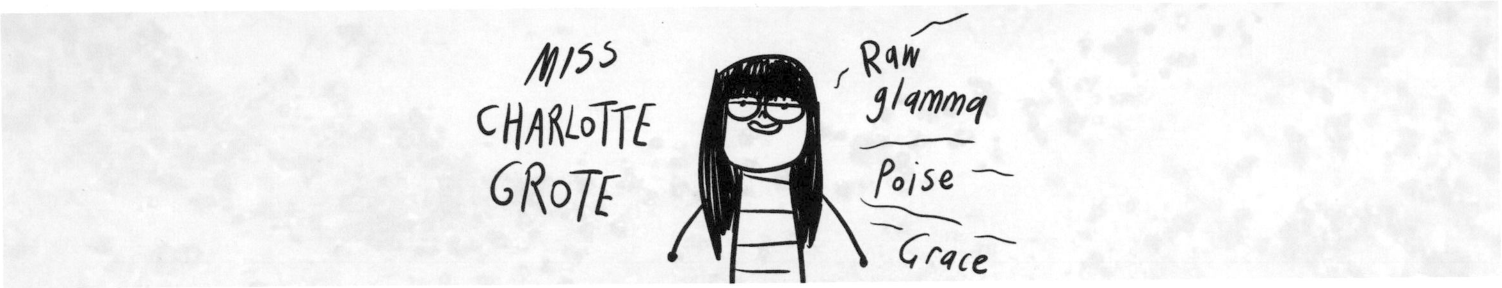
MISS
CHARLOTTE
GROTE
Raw
glamma
Poise
Grace

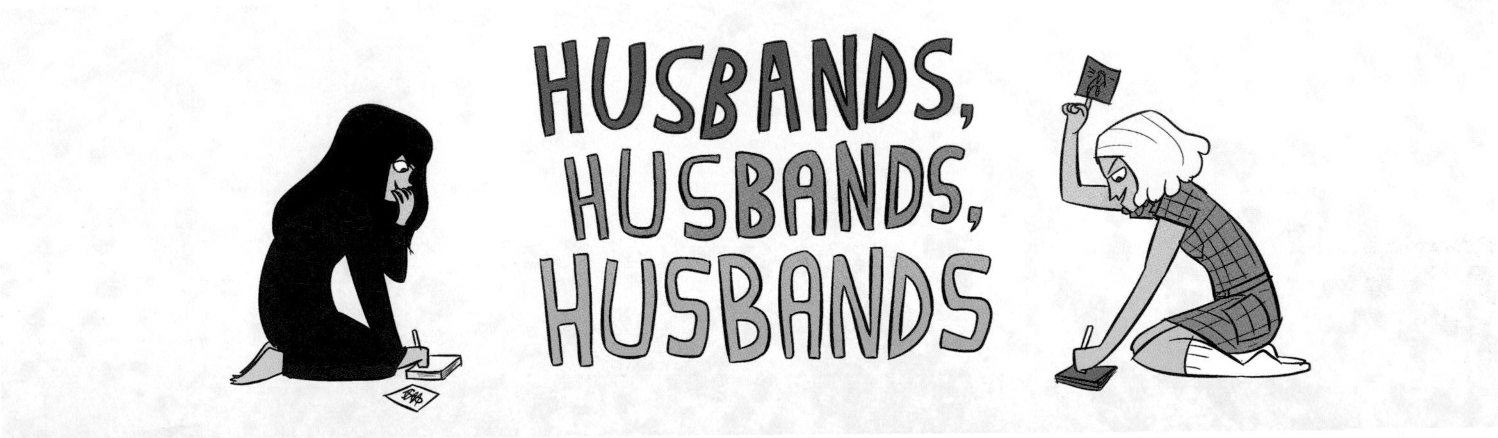
HUSBANDS,
HUSBANDS,
HUSBANDS

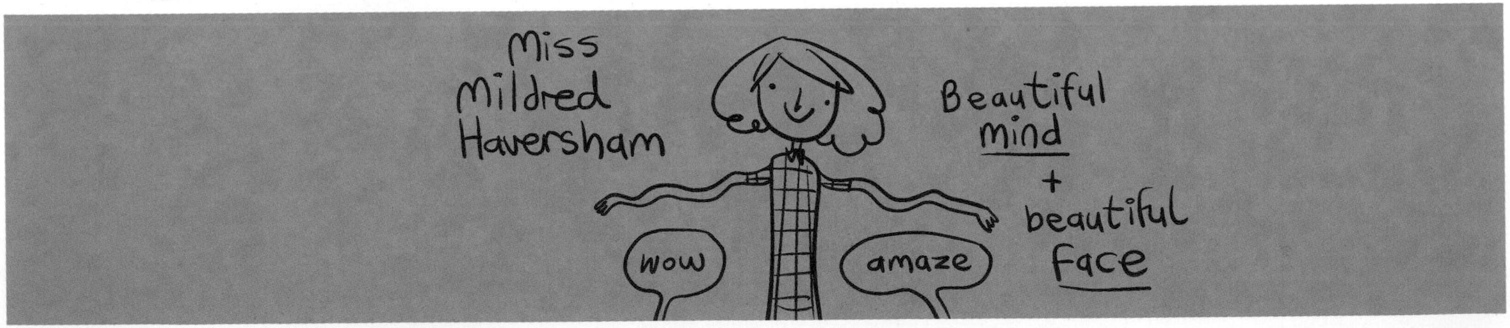
Miss
Mildred
Haversham
Beautiful
mind
+
beautiful
face
wow
amaze

FOOTBALLER HUSBAND
YES: Great wealth + strong physique
BUT: 1% chance of mental agility
PIE
kick
VICAR HUSBAND
YES: free house, listening ear, good behaviour
BUT: might grass your sins up to GOD
DOCTOR HUSBAND
YES: "in-house" expert on dropsy, penicillin and mystery aches
BUT: carries a lady's handbag everywhere with him
(even to the toilet? CHECK)
Builder husband
YES: willing participant in fancies such as bothy, gazebo, motte and bailey
BUT: hard hat leads to premature baldness, hat hair
Architect husband
YES: all the benefits of a builder but cleaner
BUT: dangerous obsession with expensive spectacles + "FRANK GEHRY"
Actor husband
YES: handsome and charismatic
BUT: in love with own reflection + sensual danger of leading ladies

SCIENCE HUSBAND
YES: powerful mind
BUT: basically a brain on legs
PRACTICAL HUSBAND
BEER TEAM
YES: good with tools
BUT: old fashioned attitudes + beer belly
ACADEMICAL HUSBAND
YES: wise and learned.
Access to capes!
BUT: smells like the inside of an old chest of drawers
"Alternative husband"
SURFS UP
YES: relaxed ways.
Extrem muscles.
BUT: Terrible music taste.
Sand everywhere!!!
Army husband
YES: man of ACTION.
Strong discipline.
Gun play?
Semper fi
BUT: Rigid attitude to bed making
Spy husband
YES: sensual air of mystery
BUT: possibility of death
a) him
b) you

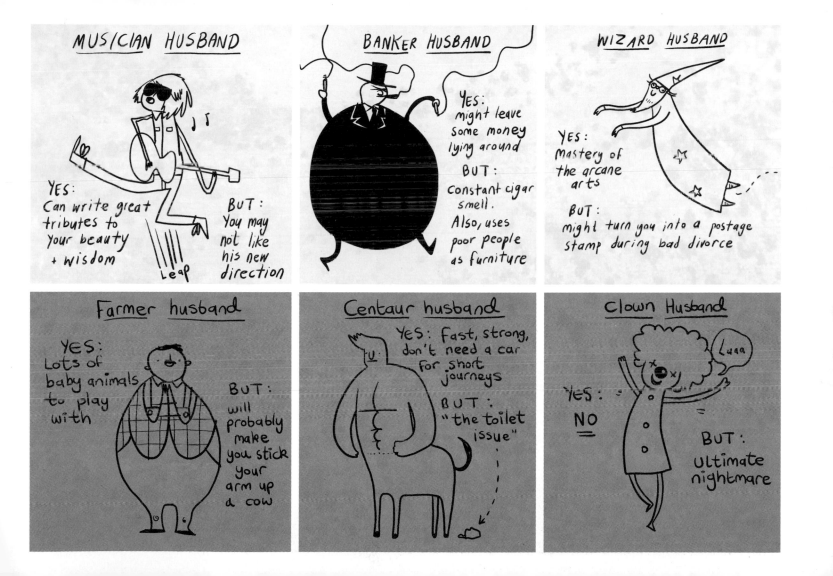

JOHN ALLISON

Born in a hidden village deep within the British Alps, John Allison came into this world a respectable baby with style and taste. Having been exposed to American comics at an early age, he spent decades honing his keen mind and his massive body in order to burn out this colonial cultural infection.

One of the longest continuously publishing independent web-based cartoonists, John has plied his trade since the late nineties moving from *Bobbins* to *Scary Go Round* to *Bad Machinery*, developing the deeply weird world of Tackleford long after many of his fellow artists were ground into dust and bones by Time Itself.

He has only once shed a single tear, but you only meet Sergio Aragonés for the first time once.

John resides in Letchworth Garden City, England and is known to his fellow villagers only as He Who Has Conquered.

—Contributed by Richard Stevens III

"THE TREASURE OF BRITANNIA"

ALSO BY JOHN ALLISON!

bad machinery
The Case Of The Team Spirit
1
JOHN ALLISON

BAD MACHINERY, VOLUME 1: THE CASE OF THE TEAM SPIRIT
By John Allison
ISBN 978-1-62010-387-6
Pocket Edition In Stores Now!

bad machinery
The Case Of The Good Boy
2
JOHN ALLISON

BAD MACHINERY, VOLUME 2: THE CASE OF THE GOOD BOY
By John Allison
ISBN 978-1-62010-421-7
Pocket Edition In Stores Now!

bad machinery
The Case Of The Lonely One
BOOKS NOT BOYS
4
JOHN ALLISON

BAD MACHINERY, VOLUME 4: THE CASE OF THE LONELY ONE
By John Allison
ISBN 978-1-62010-457-6
Pocket Edition Coming March 2018!

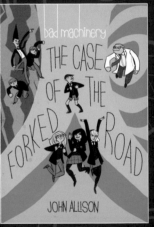

THE CASE OF THE FIRE INSIDE
bad machinery
JOHN ALLISON

BAD MACHINERY, VOLUME 5: THE CASE OF THE FIRE INSIDE
By John Allison
ISBN 978-1-62010-297-8
Pocket Edition Coming June 2018!

bad machinery
THE CASE OF THE UNWELCOME VISITOR
JOHN ALLISON

BAD MACHINERY, VOLUME 6: THE CASE OF THE UNWELCOME VISITOR
By John Allison
ISBN 978-1-62010-351-7
Pocket Edition Coming September 2018!

bad machinery
THE CASE OF THE FORKED ROAD
JOHN ALLISON

BAD MACHINERY, VOL. 7: THE CASE OF THE FORKED ROAD
By John Allison
ISBN 978-1-62010-390-6
First edition now available!

Coming Soon!
UT ROWING CHAMPIONSHIP 1999

bad machinery
THE CASE OF THE MODERN MEN

ONI PRESS
www.onipress.com